SARAH ALDERSON

SIMON AND SCHUSTER

For Tom Arnold,
an amazing writer as well as an amazing brother

A **pulse** book

Simon Pulse and its colophon are registered
trademarks of Simon and Schuster UK Ltd

First published in Great Britain in 2012 by Simon and Schuster UK Ltd,
a CBS company.

www.sarahalderson.com

Simon & Schuster UK Ltd
1st Floor, 222 Gray's Inn Road, London WC1X 8HB

Simon & Schuster Australia, Sydney

Simon & Schuster India, New Delhi

A CIP catalogue record for this book is available from the British Library.

PB ISBN: 978-0-85707-434-8
E-BOOK ISBN: 978-0-85707-435-5

1 3 5 7 9 10 8 6 4 2

Printed and bound by CPI Group (UK) Ltd, Croydon CR0 4YY

www.simonandschuster.co.uk
www.simonandschuster.com.au

"It is not in the stars to hold our destiny but in ourselves."

William Shakespeare, *Julius Caesar* (Act I, scene ii)

Prologue

'Her name is Evie Tremain. She's seventeen years old. She lives in Riverview, California. Now go and kill her.'

The stillness in the room erupted as chairs scraped the floor. There were a few hushed whispers, a stifled laugh and then the door slammed shut, cutting the noise off like a guillotine.

Lucas stood slowly, taking his time. He didn't notice that the others had left the room, or that Tristan was standing by the window watching him. All his attention was focused on the photograph he was holding in his hand.

It showed a girl – dark-haired, blue-eyed – looking straight at the camera. It was a close-up. He could make out the shadows her lashes were making down her cheeks. A strand of hair was caught like a web over one eye and in the corner of the shot he could see her hand, reaching up to brush it away. Her lips were slightly parted, like she'd been sighing just at the moment the lens snapped shut. Her expression was . . . Lucas paused. He wasn't sure what her expression was. She looked unhappy, or maybe just pissed off.

She was a Hunter, though, so what did he expect? And this one had a history that would make anyone unhappy. Or pissed off.

'Is something wrong?' Tristan asked.

Lucas looked up from the photograph, then glanced over

towards the door, realising that he was the only one left in the room. He looked back at the older man.

'No, nothing's wrong,' he answered quietly.

'Well, you'd best get going then,' Tristan said, his eyes not leaving Lucas's face. 'You don't want to miss out on all the fun.'

Lucas looked down once more at the picture of Evie Tremain, feeling momentarily ambivalent towards her. Then he scrunched the photograph up into a ball and dropped it on the floor. It didn't matter what lay behind that expression because soon nothing would. She was just another Hunter to be dealt with. Next week or next month there would be another. And then another. And dealing with Hunters was what the Brotherhood did.

Lucas didn't look back at Tristan but he could sense his eyes burning into his back as he left the room.

Moving away fast down the corridor, Lucas realised he could no longer hear the others. He was faster than any human – he knew because he'd had to outrun them many times – so it didn't take him long to reach the basement garage.

There was just one ride waiting for him. Caleb and Shula were sitting in the front seats, the engine revving, the back door flung open.

'Come on!' Shula yelled. 'What's keeping you? There's a Hunter to kill and the others are going to beat us to it!'

Lucas smiled and shook his head, ducking into the back seat and slamming the door shut.

He let his head relax back into the seat and watched the speedometer climb as Caleb slammed the Mercedes out of the underground garage and onto the highway. Lucas stared out of the window. This stretch of highway was always quiet, but at night it was more so – there were only a few factories and gas stations for at least twenty miles in each direction. The Mission was a good base for the moment. Tristan had chosen well.

'She's pretty.'

Lucas turned his head. Shula was leaning across from the front seat, waving the photograph of Evie in his face. He grunted and went back to looking out of the window.

'Think she'll put up a fight?'

Lucas looked back at Shula. She was studying the photo intently, as though she could will it to life. Her raven-black hair was spilling over her shoulders, her skin glowing freakishly in the green dashboard lights. He almost smirked. Shula tried so hard to fit in and yet here she was looking as unhuman as a Shapeshifter midshift.

He smiled softly. 'Let's hope so.'

Shula grinned back, then kicked her legs up onto the dash and spun the volume dial on the radio to high.

1

Evie Tremain was so busy inspecting the minuscule amount of change that had been deposited on the table, in the midst of a lake of ketchup next to the pile of dribbling plates, that she didn't immediately notice the man who had taken a seat at the table behind her.

'Ev,' Joe called.

She looked up at the sound of her boss calling and saw him indicate the table behind. She pocketed the change and spun around, remembering to plaster a smile onto her face as she did so.

'Good evening, what can I get you?'

The words died on her lips. The man at the table was staring right at her, evaluating her like she was discounted meat in the freezer section, his gaze travelling up and down her body. Evie shifted her weight onto one hip, resting her hand on it and waited for some eye contact.

Not another one. She sighed to herself. And he was old enough to be her dad, which was really quite gross. She raised an eyebrow and waited until the man lifted his gaze to meet her own.

'Can I get you something?' she asked, offering him a tight smile.

He sank back into the booth, seemingly unembarrassed at having been caught checking her out.

'Yes, please, I'll have a soya decaff grande latte,' the man replied, without taking his eyes off her face to read the menu.

Evie paused, hand still on hip, wondering whether she should bother pointing out that the menu had just one option for coffee. *Filter*. Always caffeinated. She didn't. She bit her lip, took the pencil from behind her ear and scribbled on the pad: *1 x coffee.*

'Coming right up,' she said brightly, and turned on her heel.

She flipped the order down on the counter and Joe took it, peering at her scrawl. Then he reached for the coffee pot sitting on the hot plate behind him.

'Was he giving you any trouble?' he asked, tipping his head in the soya latte customer's direction.

Evie glanced over her shoulder. The man was looking out of the window now. He was about forty she figured, maybe older. Black, with a goatee. He was wearing a solid chunk of gold on the little finger of his right hand. Evie noticed only now she looked at him again that he was dressed kind of weirdly for round here. She looked closer.

The last time anyone had worn a suit in town had been at her dad's funeral, almost a year ago. And this man was actually wearing a three-piece suit, complete with a cherry-red cravat that frothed at the neck, making it look like someone had stabbed him in the jugular. Apart from that, though, the suit kind of worked on the man. Or, rather, the man worked on the suit. She wasn't sure how.

'Do you want me to serve him?'

'Huh?' Evie turned back to face Joe.

'I saw the way he was looking at you,' Joe said. 'Do you want me to serve him?'

Evie smiled as she took the cup of coffee from Joe's hand and slid it onto a tray. 'No, I got it. I need the tips, anyway.'

'Things can't be that bad, surely?' Joe asked. His grey moustache tightened around his lips like a caterpillar undergoing some kind of metamorphosis.

'Nope. I just want out of here – you know that, Joe.'

Joe pulled a face. The kind of face that Evie was sick of seeing. She grabbed the tray before he could say anything else and carried it towards the man at the table.

'One decaff latte,' she said, lowering the tray. 'Grande,' she added, looking at the little cup Joe had given him. At the same moment the door opened and Evie's attention swung towards it. The coffee cup slid sideways.

She heard Joe shout for her to watch out at the same time as she saw the boy in the doorway's eyes widen. Evie's arm shot out, rescuing the coffee cup as it bounced off the edge of the tray. She held it in mid-air, watching as the coffee stilled itself.

She placed it down carefully on the table. 'Sorry about that,' she murmured, glaring over her shoulder at the guy still standing in the doorway.

'Good reflexes,' the man said.

'Huh, yeah,' Evie muttered, backing away towards the counter. Joe was there, watching her with that look on his face again. She shrugged at him. He scowled over the top of her head at the boy in the doorway, before turning his back and starting to wipe down the counter.

Evie took a deep breath and pushed a loose strand of hair out of her face. She tried to tell herself to stay calm but she could already feel the heat rising in her lungs and scorching up her windpipe. She could feel her pulse quickening with the usual endorphin hit of rage.

She turned furiously to face the boy, catching him just as he was about to speak. 'What?' she demanded, cutting him off.

The boy shut his mouth and took a step towards her. He

glanced around. The coffee shop was empty at this time of night, apart from the guy in the weird outfit. She was thankful. The whole town had already had their noses smashed up against the windows of their business. She didn't need any more witnesses to what had happened between the two of them.

'What do you want? I'm working,' Evie hissed.

'I know. I'm sorry,' the boy began, then stopped, staring down at his feet.

Evie huffed impatiently, aware that her hands were curled into tight fists at her sides.

'I just wanted to talk,' the boy said.

'I have nothing to talk about,' Evie said, studying him, realising that her voice was shaking. If he looked up, if he looked at her with those hangdog brown eyes of his, if she allowed herself for one moment to feel sorry for him, then she would hate herself later. She turned her back on the boy and moved over to an empty table to clear the cups and plates.

She started stacking, aware that the boy had crept up behind her and was now hovering by her shoulder. She put the stack of cups down carefully on the table and turned to face him. 'Tom, I'm working. Please leave.'

'OK.' Tom nodded. He was close to her, almost brushing arms with her. 'But later, after work, can we talk then?'

She glanced up at the clock over the counter and saw that Joe was looking sideways at her, concern splashed all over his face. God, it was like living in a goldfish bowl without even a stone or some fancy plastic plants to hide behind.

'Tom, why would I want to talk to you? You killed my best friend. The best friend you were also seeing behind my back. Or had you forgotten?'

Tom took a step back, his face crumpling. 'Ev, it was an accident.'

She took a step back. 'Oh, so you *weren't* driving?'

Tom swallowed hard. It was a strangled sound. Evie hesitated for a second but all the anger and the hurt dammed behind the smiling waitress routine rushed to the surface. It made her cheeks and jaw ache; it made her whole body ache, until she felt like her muscles had calcified from the effort of holding everything she was feeling inside.

She stared now into Tom's familiar brown eyes, measuring the reaction her words had caused, thinking how strange it was that once upon a time she had run her hands through his hair, linked her fingers through his, had kissed him and thought it was possibly the best feeling in the world.

It was strange because now she hated him.

She drew in a breath. 'She shouldn't have even been in the car.'

Tom dropped his eyes to the floor again. Evie felt the anger subside like a break in the storm. She was suddenly overwhelmingly tired. She just wanted to not have to go through this scene every day like she was living on repeat.

She wanted to have someone wipe her memory clean. But seeing as she wasn't likely to get hit on the back of the head and wake up tomorrow with amnesia, the only alternative was to get the hell out of this small town filled with small-town people where the gossip about her and Tom had kept the knitting circle busy for so long they had knitted enough blankets to see the Salvation Army through a nuclear winter.

She wanted to be able to walk down the street among strangers – people who didn't know her and who didn't look at her with crinkled eyes and tilted heads and ask her how she was doing with that strange inflection in their voices that made her want to scream until she was hollow.

She wanted out. So she picked up the stack of cups, walked past Tom and set them on the counter. She kept her back to him until she heard the door jangle behind her.

'You all right?'

Evie looked up. Joe was standing in front of her, his face folded into a frown.

She sighed. 'Yeah, I'm fine. I just . . . you know, I'm just sick of him apologising, as if an apology can ever make up for what he did.'

Joe nodded, taking the tea towel from where he'd flung it over his shoulder and starting to wipe the counter. 'That kid's sure got some guilt to live with.'

Evie glared at Joe. 'Well, he should be living with it in jail.'

Joe pressed his lips together and nodded non-committally. 'This one's sure taking his time,' he said, changing the subject and nodding his head at the man in the red cravat.

Evie shot a glance over her shoulder. The man was still looking out of the window. 'Listen, if you want me to lock up, I've got it,' she said to Joe.

'Are you sure, Evie?' he asked, taking the cups and placing them one by one into the dishwasher below the counter. 'Don't you have a home to get to?'

'No, it's OK. I need as many hours as I can get.' She shrugged.

'Still planning on leaving town, then?' Joe asked with a sigh.

Evie considered his face before answering. He reminded her of her father, the same ridge-lined face and deep-set eyes, the same soft tone and silvering hair.

'Sorry, Joe,' she said finally. 'I've got to get out. Only bad stuff happens here.'

Joe nodded slowly. 'I hear you,' he said. 'Listen, if you get any trouble from this one,' he indicated the man drinking coffee, 'then you just call me.'

Evie smiled at him. 'I've got it, Joe. I can take care of myself.'

'I know, I know,' Joe said, reaching for his jacket on the peg behind him. 'One thing your father did right was seeing you could take care of yourself.'

'Just one thing?' Evie asked, smiling, her eyebrows raised.

'Oh, you know what I'm saying,' he mumbled. 'Your father was a good man, Ev Tremain.' He paused a moment. 'And speaking as his best friend I know that he'd be real proud of you.'

Evie's stomach muscles contracted violently, forcing all the air out of her lungs, and leaving her feeling like she was underwater, drowning silently. She swallowed twice and tried to smile at Joe. He reached over and patted her hand before leaving.

When she heard the clang of the door, she reached forward, resting her palms on the counter, and took a deep breath and then another. She pushed her hair back out of her face and straightened up before turning around with a smile.

'Can I get you anything else?' she asked the man at the table by the window.

He was looking straight at her, as though he'd been watching this whole time. Her back straightened and her shoulders tensed.

The man's face suddenly split into a wide smile. 'Just the check,' he said.

Evie ripped a page off her pad and went to place it in front of him, then hovered by the table with her arms crossed over her chest.

The man rummaged for his wallet, then drew out two crisp ten-dollar bills. He dropped them onto the table and Evie frowned before looking up. The coffee only cost a dollar something.

The man caught her eye. 'Sounds like you could use the extra tips,' he said.

She narrowed her eyes at him. Nothing came for free. That had been one of her father and Joe's favourite sayings. Her dad would walk in here, pull up a counter stool and demand a free coffee. Joe would laugh, pour him one and tell him nothing came for free, before setting the bill in front of him.

Evie stepped forward and, with her eyes still on the man, picked up the notes. She folded them and put them in her apron pocket. 'Thanks,' she said, reaching for the empty coffee cup.

'I'm opening a store just over the road there,' the man said. Evie looked at where he was pointing, over the street at Cardman's Old Bookstore. It was boarded up and had a *To Let* sign hanging off it.

'Really?' Evie asked, unable to contain her surprise. Her mum usually knew everything going on in this town before the people it was happening to even knew it themselves, but she'd said nothing to Evie about a new shop opening up.

'Yes, it's more of a boutique than a store, really,' the man said and Evie noticed for the first time that he had an accent, though she couldn't quite place it.

'What kind of a boutique?' Evie asked. Her mother would want to know.

'Clothing. Fashion,' he said. 'Seems like the one thing this town is missing is some good fashion.'

Evie studied him again for any sign that he was joking. 'Are you expecting to turn a profit?' she asked.

The man threw back his head. 'Sometimes it's not about the money, it's about the dream,' he laughed.

'Your dream is to dress the women of Riverview in couture?' Evie laughed. 'Good luck with that. This is a farming community, the only fashion the women here are into involves denim and leather – and probably not in the way you're thinking.'

She shook her head and made to move off. Weird. This man was so weird. And so soon to be bankrupt.

'You know, I'm looking for a sales assistant, if you're interested,' the man called to her back.

Evie paused. She put the coffee cup down on the counter and turned to him. 'What are you paying?'

The man shrugged. 'Thirty dollars an hour.'

Evie's eyebrows shot up. Thirty dollars *an hour*? Was the man insane? That was almost four times what she made here.

'Forty,' she replied, blanking her face.

An amused smile seemed to be skirting the man's mouth. 'Thirty-five.'

She wanted to burst out laughing but she held it in, biting the inside of her cheek instead. 'Deal,' she said. 'When do I start?'

'Tomorrow.'

Evie thought about it. 'I work two other jobs – this one three evenings a week from five till ten and then I help my mother out in my dad's store on Saturdays and Wednesdays. Other than that, I'm all yours.'

The man appraised her. 'When do you find the time to sleep?'

'I'm trying to save as much money as I can right now, so any extra work is good.'

'Well then, Evie, I guess we have a deal. Tomorrow is Tuesday, so I'll see you at ten a.m.'

She frowned at him. How had he known her name? She guessed he must have heard Joe or Tom say it earlier. 'OK.' She nodded. 'Can I know who I'm working for?'

The man stood and Evie stepped back involuntarily. He was

13

enormous – solid muscle underneath his suit – and the seams looked fit to burst on his inside thigh, not that she was looking. But she sure as hell noticed that he wasn't built like the farmers around here, who were wiry and tough – he was built more like a body builder.

'My name is Victor,' he said, holding out his hand. 'Victor Lassonde.'

2

Evie turned the lock in the door. Main Street was dead. All the stores were dark – only the yellow street lights were eclipsing the darkness now. Two cars were parked up in the shadows out front. Someone climbed out of the passenger seat of one and walked in her direction. She flipped the *Closed* sign quickly. There was no way she was serving another customer tonight. Not even if they waved a twenty-dollar tip in her face.

She backed away from the door and flipped the light switch, collapsing the whole place into blackness, and then she headed behind the counter to gather up the trash bags. The sound of someone trying the door made her jump. She looked around, irritated. Couldn't they read? That was a *Closed* sign on the door.

There was a guy standing in front of the glass looking in, staring directly at her. His hand was still on the door handle. He was about six feet tall and wearing a floor-length black leather coat. Evie took in the whole of him in one glance and felt something similar to a rock settle on her stomach. Something wasn't right about him. In fact, something was most definitely off. Then she realised it was the sunglasses he was wearing. Ray Bans. In the middle of the night.

'We're closed,' she mouthed, wondering whether he could even see her, shrouded as she was in the shadows behind the counter.

The boy didn't respond or smile or act in any way as if he'd seen her, though his hand did drop from the door handle. He turned on his heel and strode back towards his car, coat flapping like a windsock behind him.

Evie stood there a full minute, trash bags clutched in her hand, waiting for the sound of a car engine turning over and accelerating away. Nothing. The street stayed fathomlessly silent. She edged towards the door and peered through the glass. The cars were both still sitting there; empty as far as she could tell. The guy in the long trench coat was nowhere to be seen.

A feeling of unease crept through her but she couldn't stand there all night like a total wuss, hovering in the gloom. So she took the bags and walked to the back door and opened it, annoyed with herself for getting so freaked out over a boy who looked like he'd gotten lost on the way back from Comic Con.

The back lot was empty except for the giant metal dumpster just to her right and her dusty old Ford parked a few metres to her left. There was a single light blazing above her head, illuminating the door and the concrete step she was standing on. She headed straight towards the dumpster with the bags in one hand and a tin of coffee grounds in the other – and that's when she saw him, on the periphery of the shadow line, his coat splayed out behind him.

The hairs on the back of her neck bristled. She drew in a breath and did a quick calculation of the distance between her, the boy and the door.

But before she could figure out where to run to, the boy in the sunglasses stepped forward into the zone of light. She saw that he was a little bit older than her, maybe twenty or twenty-one. He was wearing black jeans and leather biker boots, and a black wrinkled T-shirt with some kind of slogan on it. A part of her brain registered that he looked ridiculous, like an extra from *The Matrix*, but the other part warned her not to tell him so.

At least not yet.

He stopped just in front of her.

'Evie Tremain?' he asked.

She froze, her mouth falling open. How did he know her name? Who the hell *was* this guy? As she studied him, she suddenly heard a voice in her head start screaming at her to run. She could hear her own heartbeat – it sounded like a horse smashing its hooves against a stable door. Her eyes darted instantly over the lot, looking for her exits.

'Evie Tremain?' the boy asked again, impatient now.

'Who wants to know?' Evie asked, buying time. The back door was about ten metres behind her or she could try to get around him and head down the side alley and out onto Main Street. She took a small step backwards. The diner was closer.

'The Brotherhood,' the boy replied tonelessly, closing the distance between them in a single stride.

Evie couldn't rein in the laughter that erupted out of her. 'The Brotherhood? *Seriously?* What is that? The name of your death-metal band?'

The boy – whose face had been expressionless until then – suddenly frowned in confusion, as though he didn't know how to answer her. The sound of crunching gravel broke the silence. Evie's eyes flew to the far end of the lot, which was sunk in darkness. Was someone else there? The boy followed her gaze, looking over his shoulder.

Adrenaline pumped through Evie's body in one giant surge. She dropped the trash bags and took a step back, twisting her body as she moved. She brought her arm up like her dad had taught her, fingers curled into a fist, and in the second that the boy turned back to face her, she smashed it into the side of his head.

The boy's head spun with the force of the punch, his sunglasses flying across the lot.

'*Hit first, ask questions later*,' she murmured to herself. Her dad had always said it was better to be safe than sorry.

She turned to run back towards the door but the boy lunged for her, shrieking. She raised her arm instinctively, ready to smash it into his face again, but then stumbled backwards letting out a cry. The boy's eyes were inches from her own, his pupils fixed and dilated. And the thing that had stopped her, and made her stomach scrape the floor, was the *colour* of them. They were bright, carnation-red and totally unseeing. The boy flailed his head from left to right, as though someone had thrown acid in his face, his outstretched hand groping blindly in her direction.

He's blind, Evie realised, her thoughts assuming some sense. *He can't see me.*

Out of the corner of her eye she saw a dark shape wavering behind the boy. It seemed to extend and stretch out, like a time-lapse sequence of a shadow lengthening. And then it coiled like a whip and lashed towards her.

Evie dived. She threw herself hard to the left, out of the boy's grip and out of the way of whatever was coming towards her. She heard a crack as it smashed into the tarmac and another frustrated shriek from the boy.

She staggered backwards, her eyes on the space that had opened up between her and the guy in the coat. The whip or rope or whatever it was was lashing back and forth between them. Evie's brain refused to process the possibility that what

18

her eyes were actually looking at was neither a rope nor a whip but a tail. There were scales on it and it moved like a rattlesnake. Ropes didn't look like that.

The boy dropped to the floor now, and started scrabbling around on the ground for something. His glasses, Evie thought, spying them lying cracked in half on the asphalt by her car.

'Need some help, Caleb?' A girl's voice called out from the edge of the darkness.

The boy with blood-red eyes swore at her in reply.

'If you want help you need to put your tail away and ask nicely,' the girl added.

The word punctured Evie's brain like a poison dart. *Tail.* She tripped backwards, trying to feel for the door behind her. She stumbled on the step, and felt herself bump up against something solid. It wasn't the door.

She spun around and found herself stepping on the toes of a white-faced boy. A girl in a neon pink minidress stood next to him, smiling *surrrrprise.*

Evie skittered backwards, letting out a yelp. How many of these freaks *were* there?

These two weren't wearing sunglasses and their eyes weren't red. The boy was dressed in scruffy jeans, bashed-up Converse and a Nix cap. The girl was tall with long black hair, and the bright pink of her dress clashed with the green tinge of her skin.

'We've got this, Caleb,' the girl in the pink dress called out to the one with the tail, not taking her eyes off Evie.

'Well, hurry up, would you, I don't want to be here all night,' another boy's voice answered from the darkness.

So there were more of them over there, Evie thought, panic

starting to weave its tentacles around her limbs. How many did that make? Four or five at least.

'What do you want?' Evie asked desperately, spinning around to face the girl and boy blocking the back door.

'We want *you*, Evie Tremain,' the girl in pink said, striding forward. She put her hand on Evie's arm and Evie looked down, as her skin began to burn intensely.

She screamed and, with a final injection of adrenaline and anger, swung the tin of coffee grounds she was still holding at the girl's head. The girl let go of her instantly and started yelling.

Evie skittered back out of her way, skidding towards her car, dodging around the boy on the ground with the tail.

With the tail! Her brain screamed at her as though it wanted her to pause awhile and figure it out. But her arm was still burning, as though the bone itself had caught alight, and the skin was blistering and it was all she could do not to faint right there and then. She started fumbling with her one good hand for her car key, buried in the pocket of her jeans, and felt the sob start to burst in her chest.

The boy in the Nix cap was bent double, pointing and laughing at the girl Evie had hit. And the sound of it, the childish hysteria of it, was like a shucking knife opening Evie up. She glanced upwards even as she scrabbled for her keys. The girl was holding the side of her head, screaming and trying to scrape the wet coffee grounds off her face. She spat a gloop of saliva and glared furiously at Evie.

Evie's fingers closed on her keys. She yanked them from her pocket, watching as the girl and boy moved in on her. She was just prey, she realised. She was completely cornered. There was no way out.

And then the sun came up. Or it felt like it. The whole lot lit

20

up as if someone had flipped on some floodlights. The shadows wiped out and Evie was blinded. She threw an arm up to cover her eyes, trying at the same time to squint for the source of it. She could hear screaming and a hissing noise – the sound of wet meat hitting a flaming grill.

When her eyes adjusted she saw the boy in the Nix cap collapsed on the ground in front of her. He was sizzling and smoking and screaming like a stuck pig. The girl in the pink dress had him by the arm and was dragging him towards the trash container and the thin shadow it made on the ground.

'Evie?' a man's voice yelled, snapping her out of her frozen state.

She looked up. She recognised the voice – the accent. 'Yes,' she answered, scrambling to her feet.

'Get over here!' he yelled.

She ran towards the source of the light and saw who it was. Victor Lassonde. He was standing there in his suit holding what looked like a torch in his right hand. In his other hand was something that looked remarkably like a gun.

Probably because it *was* a gun.

Evie jumped behind Victor, clutching at his arm, her heart rattling at a hundred beats a minute. A million questions ran through her head, the first of which was *What the hell are you doing here?*

She heard herself voice it.

He didn't answer her.

'Half-and-half, get the Hunter!' someone screamed.

Evie looked over Victor's shoulder. The girl in the pink dress was the one screaming. But who was Half-and-half? And who was the Hunter?

The girl dumped the boy in the Nix cap by the dumpster.

He curled up in a tight ball, whimpering and steaming in the shadows.

The girl looked up at Evie, her eyes glinting. 'The girl's mine,' she hissed.

Evie cowered backwards. She felt Victor edging sideways towards the door of the diner and followed his lead. But the girl in the pink dress with the greenish skin was blocking their way to the back door.

Victor had his back to Evie, his gun raking the parking lot in front. Why wasn't he firing at these crazy people who were trying to kill them? thought Evie. Why wasn't he aiming at the girl in the pink dress for starters?

Just then the girl lunged towards her. Evie let out a scream, and stumbled as though someone invisible had shoved her. Evie flinched backwards as she heard a gunshot. She watched the girl reel backwards, clutching her arm.

Evie reached for the handle just as a shadow sprang across it. She teetered as though on the brink of a waterfall, sound rushing her ears, goosebumps raking her body. Then whatever it was was gone, leaving only a reverberation in the air that echoed through her body. Evie's knees smacked the concrete step and she let out a cry, but Victor hauled her upright and flung her towards the door.

Her fingers closed around the handle and she yanked it open.

3

Evie collapsed onto the linoleum floor, breathing so hard she thought her lungs had stopped working. The images in her mind were swirling into patterns the same way that oil did when it rainbowed on water. She suddenly became aware again of the pain shooting up her arm. She lifted it up and saw the skin blistering red and popping in tiny white bubbles where the girl had grabbed her. She closed her eyes and, on three, managed to drag herself to standing, aware only dimly that Victor was in front of her, wrestling some heavy boxes in front of the door.

She turned to the sink in the storeroom and ran the tap, shoving her arm under the spray.

'Water won't help.'

She twisted around to look at Victor. 'What?'

He was done with barricading the door and was now pulling a phone out of his pocket.

'Water won't help,' he said again, dialling a number. 'It's not that kind of burn.' Then his attention switched to the person on the end of the line. 'They've left. I'm with her now. But the area needs securing – yes – and call Risper and Earl. It's time.'

He snapped the phone shut. 'You could try urinating on it,' he said over his shoulder, crossing to the window and peering out. He had extinguished the torch and they were in semi-darkness, the storeroom illuminated only by the outside light shining through one small window.

'What?' Evie said, looking at him in horror. The pain wasn't lessening – in fact it felt like the water was tearing actual strips of flesh and nerve from her arm. But she wasn't about to pee on it to see if that made it feel any better.

'Or bicarbonate of soda works.'

Evie stared at him, her teeth gritted. He had his back to her, his gun drawn. She drew her arm out from under the tap, holding it against her T-shirt.

'Who are those people?' she asked. 'What do they want?'

Victor turned around from his stake-out position by the window. He holstered his gun. 'They're leaving.'

And, as he said it, Evie heard the sound of cars revving, followed by the squeal of tyres.

'Who are they?' she asked again in a half-whisper.

'They're the Brotherhood,' Victor replied.

'They're not a death-metal band, are they?'

Victor frowned in confusion. 'Excuse me?'

Evie shook her head. 'Never mind.' Why was she cracking jokes? 'They knew my name. They were looking for me. Why?'

Victor put his gun down on the side of the sink and stretched over her head. He grabbed a jar of something and then turned his attention back to Evie. 'They wanted to kill you.'

Evie looked at him, waiting for the punchline. 'Why?' she finally asked when he didn't give her one.

'Because of who you are,' Victor answered calmly. As if that explained it.

Evie blinked. 'Who I am?' She shook her head, still not understanding. 'Who am I? Why would anyone want to *kill* me?

24

I'm nobody special. I'm . . .' She ran out of vocabulary to describe her nonentity-ness.

Victor put his hand on her shoulder. 'Come, sit down, I'll explain.'

Evie threw him off with a shrug, felt another layer of skin peel from her arm. She ignored it and strode to the phone on the wall. 'No. I'm calling the police. Are you insane? There are some crazy people out there trying to kill me.'

'You're not calling the police.' Victor was suddenly in front of her, his hand on top of the receiver, holding it in place. Evie stared at his hand in disbelief. 'Besides, they're not coming back,' Victor said.

'How do you know?' she asked, trying to squeeze the phone out from under his grip.

Victor didn't budge. 'What are you going to tell them? A Scorpio demon and a Mixen just jumped you in the parking lot? *Any distinguishing features?* Yes, Officer, he was six feet tall, brown hair, red eyes, oh and by the way he has a long tail with a razor-sharp edge. The girl? Well, she was about five eleven, wearing a pink dress and had green skin. Oh and you should wear a hazard suit when approaching her because her skin's kind of poisonous.'

Evie's hand dropped off the phone.

'A Scorpio demon . . . ?' Evie repeated his words.

'The one with the tail – that was a Scorpio demon. They have a different spectrum of vision – they're blind in this world without the sunglasses,' Victor said. 'The girl in the pink dress – the one who burnt your arm – she's a Mixen. She has a coating of acid on her skin. That's what burnt you.'

'*Acid?*' Evie swallowed.

He nodded.

25

'And a tail? It *was* a tail?'

Victor nodded again. More patiently this time.

'Demons?'

Victor shrugged. 'Well, that's one word for them. Though it's more common nowadays to call them Unhumans.'

'Unhumans?'

'Yes.' Victor nodded again.

Evie bit her lip, her head trying to analyse the words, trying to decipher them. 'I need to sit down,' she finally said.

She swayed and tripped her way into the diner and around the counter, until she made it to one of the booths in the back and collapsed.

Victor came and sat opposite her. He placed a jar of bicarbonate of soda on the table in front of her and studied her for a full minute without saying a word. She ignored both him and the jar and the pain in her arm, even though she figured she now knew what being flayed alive felt like.

'OK,' she said, finally looking up and focusing on Victor, who was sitting with his elbows resting on the table. 'I'm just trying to get my head around this – could you explain it to me in simple terms? What the hell are Unhumans?'

Victor took a deep breath. 'Basically anyone who doesn't have human DNA – Mixen, Scorpio, Thirsters—'

'Thirsters?' Evie cut in.

Victor sighed loudly. 'You know them as Vampires.'

'*Vampires?*' Evie smirked. Her head hit the leather cushion of the banquette behind her. 'Are you trying to tell me that that was Edward Cullen outside? Because, you know, I thought he was supposed to be hotter than that. And a whole lot more romantic.'

26

Victor didn't laugh. He didn't even smile. He waited until her false laugh died away and then carried on. 'They've worked hard to glamorise themselves these past few decades – to build a cult following in this world. They're really quite vain. In the Unhuman world they're called Thirsters. The boy in the Nix cap, the one who was about to drain you – he's a Thirster. His name is Joshua. There are supposedly older Thirsters, ones that have been around for centuries, who are known as the Originals. But no one has ever seen one.' He hesitated. 'Or at any rate, lived to tell about it.'

Evie stared at him blankly. 'The Unhuman world?' she asked, shaking her head slowly. 'What are you talking about? This is not some Joss Whedon television show we're both starring in.' She became aware that she was on her feet. She had somehow pushed her way out of the booth and was now in front of Victor, yelling at him. 'Listen, you have to start making some sense. Please. Tell me something I can actually understand. And while you're at it, please explain who the hell you are and what you were doing out there in the first place!'

Evie saw Victor's eyes widen and suddenly remembered she was holding his gun. She had picked it up from the shelf in the storeroom when he'd put it down to reach for that jar. She hesitated for a moment, then decided to keep it pointed at Victor's head.

'Are you one of them? C'mon, start talking!'

Victor chewed his lip, eyeing the gun with irritation, whether at himself for leaving his gun lying around or at her she didn't know or care.

'Evie, give me the gun,' he said finally. 'You don't need to point it at me. I'm not the enemy.'

She made no move to lower the gun. Instead she rolled back

the safety catch and watched his eyes flicker from the end of the barrel to her face. He definitely looked annoyed with her now.

'I don't want to have rescued you from the Brotherhood only to have you shoot me by accident,' he said.

She heard the growl in her voice as she answered. 'Oh, believe me, it would not be by accident. If you don't start talking right now I'm going to show you just how excellent my aim actually is. So, for the last time, who the hell are you?'

'I'm not one of them,' he said, his accent coming through thicker, his hands darting upwards in surrender. 'I'm fully human. My name is Victor, like I told you. I'm here to protect you.' He said the last bit with what sounded like more than a shred of regret. 'I'm a Hunter.'

'What's a Hunter?' Evie asked, anger and impatience snapping in her voice.

'Put the gun down and I'll tell you.'

Evie looked at him sitting there in his suit and frothing red silk tie, with his hands raised to the ceiling, and weighed him up. He didn't *look* Unhuman. At least, he didn't look as freaky as the others had – if you discounted the clothing. And he'd saved her when she'd really needed saving. She glanced down. He didn't have a tail or fangs or look like the Incredible Hulk, either.

Slowly she lowered the gun. Victor nodded at the seat opposite and she dropped into it. Her arm banged the table as she did so and she let out a cry.

'Here, use this,' Victor said, pushing the jar containing the bicarb towards her. She frowned as he got up and crossed to the counter and filled a glass with some water. He returned to the table and poured some of the powder into the glass to make a paste. 'Come on, try it. It'll take the sting out.'

28

She took the glass and, wincing in anticipation, poured it over her arm. At first it seemed to be making her skin sing with pain, but then the sting evaporated, taking most of the heat with it. She scraped off the gunk and was staring at the handprint-shaped burn on her arm when Victor started speaking again, quietly and quickly, as though he was worried she might jump up and fire the gun at him now that her arm was better and she could aim with two hands.

'I'm a Hunter. Our job is to keep Unhumans out of this world. We've been doing this for a very, very long time.'

'OK,' she said, 'I'm just going along with this for the sake of conversation.' She cleared her throat. 'So you're telling me you're like, what? Some kind of border control?'

Victor leant forward. He seemed to be chewing on his response. 'If you want to think of it like that, then yes,' he said, sighing under his breath. 'We keep this world safe from . . . well, you've seen what we keep it safe from. The reason we're safe now, the reason they won't come back just yet, is because they'll know more Hunters will be on the way.'

Evie frowned at him, waiting for further explanation.

Victor shrugged. 'Safety in numbers.'

'Where do they come from?' Evie asked, her voice shaking. 'These *Unhumans*? If they don't come from this world?'

'They come from other realms. There's a gateway – in LA. It's the link between this realm and the other six realms.'

Evie nodded slowly. 'Right,' she said, while surreptitiously scanning between the tables for what looked like the fastest route out of here. 'This is such bull,' she said at last. 'None of what you're telling me makes any sense. It's not real. It can't be.'

Victor smiled then. 'This world,' he said, 'the world you grew up in, Evie, this is the one that's not real. You just need to see it from our perspective.'

She opened her mouth ready to tell him where he could stick his perspective but he cut her off.

'It exists, yes. People are born, they work, they get married, they have babies. If they're lucky they live to grow old, see the next generation grow up, and then they die. But they do all that without ever knowing what's really happening around them – in the darkness, in the shadows. In the parking lot of their local diner.'

Evie felt herself suddenly go cold. She wrapped her arms around her body, hugging herself tight. Was he right? Was this all possible? Her head was screaming no, but everything else, her instinct or whatever it was, was telling her that it was the truth.

'Humans love to fight. There are always wars in the human world,' Victor continued. 'Iraq, Afghanistan, Vietnam, the Second World War, the Great War, the Crimea, the Crusades. And on and on. Wars that last a week or a year or even a decade. But the war between Humans and Unhumans has been going on for over a thousand years. Without pause and without reconciliation.'

'Why? What are you all fighting about?' Her voice sounded surprisingly together, considering the rest of her was slowly collapsing inwards like a star silently extinguishing itself.

'To keep our world safe,' he said. 'The Unhumans wish to possess all seven realms. Our world, the human world, is the seventh. The only realm they haven't been able to take control of.'

He waited a beat and then continued. 'We've fought in secret all that time. It's a tiny war in terms of numbers. There are only a few of us who are Hunters in each generation – our numbers are shrinking. But the outcome of this war is far greater, far more important, than any war ever fought among humans.'

He sat back in his seat, resting his gaze level with hers.

Evie finally cleared her voice. 'OK, thanks for the alternative history lesson and the apocalyptic vision of the future, which I'm still not sure that I'm buying, but you still haven't explained why they want *me*. What did I do?'

'You didn't do anything. It's what you *might* do. One day.'

Evie looked at him, confused. 'What might I do?'

He paused, pressing his lips together. 'You're a Hunter,' he said finally, 'and their job is to wipe out all Hunters.'

Evie bit her lip. Then stood up. 'So I'm a Hunter?'

Victor looked at her. 'Yes.'

'Don't I get a say in this?' she demanded. 'I don't *want* to be a Hunter. I just want to be a waitress,' she saw his sceptical look and hastened to finish her sentence, 'for now, anyway. Then I'm going to New York to study and I'm never coming back here as long as I live. I don't want to know about the world you're telling me about and I certainly don't want a career hunting down any of the psychos who came after me tonight. I do not have a death wish.'

Victor waited until she'd finished, his expression unmoved. 'I'm sorry, Evie,' he said. He didn't sound very sorry. 'You don't get to choose. None of us do. You're a Hunter. That's just how it is.'

'You can't tell me who I am.'

Victor hesitated. His voice dropped. 'But it's who you are. Your real name is Evie Hunter. It's the name your parents gave you. Your *real* parents, that is.'

Evie's mouth dropped open. Then, finally finding her voice, she said, 'My parents? You knew my parents?'

'I knew them, yes. We placed you with Monica and Ed Tremain when you were eighteen months old. They adopted you having no idea who you were.'

31

It was as if her heart rocketed through the atmosphere and then came crashing back to earth in a million little pieces. She'd never thought she'd know anything about her real parents. She'd just been abandoned as far as she knew and then adopted when she was tiny. But now she had a name. But why had Victor said he *knew* them? Why had he used the past tense?

'They died when you were about a year old,' Victor said, seeing the question rise on her lips.

It took the wind out of her.

'I was about twenty, I suppose,' he carried on. 'We – the other Hunters – tried to look after you for a while, but it didn't work. You can't fight Unhumans and make play dates at the same time. We found you a safe place to grow up. A normal home, with normal parents. Somewhere we thought they wouldn't find you.'

Evie was sitting again. She didn't remember sitting. How had she made her legs move? They were dead. Nothing else had registered after that.

'How did they die?' she whispered.

Victor held her gaze. 'The Brotherhood, of course. The Brotherhood killed them.'

4

Lucas was watching Caleb's tail swish back and forth and weighing up whether he was quick enough to sneak up on him, take his damn tail and wrap it around his neck, when Grace let out an audible sigh in his direction.

'You *are* quick enough but you'll still end up over there on the ground with one hand sliced open,' she said.

Lucas stared at her carefully and considered his options. He wasn't sure he wanted to risk spilling his blood with a Thirster in the room. He was half human so his blood might not be as appealing as a full Shadow Warrior's, but he didn't want to risk it. He knew the oath they'd all sworn might not stand up under such temptation. He crossed his arms over his chest and went back to leaning against the wall, his eyes on the clock.

'So, Grace, you manage to do your psychic routine here, now, but you can't haul it out of the bag when we're sneaking up on a Hunter?'

Lucas turned his head to look in the direction of the speaker. Shula was standing in front of Grace with her hands on her hips, letting everyone know, in her usual subtle way, exactly what she was feeling.

'I got *shot* because of you.'

'Hey, what about me?' Joshua's thin voice piped up. 'I got

fried – look.' He held out his arm, which looked like it had been blended on high speed, and waved it in her face.

Shula ignored him. She'd showered the coffee grinds out of her hair and her arm was bandaged, but from the way she was waving it about, it didn't seem to be troubling her too much. Mixen always did heal well, Lucas thought with a frown. It was only then that he noticed the outfit she was wearing. She'd changed out of her pink dress and into a red silk dressing gown, which had slipped down over one shoulder – deliberately, Lucas hazarded a guess. In this light her skin was a gleaming brown, not green, and her black hair hung wet and carefully dishevelled down her back.

Shula was standing over Grace, like a vulture circling her prey. Lucas would have been worried for anyone else, but not for Grace. No one ever worried about Grace.

'I wasn't expecting any other Hunters to show,' Grace answered with a yawn. 'I thought she was alone.'

'You have one easy job to do and that's all,' Shula yelled. 'You don't have to get your hands dirty, you just have to sit there and warn us what's about to happen and you can't even manage to do *that* right.'

Shula had a point, though Lucas didn't understand why she was bothering to bring it up with Grace. Why try and argue anything with a psychic? They always won.

'Let's see how psychic you *really* are,' Shula yelled. 'Did you foresee *this*?'

Lucas watched her level an elegant roundhouse kick straight at Grace's head.

Grace slid like a whisper out of her chair and Shula's leg flew right by her, grazing the air before slamming with a crunch into Joshua's face.

'Ahhhhhh,' he screamed. 'You dumb—'

34

'Oh, I'm sorry,' Shula said, putting a hand to her mouth, her eyes widening in mock horror, 'did I hurt you?' She was smirking as she said it. 'I thought you Thirsters were supposed to be practically indestructible?' She paused, looking him up and down. 'Though clearly not flame-resistant.'

Lucas eyed Joshua, whose skin still resembled plastic grilled over an open flame. His shirt had melted to parts of his back and arm, and, where he'd torn it loose in the car, red strips of flesh had come away. It looked like someone had upended a tray of pulverised meat where his shoulder and bicep should have been.

'You got a problem with the way I look, Shula?' Joshua shot back. 'Because that would be kind of like the pot calling the kettle green, wouldn't it?'

Shula strode past him. Lucas could see the rage bubbling beneath the surface of her skin.

'I just need some blood and I'll be fine,' he called to her back. 'Ain't nothing going to help you look any better though.'

Shula spun around. 'Remind me again why I saved your skinny white ass?' she yelled. 'If it hadn't been for me you'd be southern fried white trash by now, being licked off the pavement by dogs.'

There was a giggle from the other side of the room. It was Neena. Her hand shot up to stifle her laughter but it was already too late. Joshua was right there, in her face, his crackling lip curled back over yellowing fangs. Lucas could see Neena's heart hammering beneath her shirt, could feel her fear like a vibration in the air. The shimmer around her intensified and Lucas wondered if she'd shift into a lion or a bear and try to take Joshua's head off, but she kept a disappointing amount of control. The shimmer faded. Neena stayed as she was.

'You know, Shapeshifter blood's the best damn blood there

is.' Joshua spat the words into her face. 'Can't get me enough of that . . .' He smacked his lips hard.

'Shut up. As if you've ever,' Neena hissed back, her form solidifying.

Joshua's eyes were glowing. 'You wanna bet?' he laughed. 'You wanna know how it tastes?' His face was shoved into Neena's.

Lucas merged with the shadows. He moved fast, positioning himself just behind Neena's shoulder, ready to pull her backwards if he needed to, ready to slam his fist into Joshua's face. None of them were that good yet at sensing him when he was invisible, not if they weren't concentrating at any rate.

'Every mouthful of Shapeshifter blood has a different taste,' Joshua said now, his eyes dilating so much his irises were black moons and Lucas was able to make out tiny red eruptions in the white of his eye. 'You ever see *Willy Wonka*? You know that part where the girl eats an everlasting gobstopper and it tastes of everything? Like chicken soup and roast beef and blueberry pie all rolled into one? Well, that's exactly what Shapeshifter's blood tastes like – you get rabbit for starter, or maybe some sushi, then you get yourself some nice succulent pork belly for main. If you're *really* lucky you get some big cat steak, maybe a proper hot dog, then, to finish, always a bird. Funniest thing. Best you can hope for is swan. Finest damn meal I ever ate.' He smacked his lips together again.

'You're disgusting,' Neena spat. She edged backwards and bumped Lucas's shoulder and jumped. Her shimmer momentarily blinded him before she settled back.

'Oh, ignore Joshua,' Shula said from across the room. 'He's just an ignorant little hillbilly. The only thing he's ever eaten is squirrel. And the occasional human.'

Joshua swung around to face her. 'If you didn't have skin so

36

disgusting it would be like biting through a crocodile's ass, I'd have tasted *your* blood by now too.'

Shula was sitting with her legs up on the desk in front of her. 'Oh yeah? You think? You think you could get anywhere near me?' Shula kicked the desk. 'No wonder the humans don't want you in their world. Frankly, Joshua, who the hell would?'

Joshua's face contorted as though the sun was shining right on him. He flew at Shula with his teeth bared. Only the sight of Tristan, who'd suddenly appeared in the middle of the room, pulled him up short. Joshua froze mid-pounce, his teeth retracting instantly and his eyes flashing in fear towards the man in the suit standing next to him.

Lucas smiled inwardly. If he hadn't seen Neena shift right there in front of him he wouldn't have believed it was her. Gone was the short girl with frizzy brown hair and a smattering of freckles and in her place stood Tristan. And she had him down perfectly, from the polished brogues to the inch of white shirt cuff and black crystal cufflinks. Even the lip-curling sneer and the waxed centre part of his eyebrows were just this side of perfect. He glanced down at Tristan's arms. The only thing that was off was the symmetry. Shifters were always mirror images – never quite the real deal – but it took the brain a while to figure out what was off about the picture. It was Tristan's right arm that was damaged – he could no longer bend it at the elbow – but the Tristan in front of him was holding his left arm awkwardly.

'Enough! Remember the rules,' Neena said, except her voice was Tristan's voice – silky-smooth, with razor blades hidden in the seams. It was uncanny hearing it. Lucas felt his own back stiffen.

'I want explanations,' Neena shouted. 'I want to know who it was that let the girl go.'

She turned to face Shula, who swallowed hard in response and let the arm of her robe slip down another inch, revealing her bandage and a large scoop of cleavage.

'Was it you, Shula?' Neena demanded.

Shula shook her head. 'No. No, I didn't do anything. I got shot.' She pushed her bandaged arm towards Neena. 'A Hunter showed up. It wasn't our fault.'

Neena took a step towards her, the leather of her shoes creaking on the wooden floorboards. 'You think that excuses are going to wash with me, Shula? This is the Brotherhood,' she barked. 'Failure is not an option. Now, drop to the floor and give me fifty.'

Shula froze, her eyes widened and then narrowed to points. 'Neena?' she said. She took a step towards Tristan. 'Neena, is that you?'

The shape before her began to shimmer like a hummingbird. Briefly Neena appeared, her freckled face grinning, before morphing back into Tristan.

'I'm going to kill you!' Shula screamed.

Neena shifted so fast that the others caught only the sight of a small, brown, feathered creature flying past Shula's outstretched hands. Neena landed on the windowsill and tweeted victoriously.

Lucas watched her and allowed himself a small smile.

'Come here, little bird, come here,' Shula cooed, reaching out her hands.

The bird flapped its wings and took off towards Lucas. He felt the air tingle next to him and something brush his arm. He turned his head and found himself staring at a stranger – a twenty-something-year-old man, tall, with dark hair and grey eyes and a sullen stare. He looked suddenly familiar. Then he laughed under his breath. Neena laughed too, lifting an arm and running it through her hair – pushing it back off her forehead. He became aware that he was doing the same. Neena was mirroring him.

'Very funny,' Lucas murmured.

Neena raised an eyebrow.

Lucas frowned at himself. Was that really how he looked to others?

'You gotta scowl, Neena, if you want to be more convincing as Lucas,' Shula said, apparently no longer trying to kill her.

'Yeah, you gotta be all *too cool for school* and strut around in the shadows looking all moody and everything,' Joshua sneered.

Lucas lazily moved his head so he could look at Joshua. He chewed the inside of his lip while he wondered who in all the realms had ever thought that recruiting Thirsters to the Brotherhood was a good idea.

'You been studying Lucas's moves, Joshua? Maybe you should have stuck to the shadows too – then you wouldn't look like the mechanically reclaimed meat patty you do right now.' Shula laughed.

There were snorts of derision, broken by the soft sound of Grace's voice.

'He's coming,' she said quietly, her eyes flying open.

5

Joshua sniffed hard. 'It's Tristan,' he said.

Lucas wondered who else he thought it might be. Tristan was the only other person in the building apart from them. Humans couldn't get inside the old Mission. There was a huge security gate at the top of the road down to it with an *Enter at own risk: Trespassers will be shot* sign stuck on it. Which always made Lucas laugh, as it so baldly undersold the treatment.

What it *really* should say, he thought, was something like: *Enter at own risk: Trespassers may be shot, drunk, eaten, poisoned, sliced or attacked by a wild animal. The psychic will tell you which.*

Beside him Neena shifted back to herself. Lucas cast a look at Caleb, who'd slunk into the corner. He was wearing sunglasses, held together with some electrical tape where they'd cracked across the bridge. It was hard to tell what he was thinking but his tail had stopped flickering. He'd been silent all this time but that was his usual state of being: silence, flickering and the occasional bout of snarling.

Tristan opened the door – the real Tristan this time. He was dressed exactly how Neena had portrayed him – in a charcoal grey suit with a white shirt and grey tie that matched his hair. His eyes swept the room. He walked to the front, his bad arm held stiffly at his side, and stood there looking the six of them

40

over, taking in their various states of disarray and burnt flesh. Lucas could hear Shula fidgeting, Caleb's tail rubbing against the wall and Joshua's nasal breathing. At his side, he could sense Neena shimmering lightly.

Finally, Tristan opened his mouth. 'Who is going to explain to me why she's still alive?'

The razor blades were out.

There was an answering silence. No one moved and no one breathed. Everyone waited for somebody else to answer.

'There was a Hunter. He surprised us.' Shula spoke up eventually, her voice wavering.

Tristan turned on her. 'Your job is to *kill* Hunters. Not to be *surprised* by them.'

He rounded on Grace. 'How did you not see him, Grace? You told us we had a window of opportunity.'

'He slipped through.' She shrugged, the only one of them who didn't appear fazed by Tristan's mood. 'You know how it works. My visions are sometimes hazy.'

Tristan narrowed his eyes at her. 'There were six of you and only two of them. One an untrained human girl. What happened?' Tristan surveyed the room, looking for an answer.

Lucas resisted the urge to melt into the shadows. Instead he stood straight-backed against the wall, his face impassive, waiting for the rage to abate. Tristan usually went for shock and awe tactics.

'I *asked* what happened,' Tristan shouted again.

'Caleb. Caleb happened,' Shula answered, checking over her shoulder that Caleb and his tail were out of range and under control. Caleb glared at her from across the room, his tail swishing in an arc.

41

Tristan ignored them both and turned to Lucas instead. 'I want details. Lucas?'

Lucas held his gaze. 'The girl put up a fight.'

A deep furrow appeared between Tristan's eyebrows. 'She's not trained.'

Lucas kept his voice low in response to Tristan's raised one. 'She can handle herself.'

Caleb suddenly spoke up, his voice angry and breathless. 'She knocked off my glasses, damn it. They're broken. And not one of you bothered to help me out,' he hissed at the others.

'Yeah, like I'm going to help you and get sliced to salami in the process,' Shula yelled.

Tristan interrupted, his voice dropping back to normal. 'Shula, what happened to your arm?'

'I got shot.'

'By the girl?'

'No, by the Hunter. He was there. It was like he knew we were coming. I was just about to kill her when he turned up out of the blue.'

'Who was it?' Tristan asked, taking a step forward. 'Did you see?'

'Oh yeah,' Shula nodded.

'And?' Tristan said. It seemed like he was about to grab Shula by the arms but then suddenly remembered he shouldn't.

'It was Victor,' Neena cut in.

Tristan turned his head to look at Neena. '*Victor?*'

'Yes.' She nodded.

Tristan looked at the rest of them for any sign of disagreement. When no one offered any, he shook his head. 'Still, six of you and only one of them. Truly spectacular.'

'He shone one of those torch things at me,' Joshua whined.

Tristan studied him. It looked like he was thinking the same thing that Lucas had been thinking a few minutes before, questioning the worth of having a low-grade Thirster in the Brotherhood. 'I gathered that,' he said eventually. 'Here. Have some of this.'

He threw a silver Thermos at Joshua, who caught it in the one hand that wasn't fried like a chicken's claw. Lucas watched as Joshua's fangs flew out and his eyes filmed over, becoming glassy. 'Is it human?' Joshua asked as he undid the top of the flask and sniffed the contents.

Tristan raised his eyebrows as if to say, *What the hell else would it be?* 'Yes, it's human,' he said. 'You know the rules. Human blood only within the Brotherhood. You took an oath.'

Joshua shrugged and then started glugging back what was inside. Thick, red liquid started pouring down his chin and dripping onto his chest.

Lucas watched in horrified fascination. The smell alone was enough to turn his stomach, even without the added visual of a Thirster with no table manners wiping his hand across his chest and licking it clean. The fascination was with the process which saw the flesh on Joshua's arm and shoulder knitting back together even as he shook the last drips from the bottom of the Thermos and ran his tongue around the lid. It happened as quickly as a skin forming on a pan of simmering milk. The others were watching too, even Grace.

'Lucas, where were you in all this?'

Lucas tore his eyes off Joshua and looked over at Tristan. Here it came.

'Half-and-half couldn't make it across the lot without being seen,' Joshua said with his mouth full, wiping a trail of bloody spittle off his lips with the back of his arm. He paused to lick it up.

Lucas ignored him. 'Like Shula said, the Hunter turned up. Joshua was down, Shula got shot. Caleb was blinded. I figured the only option was to get out before one of us got killed. I didn't know if there were other Hunters nearby.'

'How very collegiate of you. Putting your brothers ahead of the kill.'

Lucas stayed silent. Wasn't that what the Brotherhood's oath said they should do? He bit his lip to stop himself from reminding Tristan of the fact. Tristan didn't like being spoken back to.

'What do we do now?' Tristan asked.

It was a rhetorical question but Shula answered him anyway. 'Let's go back and kick their asses,' she said, clapping her hands together.

'Tonight?' Neena asked. She had dark circles under her eyes and clearly wasn't up for a repeat session of the night's hash-up.

'Let's go back tomorrow night. Without Caleb. Even a girl – a pathetic little human girl – could take him,' Shula said.

'She wasn't *that* pathetic,' Joshua answered, discarding the Thermos with a belch. 'She kicked your ass, Shula. Hmmm,' he said, leaning in close to her and sniffing loudly. 'Mmmmm, Colombian, I think. Fresh roasted.'

Shula scowled at him. He laughed at her and started flexing his arm, admiring the pale new skin that had formed.

'I'm coming too. I'm finishing this,' Caleb said, stepping forward.

The others stared at him. No one argued, though – you couldn't argue with him when his tail was arching over his head like that.

Tristan interrupted them, his voice cutting a silent swathe through the middle of them. 'You think you get second chances in this game? The Hunters will have strengthened their protection. She's too important to them. She'll likely be untouchable now until she's trained.'

'We still have a chance. We could get her,' Shula tried again.

'No,' Tristan answered. 'We had our chance. You failed. No one's going anywhere. It's too dangerous – if she manages to kill one of you, which frankly wouldn't surprise me, we'd be in even more trouble than we are now.' He paused, looking grim. 'I need to speak to the Elders. Clean yourself up,' he said, looking at Joshua, his lip curling in distaste, 'it's nearly sunrise. I'll see you all tomorrow night.'

They glanced at each other and then one by one moved towards the door. Lucas hung back, letting the others go ahead. He wanted the chance to speak to Tristan alone.

Grace was ahead of Lucas. He noticed the expression in her cloudy blue eyes. She was somewhere a million miles away. He reached to hold the door open for her. She smiled absently and walked on through, her arm brushing his hand as she went.

He heard her gasp and for a moment thought she'd stubbed her toe on the door jamb. Then he saw her eyes. They'd widened into two big blue pools and were fixed on him in abject horror. Her lips parted and a question formed but then she seemed to come to, her gaze dropping to the floor. She frowned and was gone in the next second, racing down the corridor.

Lucas stood watching her. Halfway to the stairs she paused and looked back at him over her shoulder, still frowning, and with fear in her eyes.

Lucas stared after her. What had she seen? She had seen

something, he knew that – but what? Grace never usually reacted to the flashes she saw – of the future or the past. She never even bought lottery tickets.

He wondered vaguely if it was bad, if she'd seen his death, and noted with detachment that he felt nothing about that except maybe a fleeting curiosity about who would kill him. Not how, or where, or when, but *who*. He didn't feel scared, though, he thought with some satisfaction.

'Lucas?'

Lucas started. Tristan was talking to him.

'Walk with me,' he said, striding past and out into the corridor. Lucas followed him, his curiosity piqued. They walked in silence until Tristan stopped outside the training room and held open the door. Lucas hid his frown and stepped ahead of him into the room. Weapons were piled on a table and hung on the walls – everything from blades and swords to crossbows and machine guns, though there were more of the former and less of the latter, there being a general suspicion of human, modern weaponry amongst the Elders.

Tristan shut the door, shrugged off his jacket and strode to the furthest wall, grabbing a slender, heavily hilted sword from the table as he went. He tossed it to Lucas, who caught it reflexively in his right hand and brought it up to an offensive position levelled straight at Tristan's chest. Tristan smiled and with a flourish unsheathed another sword which he'd slid from a casing on the wall. The metal gleamed blue under the lights.

Lucas bounced onto the balls of his feet and started circling. Tristan was a Shadow Warrior like him so there was no point in fading – he'd see him instantly. Already Lucas's heart rate was raised, his palms beginning to sweat, and he took a moment to straighten his grip on his sword. They were fairly evenly matched in terms of height and build, but Tristan was injured in one arm and twenty-five years older. Even so, Lucas wasn't about to underestimate the man.

'Whose fault was it tonight?' Tristan asked, lunging suddenly towards Lucas, his sword a blur in his left hand.

'No one's,' Lucas answered, parrying the blow easily.

Tristan took another step towards him. 'It's always *someone*'s fault, Lucas. I know you're all young and,' he grimaced, 'inexperienced. I realise the situation is unusual. But if the Brotherhood can't even handle a seventeen-year-old girl without full power, who's not even been trained yet, then our situation is worse than the Elders would have us believe.' He swung at Lucas again.

Lucas swallowed his answer and spun out of the way as Tristan's blade cut the air in front of his face. Tristan's mention of the Elders had silenced him. The Brotherhood had been almost destroyed barely a year ago. Lucas and the others were young bloods, barely trained, there to replace the generation before who had all been hunted to death. All except for Tristan whose injury and age took him out of the fight.

As the sole survivor of the previous generation of the Brotherhood, Tristan's job was now to train the next generation – Lucas and the others. For a moment Lucas saw the situation from Tristan's perspective. He didn't envy him having to report back to the Elders on this one.

'Like I said,' Lucas said, feinting to the left and coming up behind Tristan, 'she wasn't exactly your average human. She fought back. She was quick. Faster than I've seen before in a human. As quick as a fully trained Hunter.' He paused, remembering how she'd surprised Caleb. 'And instinctive.' He thought of how fast she'd been when she hit Shula. None of them had seen it coming, not even Grace. 'She's a natural.'

'She would be,' Tristan said, frowning now as Lucas backed him into the corner towards one of the arched windows.

Lucas darted forwards, his blade striking Tristan's. 'I think you should send me back. Alone,' he said.

Tristan's sword dropped a few inches as he studied Lucas carefully. Lucas didn't make a move, though he could have used the opportunity to disarm Tristan with a low blow to the elbow. Instead he stood there, waiting, not breathing.

'Now's not the time for revenge, Lucas,' Tristan finally said. 'That will come later. The girl first. She's the priority.'

Lucas's own sword fell to his side. 'Let me go back,' he said quickly. 'Not for revenge. That's not what I'm talking about. I can wait for that. I don't just want Victor. I want them all.'

Tristan tipped his head to one side as though to listen better. 'What are you proposing?'

'What if one of us could get close to a Hunter?'

'You mean close as in forming a relationship with one?'

Lucas nodded. 'Yes. What if I could work my way close to her? To this girl, Evie.'

Tristan shook his head, then strode past him back towards the sword sheath he'd discarded on the floor. He bent to pick it up and carefully slid his sword into it. Finally he turned. 'You're getting better. Still, you could have disarmed me but you chose not to. Your weakness is your humanity, Lucas.'

Lucas frowned, thrown by the sudden change in the conversation. Had Tristan not heard his suggestion? But before he could ask again, Tristan spoke. 'Lucas,' he said, with something of a sigh, 'your power is unusual, you're almost as fast as your father and, despite the fact that you're diluted with human, it doesn't seem to have impaired your ability to disappear – but you're still young. You haven't been able to develop your powers of perception or judgement yet.'

Lucas tried to wipe the scowl off his face, to keep it free of shadows. Who was Tristan to tell him about judgement or perception? He could judge and perceive just fine, better than any of the others. And since when was humanity a weakness?

Lucas took a step towards Tristan, his sword still clutched in his hand. 'Listen,' he said, 'the Elders are worried. We can't fight the Hunters right now. They almost destroyed us and, let's face it, we're not putting up much of a fight at the moment. The Brotherhood isn't exactly what it was. You're right – we're young and inexperienced but we're all you've got.' He paused, trying to rein in the eagerness in his voice. 'But what if you change the pattern of attack? The Brotherhood keeps fighting the same way. For a thousand years, our attack methods haven't changed. And we keep getting beaten as a result. But what if we could use the girl as a way to learn about them? Find out how they train Hunters – what they know about us. We could find a way to beat *them*.'

Lucas watched and waited for Tristan's response, his heart beating fast, a buzzing energy racing around his body that he finally recognised as excitement. He couldn't figure out what the excitement was about though – whether it was the thought of getting away from this place and the others with their petty fights and lethal body parts; or away from Tristan's incessant lessons and training schedule; or of getting close to a Hunter without the others nearby to mess things up.

What would it be like to sense revenge like a scent on the breeze and know that it was right there – obtainable – just in front of him?

'It's an interesting idea,' Tristan eventually said.

'I'm half human. I'm the only one who can get past the Hunters without them sensing me,' Lucas said, trying to read Tristan's expression. 'You've never had that before in the Brotherhood. Maybe it's not the curse the others think it is. Maybe it's actually your way in. It's worth a shot, isn't it?'

Tristan's mouth tightened in thought. Lucas tried to keep his face blank – to act like he didn't really care whether Tristan said yes or no, when really inside he was poised on the answer as though it was a sword he was about to fall forward onto.

'OK.' Tristan finally nodded. 'You have one month.'

He didn't say what would happen after that month but it was clear, hanging there in the air. After one month Evie would be dead. She was dead either way, though – despite what Tristan had said to the others about not going back for her, the Brotherhood would want to get her before she was fully trained. Whether she was surrounded by Hunters or not.

'OK. I'll leave tonight,' Lucas said, wanting to get going before Tristan changed his mind or decided to talk to the Elders about it. He marvelled at how easy it had been to convince him.

'Lucas?'

He stopped with his hand on the door.

'Victor is not stupid,' Tristan said. 'Don't get caught.'

'He doesn't know who I am,' Lucas replied. 'Besides, I'm good at blending in.' He turned once more to leave.

'One more thing, Lucas,' Tristan called after him. 'Don't make this personal.'

Lucas met Tristan's stare head on. Around the edges of Tristan's brown contact lenses he could make out the yellow of his actual eyes. Lucas nodded at the man in the suit, the only survivor of his father's generation of the Brotherhood, and then closed the door.

6

It was the phone that woke her, not fangs. There was no one standing over her in a black leather coat, with a razor-sharp tail poised to slash her to pieces, no girl in a too-tight pink minidress lunging for her – but nonetheless Evie found herself sitting bolt upright in bed, with a baseball bat clutched in her hands, ready to swing. It took a few seconds for her brain to process that the room was empty and for her heart to stop hammering against her ribs. She fell backwards on top of the bedcovers, letting the bat slide through her fingers and clunk to the floor.

Evie rolled her head to the side and stared at her surroundings. Nothing seemed to have changed. The room was as it always was, stacked under the eaves of the Victorian clapboard house, the sloping ceiling above the bed making it look as if she was sleeping in a tent. A pink tent, which she couldn't be bothered to redecorate, scattered with the hurricane debris of her life, which she couldn't be bothered to clear up, because she had no intention of sticking around.

Dolls she'd thrown on top of the wardrobe years ago were trying to free-dive to the floor, school books were stacked on the desk among a sea of paper. Clothes were alternatively toppling off a chair and slung over the door of her wardrobe. On the night table was a picture of her dad, propped next to a teddy bear clutching a heart, into which she'd stuck pins.

Nothing appeared different. Evie slid her hand under the pillow, checking if it was there. It was. She took a breath, felt it swell her lungs.

So it was real. Last night *had* happened. Nothing was the same then, despite appearances. Everything was different. Slowly she drew the photograph out from under the pillow. Her eyes stayed stuck to the ceiling. She wasn't yet ready to look at it.

Eventually she swivelled her head to the clock on her bedside table. It said 7.03 a.m. She didn't remember sleeping. She was still in her jeans and T-shirt from last night – she hadn't even bothered to kick off her Converse. She hadn't planned on sleeping. After Victor had spent an age convincing her that the Hunters had her back and wouldn't let any Unhumans near her, he'd still insisted on following her home, which had totally undermined his efforts to make her feel safe. Yet this morning, in this room full of childhood pinks, lying on top of a patchwork quilt, with buttery sunshine easing through the blind, it was impossible to feel in danger, either.

'*Unhumans.*' Evie whispered the word.

It sounded just as ridiculous in daylight.

She lifted her arm and studied the burn on it. With her finger she traced the shape of a splayed hand.

A human hadn't done that. What had Victor called the girl again? A Mixen? Evie closed her eyes and tried to recall what the others were called. The one with the tail, and the vampires. Thirsters? How was she supposed to fight these people? She wasn't Blade. But Victor seemed convinced she was a Hunter. That she was meant to fight them. And did she have any choice in the matter anyway?

That's when she brought the photograph up to her face. She

had studied it for over an hour last night until her eyes had started to pixelate it. There she was as a baby – truthfully, it could have been a picture of any baby. But this baby did have dark hair and navy blue eyes and the same shallow dimple in her left cheek that Evie had when she bothered to smile. Once she'd established the likelihood that it was indeed her in the picture she'd started studying the other two people. These were her parents, Victor had told her. Her birth parents. James and Megan Hunter. She whispered the names aloud, feeling a rush that was followed by a cut that drained it away. She'd never had much interest in finding the parents who'd abandoned her, so she didn't know why it was hitting her so hard. The last year had been so full of loss she was on first name terms with all its parts – boiling anger followed by hissing sadness and eventually an ice-cold numbness that was infinitely preferable to either of the first two.

She could feel herself being pulled backwards out of the ice, could sense anger starting to defrost her, and she fought against it. She fought against it hard.

She swiped the back of her arm against her eyes.

It was her mother's face she was so fascinated by. Her mother was holding her tight in her arms and smiling so hard at the camera that at first Evie had focused only on the smile – but when she finally looked closer she saw her mother's eyes – blue like Evie's own – were sad, haunted even. The three of them were outdoors somewhere cold – they were all bundled up, Evie looking like a squashed duvet with a face. Her father was dark-haired and good-looking. That felt weird to say. She revised it in her head to handsome, charismatic, perhaps. He was staring upwards, not directly at the camera. His eyes were on the person taking the picture. Where had they been? What had they both been thinking? Why did her mother look so sad?

Evie turned the photograph over and began studying the words scrawled on the back, searching for some hidden meaning that she might have missed last night.

'*Evie*,' she read, her fingers tracing the words, trying to find some connection with them, with the ink that had come from the pen that her mum had once held.

'*Evie*,' she read to herself as though repeating a prayer. '*We love you more than you will ever know. You are our Evie* – always remember what you mean, to us. *We are sorry we couldn't be there to watch you grow and keep you safe. We hope one day you will understand why and will forgive us. Above all, we hope that you make the choices we couldn't. We will love you always, Mum and Dad x.*'

They hadn't abandoned her. They had loved her. They had always loved her. Evie was squinting at the words when she heard a scratching at the door. She looked up at the dog that had appeared in the crack.

'Lobo, come here, boy,' Evie called.

The husky edged the door open with his paw and leapt onto the bed beside her. Evie wrapped her arms around him and buried her head in the white patch of fur on his neck.

'Hey, Lobo,' she whispered.

He nudged her away and licked her face in reply, growling low.

'I had the craziest night,' she said, by way of explanation, wondering how a dog could read her better than most people.

'Sweetheart?'

Evie started, ramming the photo under the pillow and looking up as her mum poked her head around the door.

'Oh, you're up already,' she said, seeing Evie was dressed. 'You got in late last night, I didn't think you'd be awake yet. Joe's not working you too hard, is he? I'm going to have words with him.'

Evie looked at her mum, who had started picking up the clothes littering the room.

'No. No, he's good. I was just, um, hanging out, doing stuff.' She jumped off the bed and took the clothes out of her mum's hands, bundled them up and threw them into the cupboard.

Her mum let out a shriek. 'What on earth happened to your arm?' she said, reaching out to take hold of it.

'Nothing, nothing, it's fine,' Evie said, stepping backwards and hiding her arm behind her back. 'I just spilt some coffee. It's fine, honestly. Doesn't hurt.'

Evie's mum frowned at her and Evie noticed how much more lined her mother's face was these days. She'd always been a lot older than Evie's friends' parents but now she looked old enough to be her grandmother.

She smiled weakly. 'It's fine, Mum, honest.'

Her mum sighed as though she couldn't be bothered to argue. 'OK, listen, Mrs Lewington just took a call from her sister, the one that lives in Michigan. She's taken a turn and is in hospital, she's not sure exactly what's happened because they were less than clear on the telephone but anyway, the long and the short of it is, she's packing her bags and leaving and I've no idea how long she's going to be gone and . . .'

Her mum was talking in a rush, her eyes dropped to the carpet. Evie stepped forward and put a hand on her arm to still her. She wanted to tell her that it was fine, that it would be OK, that they'd manage without their lodger, but her mum had bustled off to the bedside and when Evie turned she found her straightening up with the baseball bat in her hand.

She held it up to Evie with a quizzical look. Evie snatched it from her and shoved it behind the door, ignoring the look.

'Mum, it's OK, I got a new job. That'll help. Until the life insurance pays up.'

She knew her mum would never take any money from her but the fact was they needed it and now she had a new job earning thirty-five dollars an hour. She checked herself. Did the job actually exist? Had it ever? Had Victor been lying to get her onside?

'What do you mean, a new job?' Her mother shook her head. 'You've got two already.'

Evie shrugged. 'I got a third.'

'Evie! What about school?' Her mum's lips were pursed.

'It's only till school starts up again. Then I'll cut my shifts back. Don't worry, I'll still help out at the store. This is just really good money.'

Her mum was still frowning. Here it came. 'What's the job? I didn't know anyone was hiring.'

Evie walked to the dresser so her mum wouldn't see her face. 'There's a new store opening in town,' she said, burrowing through the drawers, 'where Cardman's used to be. A clothing boutique.'

'A *boutique*?'

'Yeah.' Evie cleared her throat. 'It's kind of high end. I doubt it'll make any money but it pays well.' She really hoped Victor wasn't lying to her.

'Well, OK . . .' Her mum sounded annoyed at not having heard the news sooner. 'I'll maybe pop on by at lunchtime to have a look-see.'

Of course she would. Evie smiled at her. 'I gotta get ready,' Evie said, 'but, Mum, don't worry, it'll be OK.'

Her mum nodded, her eyes flittering over the room. 'Yes, yes,

I'm sure you're right.' She crossed to the door. 'Oh, by the way, I almost forgot, Tom came by last night looking for you. He said the diner was dark. He couldn't find you.'

Evie froze. 'I was round the back, putting out the trash.' Her heart struggled to find its footing. What if Tom had walked around the back looking for her? What if he had walked into the middle of it all? He could have been killed.

'Did you two sort things out?' her mum asked.

Evie looked up sharply. 'Sort things out?' she growled.

Her mother ducked out of the room. 'Well, I think you should just hear him out. And you don't know for a fact he was drunk. The police certainly didn't think so. I'm just saying. You know how I stand on this.'

Yeah, Evie knew how she and the whole world stood on this. The world just didn't seem to care how *she* stood on it. It was all she could do not to slam the door after her mother had left. Instead, she flopped onto the bed and buried her face in Lobo's fur.

She sat straight back up again. 'You stink, boy. Come on, let's go for a walk.'

7

Evie was late so she drove, parking her dad's old Ford pickup outside the store that used to be Cardman's Bookshop. The boards had been taken down and a new sign in lavish purple script already hung over the door. It said simply, *Lassonde*.

Evie doubted anyone in town would know how to say it right. Not that she expected many customers. She could see Victor through the glass front sitting on a stool by the cash register, surrounded by boxes and with a coffee cup in one hand. He was staring out of the window, chewing on his lip, but he smiled as soon as he saw her, sprang off the stool and crossed to the door to let her in.

'You're here,' he said, ushering her inside.

'Yes, why?' asked Evie, taking in the rails along both sides, empty except for a few canary yellow dresses and two red velvet chairs, each wide enough to host a dinner party in, that had been placed facing each other across a low table in the centre of the shop. 'Did you think I wouldn't show or were you worried I got eaten in the night?'

Victor put his coffee cup down and indicated the velvet chairs in the centre of the room. 'You were safe. I told you already they won't come back.'

He turned his back on her but she could have sworn he finished the sentence with the word *tonight*.

She flopped onto one of the chairs, tilting her head to look past the plastic limbs of the mannequins stationed in the window out onto the street. Old Mrs Frampton walked past, her mouth falling open in astonishment at the naked mannequins and the sheer decadence of the velvet couches within. She must think this is a brothel, Evie realised with a slight smile, wondering what that would make her in Mrs Frampton's small-town imagination.

Oh well, it wasn't like she wasn't used to being gossiped about.

'You keep saying I'm safe,' Evie said, turning back to Victor, 'but how do I know you're not just telling me that so I don't freak out?'

Victor turned around with a china cup poised in his hand and offered it to her. She noticed the pot of fresh steaming coffee on the counter by the till and looked back at Victor.

'Freshly ground Costa Rican decaff,' he said.

She took the cup with a raised eyebrow. What was the point of decaff?

Victor was wearing fresh clothes – dark suit trousers and a checked cotton shirt – no tie or frothy cravat thing. What time had he got here this morning? she wondered. Where was he even sleeping? She turned her head and glanced towards the back of the store. There was a door which she assumed led through to a storeroom, and a fitting room to the side with a black velvet drape and a gold-framed floor-length mirror in which she saw herself staring back, eyes like saucers ringed with black shadows, hair damp from the shower and scraped up into a messy ponytail while still wet.

She turned back to Victor. He was handing her a small china jug of milk now, his fingers too large to fit through the handle.

'You need to learn to trust me, Evie,' he said. 'That's your first lesson.' He paused. 'The second lesson is that you need to learn you can't trust anybody else.'

She thought about that. She didn't trust anybody any more, anyway. So that wasn't exactly going to be a problem. And Lobo was a dog so she assumed he didn't count in Victor's reckoning.

'So, are you ready?'

Evie looked up. 'For what?' she asked.

'To become a Hunter,' Victor answered with a small smile.

Evie set the coffee cup on the low table. 'Do I have a choice?' she asked.

'We always have choices, Evie.'

She shook her head at him. 'No we don't.' Her voice was angry. It took her by surprise how angry she was. 'That's a lie. This is not a choice. I either choose not to become a Hunter and get killed in some hideous manner or I choose to become a Hunter and get killed in some hideous manner.' She saw Victor trying to suppress a smile. 'What *is* the life expectancy of a Hunter anyway?' she demanded. 'How old are you?'

Victor held up a hand. 'Listen,' he said, 'it wasn't my choice either, Evie, but you *are* a Hunter and you can fight it all you like but you'll find in the end you can't deny who you are.'

She tipped her chin up so she could glare at him. 'Who am I?' she demanded.

Now he really did smile, a slow smile that warmed his face and made her soften towards him and which deflected her anger, even though he'd avoided the question as to her life expectancy. 'You're Evie Hunter,' he said, her name coming out sounding all French and mysterious. 'You come from a long line of Hunters. We're all descendants of the original Hunter family but you're a direct descendant. The blood runs strong in you, that's why you're on the most wanted list.'

She could feel herself frowning as she brought her legs up onto the seat and started hugging them.

'The rest of us are alley cats,' Victor continued, 'bastards, distant cousins – the genes turn up all over the place, sometimes,' he winced a little, 'in the most unlikely places – but the important thing to remember, and I wish someone had told me this when I was first discovered . . .'

Discovered? What was he? The New World?

He held her gaze intently. 'You are still the same person you were yesterday.'

Evie considered this for a few seconds then stood quickly. 'The same person I was yesterday?' she demanded, her voice more shrill than she'd been aiming for. 'Except I'm not, am I? I'm not some seventeen-year-old girl living in a small town dreaming of getting the hell out of it. I'm some kind of demon hunter.'

'You're not a *demon* hunter, Evie. You're a Hunter of Unhumans – or you will be when you're trained. At the moment you only have half the power you will eventually have, if that.'

'Oh great.' Evie threw her hands up in the air. 'I'm an untrained demon hunter with only crap half-powers, suddenly expected to go all Buffy and save the world.'

She could see him biting the inside of his cheek to stop from laughing at her and it made her stomach muscles clench.

'Evie,' he said quietly, his voice a *shush* in itself, 'relax. It's not as terrifying as it seems.'

Was he joking? Had he forgotten that she'd been there last night? That she'd come face to face with terrifying and his best friend horrifyingly deadly?

'You get help,' Victor reassured. 'There are quite a few of us. There are three Hunters patrolling the borders of the town as we speak. You'll meet them soon enough. You're well protected and you will continue to be until you're trained.'

Something pulled in her, a certainty, a thrill even, when he said the word *trained*. She frowned at herself. She wasn't even sure she *wanted* to train. She wasn't about to get excited about a career path that could lead her to an early grave. Yet, there was a *yet*. Something was pulling her towards that path – something undeniable. She had a feeling in her gut that she couldn't ignore, even though her head was still trying to find excuses.

'If there are so many of you, then why do you need me?' she asked, feeling the lift of her chin as she said it, knowing at the same time that it was futile. There was no going back from this. There was no choice. The memory of her parents' faces leapt into her mind.

Victor put a hand on her shoulder. 'I'll tell you all you need to know but first things first.' He swivelled her easily towards the empty railings. 'Start unpacking that box over there.'

Evie glanced at him then back at the six or seven sealed boxes in front of her. On the side of one *Marc Jacobs* was stamped. Her eyes flew to the others. *Stella McCartney, Alexander McQueen, Valentino, Chanel, Philip Lim.* She stared at Victor. 'We're actually opening a store?'

Victor looked at her in bemusement. 'Yes, what did you think we were doing?'

'Er, I thought you were here to maybe teach me how to kick some demon butt or something. Because forgive me if I got this wrong but I don't think Chanel garments are going to do it – unless I'm missing something. Are demons allergic to fashion? Am

I supposed to blind them with sequins? Give them a cardiac arrest by showing them the price tags?'

'Unhumans, Evie, not demons. We're not living in Biblical times, let's update our language please.'

She shook her head. 'Well, whatever, do you want me to unpack dresses or do you want me to be a Hunter – because a second ago you were all about the Hunter and now you're all about the fashion, so please choose. And, by the way – you are still paying me, right?'

'Yes. Thirty-five an hour. And right now I want you to unpack those boxes over there and start filling these rails with New York's finest designer offerings.'

Evie took a step forward and dropped to her knees in front of the first box. 'Is this like *Karate Kid* where I learn how to do martial arts moves by hanging clothes up?'

She heard Victor sigh. 'No. This is our *cover*, Evie,' he said. 'You don't think people would start asking questions if you started hanging out with the only black man in town?'

'Hey,' she replied indignantly, 'I know it's Smallville but we're not racist.'

He looked at her with heavy lids. 'I'm also twenty years older than you and I know how people can talk.'

She shut her mouth. He was right about that much, especially in this town.

'Besides, I don't want my reputation destroyed,' he added.

'Your reputation?' she blurted.

He winked at her and she pulled a face at him. Out of the corner of her eye she saw a silver glint, something dancing through the air, and instinctively threw up her hand to catch it.

'Ow,' she said, as the scissors caught her palm. 'Did nobody ever teach you not to throw scissors? You could have blinded me. I could have lost a finger. Does this job have benefits?' she asked as an afterthought, rubbing the palm of her hand.

Victor arched an eyebrow. 'You caught them, didn't you? And yes, working with me. That's benefit enough.'

Evie grunted in reply and started slicing into the first box.

'You have natural instincts, Evie. We'll improve them, yes, but you're a natural. Let me hazard a guess – state athletics champion? Dropped out of cheerleading at fourteen?'

He was hazarding a guess? She narrowed her eyes at him. How did he know all this?

'Too bitchy?' he continued. 'Too competitive? Or just too easy? You excelled in track but also ball games. Your reflexes are top of the range, your hand/eye co-ordination unparalleled. My guess is you found it all pointless but that you're not naturally competitive when it comes to games anyway. In things that you don't think are important.'

She could feel her face flaming but Victor seemed to be enjoying his little game of psychoanalysis. He tipped his head to one side, studying her with interest. 'You weren't interested in the medals or the glory because it was no competition for you. Other things interested you more.'

She glared at him. How did he know this? Even she wouldn't have been able to put this into words. She'd cheerleaded until the point had come where she'd wanted to shove the pompoms up the cheerleading coach's butt. And she had always been fast. She had been state running champion until last summer when her dad had died. Then she'd decided the only running that mattered was the running away kind. There was irony in that, she saw now.

Victor carried on, oblivious to her stare and dropped jaw. 'You're bright – brighter than your classmates – but you hide it because you don't want to appear different but you are and you've always felt that way, haven't you? An outsider? Like you didn't quite belong. And now,' he said as an aside, 'now you know why. But before, before you didn't want to appear ungrateful to your parents or those around you by acting like you wanted to leave. You didn't want to disappoint your parents by making them think this life – this town – wasn't good enough. After everything they've done for you. You didn't even go looking for your birth parents. I found that surprising.'

Evie felt the pinprick of tears behind her eyes and swallowed the lump in her throat. There was no way she was crying in front of him. She kept her head down, her fingers gripping the scissors, stopping herself from hurling them at him to stop him from talking. The last six months she'd suffered an intrusion into her privacy, but this was an intrusion into her soul. This was all her most private, unspoken secrets and fears laid out on a mortuary slab and dissected with clinical detachment.

'How do you know all this?' she asked under her breath.

'We've been watching you, Evie. You didn't think we'd leave you here as a baby and forget all about you, did you?' He looked at her in wide-eyed bemusement. 'We were waiting until we felt you were old enough – ready – before we broke it to you.'

She chewed her lip. It was too much to comprehend that her whole life had been a science study. Strangers had been watching her. It made her feel a little unreal, as though she had just discovered she was a character in a film, that everyone in her life was just an actor, all in on a joke she was the butt of.

'So,' she smarted, finally looking up and trying to act like his words had meant nothing, even though her head was a spinning teacup ride, 'you've been spying on me and now you think you know me because you once read a book on pop psychology. Great. Shall I get on with opening the boxes?'

Victor seemed merely amused with her little outburst. He nodded at her to go ahead. He was observing her every reaction, she thought, as she bent down, feeling his eyes burning into the back of her head. He was weighing her up. But so far he didn't seem disappointed and she realised with a pang that a part of her was glad. Then she got angry with herself. Why did she care about pleasing him?

She ripped open the first box and tissue paper cascaded over the sides. Evie rummaged through it, her hands sinking into watery silks. She drew out a long, pale grey evening dress, with a full tulle underskirt, and held it up.

'Oh, just the thing for all the balls we've got happening around here,' she commented with a sarcastic glance in Victor's direction. Then she flicked over the price tag. 'This has got a three-thousand-dollar price tag!'

She looked up at Victor in astonishment. That was almost twice as much money as she had earned the entire summer working two jobs. She dropped the dress and rifled through the box, pulling out another one – this time a knee-length, blue silk cocktail number. The price tag had just as many zeros as the first one. 'No one in this town can afford to buy this stuff,' she said, looking up at Victor.

Victor was watching her from his vantage point on the red velvet chair, one leg resting on the other knee. 'Exactly,' he said. 'That's the point.' When she continued to look at him dumbfounded, he explained. 'No one will come in to bother us while we're training.'

'Except Mrs Lovell,' Evie said, her attention drawn to the mirror at the back of the shop and its reflection of the street.

'Mrs Lovell?' Victor asked, confused.

The doorbell dinged. Evie leapt up from her tissue paper mound and greeted her mother's oldest friend. 'Mrs Lovell! Good morning.'

She gestured with her hand at Victor who was still reclining on the chair, eyeing Mrs Lovell's polyester jumper and shin-length skirt. 'This is Victor Lassonde.' She enunciated the Lassonde, making it sound as French as she could.

Victor raised himself, putting down his copy of *Vogue* and reaching out his hand. Mrs Lovell stared at it like it was a wild animal, one she wasn't sure she should pet, before taking it briefly and giving it a meagre shake. She stared at her surroundings, her mouth falling open and her eyes widening at the red and black velvet decor and at Victor's beaming white smile amid it all.

'Feel free to browse,' Victor said, spreading his arms wide. 'We're still unpacking, I'm afraid. If you need any help, just give Evie a shout.'

Mrs Lovell murmured her thanks and started flicking through the three yellow dresses hanging up. She glanced over her shoulder at Evie and beckoned her with a motion of her head.

'Is this a size 00?' she asked in a stage whisper.

Evie looked at the tag she was holding up. 'That's the price tag not the size,' she said. 'But it's a 2 if you're interested.'

Mrs Lovell looked at her over the top of her spectacles. 'Do I *look* like a size 2, Evie Tremain? And do I look like I am going to spend thousands of dollars on a scrap of material no bigger than a tea towel?'

Evie bit her tongue, wondering what she was supposed to say

that wouldn't get her fired. 'It's Marc Jacobs,' she offered with a small shrug, 'and that colour would really complement your hair,' she added as an afterthought, looking in Victor's direction. He glanced up at her over the top of his magazine and gave her a look she couldn't read.

'Nice try, Evie. I may not know much about fashion but I *do* know that custard yellow is not that flattering to red hair,' Mrs Lovell answered. 'You just wait until I tell the knitting circle about this.' She lowered her voice once more. 'You'd best not give notice on your other jobs.' A pause. 'Does Joe know you're working here?'

'Not yet,' Evie answered.

Mrs Lovell drew closer. 'Well, you hold on to that job; this one isn't about to last.'

She left, muttering as she went about people with too much money and not enough sense, and Evie went back to unpacking and hanging clothes, getting more and more irritated as she did so. Victor steadfastly refused to answer any questions about anything other than what dresses went on which rack so eventually she gave up trying to find out about her parents and the other Hunters and when she'd learn how to fight as opposed to how to hang strapless dresses. She focused instead on trying to clothe the two mannequins which, after thirty seconds, she estimated was probably more challenging than fighting a demon with a tail. All the while she was thinking back to what Victor had said about her not wanting to disappoint her parents and feeling like she didn't fit in around here.

Even if the Hunters *had* been watching her, it didn't make sense that Victor could know things that she'd never been able to voice herself, stuff that had just been unformed, foggy thoughts in her

69

head. She hadn't wanted to tell her parents that she dreamt of leaving this small farming town and moving somewhere busy and frantic and completely the opposite of here. She couldn't tell them she wanted to move to the other side of the country and maybe become a journalist, because her father had spent her whole life teaching her how to ride horses and shoot rabbits and run a farm, and how could she repay him by telling him that she didn't care about horses and cows' udders and the price of peaches?

Halfway through trying to pull a navy jumpsuit onto one rigid mannequin, still puzzling angrily over what Victor had said, Evie felt the heat of someone's eyes on her. She spun around. The street outside was empty, yet she could have sworn someone had just passed by the window. She had seen the shadow cross her and caught the dark reflection of something in the shiny plastic shoulder of one of the mannequins. The hairs on the back of her neck were raised. She stood there, holding the mannequin's hand for balance, scanning the street.

Maybe she was just paranoid. Maybe that was par for the course. She saw a couple of kids she recognised from her class walking into Joe's Diner opposite but nothing else was out of place on the street.

'Are you OK?'

Evie turned from the window and manoeuvred around the mannequin. Victor had come to stand by her, his face concerned.

'Yeah, I'm fine,' she said. 'I just thought I saw something.' She paused, glancing back over her shoulder at the street. 'You're sure no one is coming back?'

'Well, I don't think there's anything in Mrs Lovell's size.'

'No, I mean the others, the Unhumans.'

Victor sighed loudly. 'They aren't coming back.' His tone said

Stop doubting me. 'They can't get into town. The Brotherhood is small right now and weak. They won't risk it again. And besides, we'd know as soon as they tried to get near.'

'How?' Evie asked, hoping that he'd finally start telling her some of the stuff she needed to know in order to, say, stay alive.

'We can detect Unhumans. We sense them.'

Evie arched an eyebrow.

Victor's voice took on a softer tone. 'Have you ever walked into a room and felt something – a change in the atmosphere – as if it's charged with something? A movement that's out of place? Something that makes your ears prick up or your gut tighten?'

Evie nodded slowly.

Victor's eyes held hers, a dark caramel colour that was hard to look away from. 'That's your instinct. It's the voice in your head that warns you to run if it senses danger.'

She thought back to the night before, when the crazy one with the tail had approached her in the lot. The voice in her head had been loud and clear then.

'Humans do this automatically,' Victor went on, 'subconsciously. We're programmed from childhood to read body language all the time. True, some people are better at it than others. Your instinct, your ability to read a situation is strong, Evie, but with training we'll make it stronger still. Eventually you'll be able to sense an Unhuman within a two-mile radius.'

'How? Do they smell or something?'

'No. Some of them look unusual – Mixen, for example – which helps. But some – Shapeshifters, in particular – can blend and look as normal as you or me. A normal human being wouldn't be able to tell them apart. As a Hunter, your instinct will flare immediately. You'll learn to read the atmosphere around you, to sense the shifts and the changes in energy. It's the same instinct that allows me to read you. I know right now that you're wondering how I know so much about what's going on inside your head – things you probably didn't even know you were feeling.'

Evie froze. Her breathing stilled.

'I can read you,' Victor carried on. 'Not your mind – we're not telepaths – but I can read your body language: the expressions on your face, the way you cross your arms over your chest when you're feeling defensive, the way your breathing goes shallow when I mention your father, the way your jaw sets when you're angry and the way your nostrils flare when anything or anyone annoys you – which is most everyone in this town, myself included.'

Evie swallowed and tried not to flare her nostrils. She uncrossed her arms and willed herself not to move.

'You'll learn to listen to the voice in your head,' he said, tapping the side of his shaved temple, 'and to heed it, because that voice is going to be what keeps you alive.'

Evie sank into the seat. 'It didn't keep my parents alive though, did it?'

Victor's face fell, his lips pursed and a crease line took up residence between his eyes.

'How did they die?' Evie asked in a broken voice. 'I want to know. I *need* to know. I need to know everything. How do I fight these things? When are you going to tell me?'

Victor drew in a deep breath. Then he turned on his heel and walked over to a battered leather trunk that Evie had noticed standing in the corner of the room. He opened the padlock on it and she slunk closer for a better look – wondering if it was going to be full of medieval-looking weapons or something more modern, like guns – but Victor's broad shoulders hid the contents from view. He snapped it shut before she could get a look and turned around holding something in his hands.

He offered it over to her and she saw it was a book. An old, stiff-paged, heavy-as-a-brick book.

'Everything you need to know is in there,' he said, handing it to her.

8

Victor disappeared off to Joe's Diner for lunch, leaving Evie manning the fort. No one had stepped foot inside since Mrs Lovell. They'd watched two dozen or more townspeople stand slack-jawed in front of the window, gaping and pointing at the price tags that Victor had assembled by the mannequins' feet. Then they'd watched every single one of them wander off down the street shaking their heads and laughing. One person even stopped to lean against a lamp post, bent double and heaving with laughter until Evie thought she was going to have to call the paramedics. But Victor had just watched happily, coffee cup in hand, from the door.

Evie sat cross-legged and rested her hands on top of the book as though she could read it through her palms. She closed her eyes and took a deep breath, then opened her eyes and turned the first page.

It was a handwritten book. The ink was red and so faded that it looked to Evie like someone centuries ago had run out of ink and decided to open a vein. The pages were warped and dry as tinder. She had to peer closely to figure out if it was even written in English because the words were so curlicued and ornate they looked like pictograms. Her finger traced the first line, deciphering the letters one by one.

The lore of the Hunter, she read.

O-K, she thought.

Hunters are the defenders of the human realm. Since the early 900s we, the descendants of the Hunter family, have fought to keep this world safe from demons.

Hah! Evie thought, they called them demons back in the day! Maybe she'd stick with that rather than this postmodern Unhuman nonsense. And then she noticed that her hands were trembling.

Taking a sacred oath to protect all humans, Hunters have sacrificed their lives in the name of the oath throughout the last thousand years.

Evie could feel the earthy taste of panic filling her mouth.

To be a Hunter is to be chosen from among the many. It is an honour.

Honour schmoner. Evie swore out loud and turned the page. She'd had enough of her ancestor and his talk of death and duty.

The next page was covered in an intricate drawing of a man in funny-looking clothes – puffy trousers that ended at the knee, a top that looked like a woman's blouse and a long dark cloak that trailed behind him. She peered closer. That wasn't a cloak behind him. It was a tail. She felt her stomach tighten into Medusa knots. The ink had dried to a dull orange but the eyes had been carefully drawn and once upon a time they had been bright red.

Above the picture were the words *Scorpio Demon*. In the corner were a few scratch marks and the number 23. Evie ran her finger over the marks, wondering what they meant.

On the facing page was another page of script. Evie scanned it quickly.

Scorpio Demons are marked by their blindness in this world – we were able to hunt them almost to extinction.

Evie guessed that since the invention of sunglasses they'd been brought back from the brink. But why did they even *want* to be in this world in the first place? Evie didn't understand why any demon would want to come here. Demon realms must really suck if they were willing to fight a war over centuries just so they could hang out in Riverview. What was so good about here? She made a mental note to ask Victor once he was back from lunch.

She turned the page, anxious to swallow as much information as she could before he came back.

A picture of another man, this time slighter and slightly greener. Someone had obviously redone the colour at some more recent point in time because the green shade of the skin leapt off the page. Once more she noticed the fine strike lines at the bottom of the page – about twenty or so. And the number 17 next to them.

Mixen Demon, she read. Do not engage in hand-to-hand combat.

'You don't say', Evie muttered, glancing at the handprint on her arm.

She flipped the page.

Here was a normal-looking demon for a change. Actually quite a good-looking one, if she was allowed to think that, despite the medieval fashion and the glowering face. It looked like someone had taken an eraser to the picture because it was smudged in places, fainter in others, as though it was disappearing off the page, and the ink for the eyes had yellowed somewhat. There was one strike line in the corner of the page, and next to it the number 33. Above the picture it read:

Shadow Warrior.

She could remember Victor mentioning Shadow Warriors but to her knowledge she hadn't come face to face with one yet.

Shadow Warriors are among the most lethal demons in the realms. Their speed and ability to vanish into the shadows makes them a formidable opponent in battle.

Maybe that was why she hadn't come face to face with one yet. Evie kept reading, hoping to find something positive, perhaps a way to avoid meeting one, but there was nothing else except for the comforting words that only one Shadow Warrior had ever been killed or captured by a Hunter. She wondered if the text had been updated since it was first written or if this was the only edition. Another question for Victor. Along with how the hell was she supposed to pick a fight with any of these demons and actually win.

She flicked through the pages until her eyes fell on a page with what looked like a poem written on it. Written in large letters over it were the words, White Light Prophecy. She drew a breath and started reading out loud. 'Of two who remain, a child will be born.'

The doorbell jangled. She looked up. It was Tom.

'Whose child will be born?' he asked, looking at her slightly fearfully.

Evie pushed the book under the seat cushion and stood up. She glowered at him, standing there in his slouchy jeans and marl grey T-shirt with his brown hair ruffled just so and his mouth twitching in a nervous smile.

'English assignment,' she mumbled, 'it's nothing, just some stupid poem.'

She waited as he hovered there, refusing to smile back at him. When was he going to take the hint and leave her the hell alone?

'Joe told me where to find you,' he said, by way of explanation, even though she wasn't interested. She noted though that the gossip about her new job had wended its way to Joe, which at least saved her a conversation, she supposed.

She rested a hand on one hip. 'Feel free to browse. If you don't see something in your size just ask and I'll see if we have it in stock.'

Tom looked around the store, then back at her, his brown eyes both amused and wounded at the same time, though she wondered how that was physically or optically possible.

'Ev, when are you going to give me the chance to explain?'

She turned her back on him and headed to the nearest rack where she started shuffling hangers around and rearranging dresses. How many times could she say *never*? How much longer could she keep up the stonewalling?

She felt him come up behind her, his breath warm on the back of her neck, and for the time it took her heart to beat just once she fought an epic battle against her better instincts not to lean back into his chest. Then Anna's face flashed in front of her, her big, wide smile and her crazy tumble of auburn hair and she saw her clear as day in her mind throwing her head back, clutching one hand to her chest as though she was stopping her heart from bursting out, and heard her laugh, a loud, cackling eruption. A laugh that Evie would never forget, not for as long as she lived, though now when she remembered it she imagined Anna laughing *at* her. Laughing at her for being so stupid and not seeing what was happening right under her nose between her boyfriend and her best friend.

It kind of soured the memory.

She swung around and pushed Tom away. 'Stop harassing me.'

Tom stood his ground. 'No,' he answered, shaking his head. 'Not until you listen to what I have to say.'

Evie grimaced. 'I wasn't interested then and I'm not interested now. I don't need to hear your lies.'

'I'm not lying. Ev, for God's sake. Is that honestly what you think?'

His voice was strained. She regarded him coolly, trying to stay objective, but it was hard when her body was insisting she walk over to him, take his hand and tell him it was going to be OK. God, she wished her brain and her body would connect more cohesively. He looked thinner than he used to, his solid football physique gone. She refused to allow the pang of worry to surface on her face. She didn't care how much weight he lost or how genuine he looked. In fact, overall, it was better if she didn't look at him. She turned back to the clothes she'd been rearranging and started randomly arranging them again, this time by price, her eyes going fuzzy over the zeroes as she tried to concentrate while simultaneously ignoring Tom's breath on the back of her neck.

'Ev, I'm *not* lying to you,' he said. 'I'm sorry about Anna. Her and me, it was nothing, a mistake. A one-off. I never meant to hurt you.'

She felt her blood starting to boil. A crimson streak flashed up her throat like fire, searing its hotness into her cheeks. All her feelings of tenderness and worry evaporated with the heat. She turned to face him. God, how could she ever allow herself, even for a split second, to look at him again in that way? She loathed him. She absolutely, utterly and completely loathed him.

'I'm sorry for everything that happened,' he said, his voice barely above a whisper, 'and I can't bring her back and I'll regret that for the rest of my life. But I didn't kill her.' He took a step towards Evie and she felt her stance harden, her arms locked across her chest. She struggled to keep her face impassive.

'I wasn't drunk, Ev, believe me,' he pleaded. 'Something jumped in front of the car. Some kind of animal.'

The doorbell jangled. Evie dragged her eyes away from Tom's face, away from his begging, haunted expression and over to the door.

'I'm thinking of opening a menswear boutique just next door once Mrs Milner decides to retire. What do you think? Will it do well?'

Evie watched Victor as he dropped a take-out bag onto the counter by the till and then turned to study Tom. Tom's eyes still hadn't left Evie's face, his expression begging her to answer him, to show some sign that she'd heard him or even forgiven him. When her expression didn't soften he let his gaze move off her unwillingly. He turned to Victor.

'Yes, I'm sure it'll do great,' he said quietly.

He ducked his head and left quickly, throwing one last glance in Evie's direction. She couldn't be sure but she thought she saw resignation in it. A turning point – as though he'd finally given up. On her, she realised. He had finally given up trying to persuade her. He'd figured out forgiveness was never going to happen. A well of sadness sprang up in her as though a stopcock had broken. It took her by surprise and she turned away from Victor. She didn't want him to see how she was feeling. She was furious with herself for feeling anything at all. She had sworn to herself no more: no more boys, no more forgiveness. If she stuck to that she'd make it out of here. If she didn't, if she gave in to her sadness or her anger, to Tom's lies and pleading eyes, and forgave him or, worse, believed him, then she'd never leave.

For six months she'd held it together and now Tom had gone and tugged at a loose stitch and all her resolve was in danger of unthreading.

'What was that all about?' Victor said.

Evie spun around. 'Don't act like you don't know,' she snapped.

Victor opened his mouth to say something, thought better of it and took a sip of coffee instead. 'What makes you most angry? That your friend betrayed you? That she died?'

'Yes!' Evie cried. 'No!' She shook her head. 'I'm angry that he lied. I'm angry that he got away with murder. I'm angry that he killed my best friend and he gets to walk around town still flirting with girls that are way too young for him.'

'*Did* he lie?' Victor interrupted.

Evie looked up, startled. 'Yes.'

'He lied about Anna, sure. He betrayed you. But is he lying about the accident?' Victor pushed.

'I . . .' She faltered, feeling as though the ground had just given

81

way under her. She stared at Victor. What was he trying to get at? Why was he staring at her so intently? 'I – I don't know,' she finally stammered.

He took a step towards her, his voice dropping in its urgency. 'Listen to your instinct, Evie. It's been trying to tell you something this whole time. Is he lying?'

'No,' she answered, unthinking. She shook her head, trying to think straight. The words were becoming tangled. 'I mean, yes. I mean . . .' She paused, her stomach lurching. It was as if the view had suddenly become clear. 'I don't know,' she murmured.

'He's telling the truth. You know it. If you listen to your instinct you'll know it too.'

'What?' Evie demanded. 'How do you know?'

'Six months ago, when the Brotherhood first became aware of your existence, they came here looking for you.'

Evie stared at him, a wave of shock riding through her body. 'What?'

'They came here looking for you. To kill you,' Victor said, scrunching his paper coffee cup into a ball and chucking it over his shoulder into the bin.

He almost didn't need to continue. The pieces were sliding sickeningly into place.

'We don't know how they found you. But they did – and they came after you,' Victor said with a sigh. 'And we stopped them.'

'So what?' Evie asked, praying silently that the pieces were sliding into the wrong places. That she was wrong. Her voice shook when she finally managed to find it. 'What's that got to do with Tom or Anna?'

'We stopped them from getting to you,' Victor said, watching her closely.

There was a silence so steep she felt she had vertigo and was going to fall into it.

'But you didn't stop them from getting to *her*?' The tears welled out of nowhere, spiking her eyes. An image of Anna on the last day she'd seen her, waving at her through the window of Joe's Diner as she worked, flashed through her mind. 'It wasn't an accident. Is that what you're saying?'

'No,' Victor answered. 'It wasn't an accident. And we weren't in time.' He shrugged. 'The Brotherhood didn't know what you looked like. They thought it was you in the car with Tom. As it probably would have been if the two of them hadn't been . . .'

Oh God. Oh God. She sucked in a breath, and then another, felt like she was falling, reached out an arm to steady herself and banged into the rail. She felt sick. She was going to be sick.

'Evie. It's not your fault.' She felt Victor's hand on her back and shrugged it off.

'How can you say that?' She whipped around. 'Of *course* it's my fault.' Her yell broke into a sob. 'It should've been me. And all this time, all this time,' she shook her head, her eyes automatically moving to the door through which Tom had just left, 'I've been – blaming him. Not believing him. *Why* was she in the car? It should have been *me*.' She slammed her fist into the couch as she collapsed down onto it.

'Well, it wasn't you. Fate has other plans for you,' Victor said. 'And you can't go forward blaming yourself, either. You have to let it go.' He knelt down and took her hand in his own enormous one. 'You will learn to only blame the Brotherhood for her death. Do you understand?'

She frowned at him, not comprehending. There was only one thing she could focus on, one thing that her brain kept tripping over on.

She looked at Victor. 'Tom wasn't lying?' she asked again, like a simpleton.

'No,' Victor replied, like she *was* a simpleton. 'Evie,' he continued slowly, 'the score was settled. What the Brotherhood did was kick-start a battle, the worst battle I've ever been in. We came after them in numbers – we needed to protect you. We fought them and we killed them. All except for one – Tristan – a Shadow Warrior. For the last six months the Brotherhood has been finding and training a new generation to replace the lost ones. And now they're back. They're who you met in the parking lot.'

'Well,' Evie yelled, 'why didn't you stop them when you had the chance? When they were weak? Why didn't you go after them and finish them off? Why didn't you stop them from recruiting more?'

Victor shook his head at her before answering. 'We couldn't find them.'

Evie stood up and crossed to the window, looking out at the half-empty street. Just a handful of farmers going about their business. Some high school students messing around outside Joe's Diner. A woman pushing a child in a stroller across the street. How could all this still be going on? How could the whole world be oblivious to the reality of what was happening around them? Unaware that there were other realms in the same way that there were other planets? She scrunched her eyes shut but when she opened them again the street was exactly the same, the sun still shining, her beaten-up pickup still parked with one tyre up on the sidewalk, Victor still standing behind her, ominously silent.

She turned back to him. 'So, this war – it will never end, will it? Because even though you destroy them they keep coming back.'

Victor said nothing, only continued to hold her gaze.

'All you're doing is stemming the tide,' she said, almost to herself.

'For the moment,' Victor said.

'Well, you're wrong about one thing,' Evie said finally. 'The score isn't settled.'

9

He didn't lie. He didn't lie. He didn't lie.

The words played in an endless loop in her head. She was mired in guilt, sinking in it fast, barely able to keep from veering off the road every time she thought about yet another incident when she'd told Tom to go to hell. God, just remembering the look in his eyes when he'd left the store this afternoon forced the guilt deep into her lungs, making her choke. She hit the steering wheel with the flat of her hand and tried to tell herself that he'd still been cheating on her, with her best friend too, but somehow that didn't matter any more.

By the time she had driven the two miles out of town to her house she felt exhausted, her body aching all of a sudden from yesterday's fight. She'd been ignoring it all day but the burn on her arm was stinging and her shoulder, where she'd been pushed or pulled – she couldn't remember which – felt like it had been dislocated and slammed back into its socket with a sledgehammer.

Evie pulled up into the driveway and killed the ignition. The house was dark, the white clapboards glowing like bones in the purple dusk. Her mother would still be at the store. The house was on its own plot, the nearest neighbour half a mile down the road. The river bordered the back of the house, just beyond the orchard her grandfather had planted. It had been a hot summer and the peaches were dropping to the ground and rotting, unpicked for the first time in years.

A tyre swung from the oak tree out front and every time Evie looked at it she was reminded of her dad swinging her, her hair trailing the ground, her screams echoing all the way to the river, scaring the birds better than a scarecrow.

She noticed she was crying and swiped at her eyes. No more tears. That was the vow she'd made. Damn memories and damn Victor and damn her dad for dying and damn Tom for not lying and damn the whole goddamn world for not being the world any more. She looked up at the house standing quietly, the first leaves of fall starting to chase each other around the driveway. The grass was scorched a golden brown. She sighed loudly and then opened the car door, but made no move to get out. She was trying to test her instincts, to see if she could sense anything in the vicinity. She couldn't hear anything except the wind in the oak tree and the rattling of the whirligig she'd made in third grade, which still lived in the pot by the front door. She jumped out the car and made a dash for it.

She tried telling herself that she was safe, that the Hunters – whoever they were – had her back, but her heart was pounding in her ears louder than the sound of her feet on the gravel and only when she was inside the house, with the door locked behind her, did she let out the breath she'd been holding. Lobo was scratching against the kitchen door so she let him out, flipping on all the lights as she went.

She dropped to her knees and let the husky nuzzle her for a minute. He kept knocking his head into her jaw until she scratched him under his chin. 'What's up, boy?' she asked.

He uttered a howl in response.

'OK, I'll feed you in a minute, I just need to shower,' Evie said, getting up and heading up the stairs.

Lobo sat at the bottom watching her, a low whine settling in his throat. Evie paused halfway, her senses suddenly alert, her gut tightening. Was this the instinct thing Victor kept going on about? She put her finger to her lips and Lobo stopped howling and began pacing instead. Evie took the next few steps soundlessly, creeping down the corridor to her room.

The door was slightly ajar and she felt the first shiver of fear run up her spine. She nudged it with her foot. It fell open. The room was empty. Of course it was. She was under protection. There were Hunters all over town making sure she was safe. There was nothing to worry about. Nothing at all. She turned on the light and threw her bag on the bed, shaking her head. She needed to work on her instincts – they were about as accurate as the weather channel.

First she was going to take a shower to ease some of the aching in her body, then she was going to finish reading that book. She reached across the bed for her bag and took it out, feeling the weight of it in her hands.

She pushed the book under her pillow and pulled off her T-shirt, loosening her denim shorts and stepping out of them so she was standing in her underwear.

As she bent to pick them up, a sudden rush of warm air ran over her, leaving a trail of goosebumps. She shivered and crossed to the window, ramming it down and drawing the curtains.

A creak.

Her head spun towards the door, her breath catching in her throat. There it was again. Another creak. Someone was in the house. Evie's senses seemed to magnify in that same instant, her hearing pinpointing the sound and her head clearing instantly. A low energy started buzzing at the base of her spine, travelling in rushes up and down her limbs. She noticed her legs and arms were tingling, the aching completely gone. She glanced around her room for a robe or something to throw on over her underwear. She wasn't about to tackle a demon in her bra. She didn't want her mother finding her unclothed body and figuring the worst.

She unhooked her robe from the back of her door, slipped it on and picked up the baseball bat, then tiptoed barefoot down the hall.

The creaking stopped instantly, it sounded just like footsteps hesitating. Evie thought she could hear breathing but that surely wasn't possible. She stopped outside Mrs Lewington's room. There was a light shining under the door. Maybe their lodger hadn't left after all. Maybe her sister was fine and she'd decided to stay on in Riverview.

Evie weighed it up for one second. She was certainly going to look crazed and was risking giving the old lady a heart attack by bursting in half-naked and brandishing a baseball bat, but what the hell, Evie thought, smashing back the door and rushing into the room with a yell.

She wasn't sure what she'd been expecting but he definitely wasn't it.

Evie froze, almost dropping the bat, coming to her senses just in time to make a grab for it. She swung it up high behind her head, ignoring her gaping robe because she needed both hands to hold the bat.

'Who are you?' she yelled at the boy standing in front of her.

His graphite eyes were focused on the baseball bat. When he

shifted them to look at her she felt the adrenaline score through her body. He had a thick shock of dark hair falling over his forehead, straight black eyebrows and cheekbones so sharp they cast shadows over the rest of his face. Her eyes flashed to his butt checking for a tail, then to his mouth for any sign of fangs. No tail. No pointy teeth.

'Who are you?' she yelled again, waving the bat at him.

'Whoa,' the boy answered, his voice soft and commanding at the same time. 'Do you want to put the bat down?'

'Don't tell me what to do,' Evie hissed. 'Who are you and what are you doing in my house?'

He took a step towards her, his hands held up defensively. 'I'm Lucas, Lucas Gray,' he said with a half-smile that almost made her drop the bat again. 'I'm your new lodger.' His eyes had settled on her and she felt them like a butterfly dancing on her skin.

'You're *what?*' Evie asked, shifting her body slightly to the side so that he wasn't getting quite such a full frontal. She daren't take a hand off the bat to close her robe but he didn't seem to have noticed anyway, his eyes hadn't once left her face.

'I'm your new lodger. I just moved to town and someone told me your mum was looking to rent this room so I called her and here I am. You're Evie, right?'

Evie's mouth fell open. She narrowed her eyes at him. Could he be a Shapeshifter? Or, what was it? A Shadow Warrior? God, she wished she'd finished the book. What had Victor said about trusting her instincts because that's what would keep her alive?

She paused, trying to get a reading. No. She couldn't trust them. She hadn't a clue what they were telling her.

'Where did you come from?' she asked, hefting the bat again.

'Iowa,' he answered slowly.

It wasn't another realm, true, but that wasn't enough to convince her.

'What are you doing in Riverview?' she demanded.

He glanced at the baseball bat nervously, then she was sure she felt him glancing down at her body, could feel the heat of his gaze across her legs, sweeping up the length of her, but his eyes didn't seem to have left her face. She used her left hand to close her robe together across her chest, holding the bat out in front of her with her other hand.

'I'm working at the Del Rey ranch,' Lucas said, with a hint of a smile.

'You're a farmhand?' Evie asked with suspicion, ignoring the smile.

'I'm working with the horses,' he shrugged. 'Whatever you want to call it.'

Evie's eyes flew to the bed behind him. There was an open suitcase on top of it, clothes piled neatly inside. On the rug was a pair of dirt-splattered boots. She glanced at his hands. There were calluses on the thumbs. He was wearing well-fitting, worn jeans and a black-and-grey checked and rumpled shirt over a white T-shirt. He *could* pass for a farmhand, but then again so could most boys in this town.

'Sorry to have scared you,' Lucas said. And there was that smile again. Disarming her, making her pulse speed up and her head fog over like a summer day in the bay.

'It's OK,' Evie said, slowly dropping the bat. She edged backwards towards the door, keeping her eyes on the boy in front of her in case he made a move. She didn't know if he was telling the truth but she couldn't take the risk that he wasn't and smash him over the head in case he *was* just the lodger. Her mother wouldn't be pleased.

Lucas followed her to the door, watching her as she walked backwards down the corridor. Then he turned back into the room. She took a deep breath and ran the last few steps to her room, slamming the door behind her and shoving a chair in front of it.

10

Lucas stood outside Evie's door, listening to her hefting what sounded like a chair in front of it as a barricade, and smiled despite himself. A chair? He shook his head. It would be so ridiculously easy to finish her right now. She had no idea.

But it would have been just as easy the other night, in the parking lot, to finish her. Shula had been just about to. But for some reason he'd acted before he could think and had pushed her out of the way. And he still wasn't sure why he had, except at the time he'd just known that he hadn't wanted Evie to die. At least, not yet.

And before he knew it, he was making up a plan to come back to Riverview on his own. And that's why, he told himself, that's why he'd pushed Evie out the way and saved her. It was because Evie's death wasn't enough. It was because, as he'd told Tristan later that night, he wanted to find a way of bringing the Hunters to their knees, just as they'd done to the Brotherhood.

He thought he heard Evie pausing, her breath sounding shallow, and he imagined her inky blue eyes fixed on the back of the door, wondering what or who stood on the other side, wondering if she was paranoid or going mad. Maybe she'd even picked up the baseball bat again.

He knew his shadow wouldn't give him away, and she wouldn't be able to hear him – he was far too quiet for that, and her senses weren't that developed – they couldn't be or she wouldn't have set foot in the house in the first place. Even the dog had been more wary than she had been, refusing to come near him until he knelt down and murmured to him that he wasn't going to hurt him. It was the same with horses – they picked up on him immediately, sensing he wasn't quite human, but once he got close, and reassured them, they stopped stamping their feet and snorting hot air, and became putty in his hands. He frowned at the door, hoping he could do the same to Evie, get that close to her, convince her to trust him, open up to him. He sensed, however, that somehow it was going to take more than a few tickles behind the ears and a quiet whisper to get her to trust him.

He'd been in her room, searching for any information she might have lying around about the Hunters, when he'd heard her pulling up in the driveway in that old Ford pickup of hers. The engine was so grizzled that a deaf person two counties away could hear her coming. From the window he'd watched her as she sat in the car with her head in her hands. When she'd finally looked up there had been a fierce frown on her face. It had made him curious. It was only when she finally flung open the car door and raced up the porch steps that he'd understood she was afraid.

After she'd slammed the front door behind her, he'd wondered how long it would take her to pick up on his presence. When it had seemed like she never would he'd chucked her a clue, opening the window in her room, thinking that she'd pick up something on the breeze – a scent or a change in temperature. But no, she'd come rushing into her room oblivious as a Mixen was to anyone else's feelings.

He'd been hiding in the shadow behind her door when she came in and tossed her bag on the bed. His first good look at her had surprised him. She was taller than he remembered, only a few inches shorter than him, and the blue of her eyes was more intense than the washed-out colours of the photo had suggested. In the back lot of the diner he hadn't got a decent look at her. And he hadn't managed to get much more of a look at her in her bedroom before she had stripped to her underwear, at which point he had slipped silently from behind the door and out of the room.

He hadn't been expecting the baseball bat. She had surprised him with that and he was angry at himself for being distracted enough not to hear her coming. She could be stealthy when she wanted to be. He'd gotten a much better look at her when she'd come bursting into his room though. He had seen straight away that once she was fully trained she'd be strong. She had the Hunter genes, no doubt. There was speed and grace in her movements, even when she'd almost dropped the bat and had to make a lunge for it. She had hair a shade darker than his, skin much paler and a wide mouth, and her dark blue eyes, which flashed furiously at him, had been as haunted as the shadow realm.

It had taken him a tenth of a second to take in the rest of her body, to notice the mark the colour of bruised fruit on her right hip bone and the graze on her left knee, but the injuries looked week-old rather than day-old, which meant she was healing quickly. She was athletic, too, he could see that from the shape of her legs and the flat of her stomach. She wouldn't need much in the way of strength-training.

He heard Evie's voice on the other side of the door and edged closer. It sounded like she was arguing with herself.

'You don't think that's weird? Or slightly suspicious?' he heard her shout in a loud whisper.

A pause of a few seconds.

'Well, have you checked with them? Maybe one got through. Maybe there's some kind of error system with your instincts . . . Mine? I don't know. I'm not trained. How should I know if he's Unhuman or not? That's your job, not mine.'

Lucas smiled faintly to himself as he heard her groan. She must be on the phone to Victor. The others hadn't picked up on him then. He had been right. Being half human was playing in his favour for once. The Hunters couldn't sense him. That was a relief because his story was hanging by a thread as it was. All he needed was Mrs Lewington to come traipsing back from Michigan with talk of a hoax call. He had a few days' grace while her bus made it across the country before he had to deal with that loose end though.

'No, OK, OK.' Her voice came through louder now. 'Tomorrow then, at Joe's. If I'm still alive I'll see you there.'

He heard her flop onto the bed and, after a few seconds, the sound of stiff pages turning. Later, when she was sleeping perhaps, he'd take another look around and try to find whatever it was she was reading. If she didn't barricade the door again, that was. Though there was always the window.

From up the road he heard the sound of another car engine. He turned his head to listen. It was Evie's mother – he could tell by the sound of the tyres and the country music she had playing. He glanced back at Evie's door, wishing he could see through to the other side, and then disappeared.

He sat down on his bed and glanced at the dresser where he'd placed a photograph in a silver-coloured frame. His mum and his dad. One human, one Shadow Warrior. Both dead. His mum, fully human, incapable of defending herself, killed by Hunters as though she'd been nothing more than a dog that needed to be put down.

His father, from the Shadowlands, a warrior and member of the Brotherhood, had died six months ago, killed by Hunters in the reprisals following the death of the girl they'd believed was Evie.

The sum of his parts. Half human, half Unhuman.

Lucas suddenly stood up. He tore his shirt off over his head. Then he stood in front of the mirror staring at the amulet lying against his chest. He lifted it up and traced the twisted silver, six strands twined into the shape of one dagger. This was his promise to the Brotherhood, his oath to fight with his brothers from the other realms until either the war was won or he was dead. But more than that, much more than that, it stood for his promise to his father and his mother that he would make the Hunters pay.

He let the amulet drop.

'Evie!'

It was her mother calling her. He heard Evie open her door and bound down the stairs and he walked silently along the corridor to watch from the shadows in the landing.

'Did you get a new lodger?' Evie demanded as soon as her feet hit the bottom step.

Evie's mother, who was dropping her bags onto a chair by the door, looked up, eyes aghast. 'Yes, oh dear, sorry, I totally forgot to call you, didn't I? Did you get a fright?'

'A fright?' Evie screeched. 'Mum! You could have warned me. I almost smashed in his head with a baseball bat.'

Evie's mum pressed her hand against her mouth. 'Oh no! No, don't do that. Sorry. I just had a call at the store from Janet Del Rey, she said she had someone there working for them who was looking for a place in town to stay for a while.' She shrugged. 'Well, it was just perfect timing.'

Evie had her back to him but he could see she had her hands on her hips and it was easy to imagine the expression on her face, the same furious frown she'd had in the car. The one where her eyes turned deep ocean blue and she pressed her lips together in a firm line.

'Perfect timing,' he heard her say. 'Exactly. Did you check his references or anything?'

Her mum turned back to her bags and started rifling around for something. 'Well, um no, but he's working at the Del Rey ranch, I'm sure they have.'

Evie took a step closer to her and he could see her in profile now. He was right about the expression.

'How do you know he is who he says he is?' she hissed at her mum, lowering her voice as though scared he might hear her. 'He might murder us in our sleep.'

Evie's mother let out a laugh and put a hand on her daughter's arm. 'Oh, don't be so silly, Evie. Did you get a good look at him? He's rather gorgeous, isn't he?'

Lucas slunk further back into the shadows.

'I think you might get to like him, Evie, if you gave him a chance,' she said, squeezing her daughter's arm and walking through into the kitchen, leaving Evie standing open-mouthed, barefoot in her robe, staring after her.

Then her head suddenly whipped around and she was staring right at him. Or, rather, she was staring right *through* him, unable to see him, even though he was standing right there and if she'd been properly trained she might have been able to notice the outline of him, feel him standing there, his eyes burning into her, but she couldn't and so her gaze flitted over him and past him and then back to the kitchen before she huffed loudly and stomped up the stairs.

She brushed his shadow as she passed and, for an instant, seemed to feel him, pulling her robe closer around her, before hurrying into her bedroom and slamming the door.

A half-hour later he heard his name called from downstairs and wandered out of his room.

'Oh, Lucas,' Mrs Tremain said from the hallway beneath. 'Would you like to join us for some dinner?'

He heard the sound of a door opening behind him, Evie's footsteps stopping just at his shoulder. He could sense her pulling a face at her mother, could smell her skin – she'd just come out the shower – but he didn't turn around.

'That would be lovely, Mrs Tremain,' he answered. 'If you're sure.'

'Oh yes, yes. Please, do join us.'

Evie rocked past him at that point, her shoulder bumping his. He stepped aside and watched her as she walked down the stairs. She was now dressed in jeans and a faded black T-shirt that was rucked up at the back, exposing a pale strip of skin at the base of her spine.

He sat opposite her at dinner, aware of her glowering at him, though he refused to look at her directly. Maybe she was picking something up after all. Or maybe she was just like this with everyone. He didn't know why but he found it mildly amusing.

'I think you've met Evie,' Mrs Tremain said, with a smile at the two of them.

'Yes, we met.' He shot her an upward glance through his lashes and received only a stony glare in response. She was still suspicious, then, despite her conversation with Victor. He realised he would have been disappointed if she wasn't.

'So, Lucas,' Mrs Tremain said, once she'd laid their plates

in front of them. 'How are you finding things? Do you have everything you need?'

Lucas turned to her and gave her his most charming smile. 'Yes,' he said. 'Yes, everything's great, Mrs Tremain. And this,' he said, indicating the meat loaf and carrots she'd placed in front of him, 'looks amazing.'

She flustered under his smile, blushing pink and muttering something about him being silly and old recipes which he only half heard because he was tuned to the groan he heard from opposite. Out of the corner of his eye he saw Evie rolling her eyes. Maybe he needed to try his smile on her. But he couldn't bring himself to. He suspected it would have the opposite effect on her anyway.

'So where are your folks from, Lucas?' Mrs Tremain asked, shooting a sharp glance at Evie, who was stalking the food around her plate.

'My parents are both dead,' Lucas said quietly, reaching for a glass.

There was a clatter of silverware against plate. He heard Mrs Tremain gasp and felt Evie's eyes on him. A stillness descended.

'Oh no, I'm so sorry. Evie's father passed away just a year ago,' Mrs Tremain said, reaching a hand over and squeezing his arm.

He winced at her touch. She must be talking about Evie's adopted father because he knew her real parents had been killed fifteen-odd years ago.

He cleared his throat. 'I'm sorry to hear that.'

'When did your parents die?'

It was Evie asking. Her mother shot her another look. 'Evie!' she said in a warning tone but then she turned and looked at him expectantly.

100

He cleared his throat. 'My father died recently, my mother ten years ago.' There was a pause, so he filled it. 'It was a car accident.'

Evie put her knife and fork down on the side of her plate and he heard the intake of air.

'Anyone like more potatoes?' Mrs Tremain asked, her voice unnaturally strained.

He nodded and let her pile his plate high.

'So, Lucas, you come from Iowa, then? Originally, I mean. Were your family from around there?'

'Er, around and about.'

'What's it like there?' Evie piped up.

He looked across at her. Her blue eyes were fixed on his. 'It's cold and dark,' he answered. 'In the winter, that is.'

'And in the summer?'

He held her gaze. 'I don't spend much time there any more. It's not home.'

'Oh,' said Mrs Tremain, shooting Evie another warning glance. 'So where *is* home?

'I don't know,' he said quietly. 'Guess I'm trying to find that out.'

'Oh, you sound just like Evie,' Mrs Tremain said. 'She can't wait to leave here. She says this doesn't feel like home, either, don't you, dear?'

'Mum,' Evie growled, widening her eyes at her mother.

Her mum ignored her. 'She wants to go to New York as soon as she's through with school.'

Evie's eyes had dropped to her plate. She seemed suddenly introverted, defensive. She was sitting down, otherwise he imagined she'd be standing with one hip jutted forward, her hands fisted at her sides, as though ready to do combat with anyone who came too close.

He observed the way Mrs Tremain looked at Evie, saw the pride tinged with sadness in her eyes, and felt a rush of affection for the old woman. Because she *was* an old woman – almost old enough to be Evie's grandmother. In fact, she reminded him of his own grandmother, the human one that is, the one he'd spent a few years living with in Iowa. White-haired and broad-faced, serving up steak and potatoes for dinner, along with a generous helping of town gossip. He smiled to himself at the memory. His grandmother hadn't wanted *him* to leave home either. Mind you, she knew of a lot more reasons than Evie's mother did why staying home would be a good thing.

'In a year's time you'll be gone,' she sighed at Evie. 'Living in New York. And it's such a long way away. I honestly don't know why you want to go there when there are perfectly good state universities in California. And I'm sure you'd get a good scholarship too – if you would just take up sport again.' Mrs Tremain looked at him. 'Evie used to be state running champion, you know,' she said proudly.

Across the table Evie was looking at her mother pleadingly.

The running made sense, Lucas thought. She looked like a runner. Had she stopped because of her father's death? Or maybe because of her friend's death – the girl who'd died in the car crash? He tried to imagine Evie in New York, pictured her on a crowded sidewalk in the shadow of enormous skyscrapers under a fall sky, and couldn't. And then he remembered with a slight start that she would never set foot in New York. She would be dead in a year. In a month, in fact.

He glanced quickly away, aware that he'd jolted the table with his foot. He looked at Mrs Tremain, who was watching him with her transparent concerned face, smiling at him, oblivious to the future. First a husband, then a daughter. He couldn't meet her eyes for long.

'How long will you be staying, do you think?'

He realised she was talking to him, was waiting for him to answer, and he cleared his throat. 'I don't know, maybe just a month,' he answered. 'If that's OK?'

'Yes, yes, of course,' she said, smiling so warmly at him that his stomach tightened. 'I'm not sure Mrs Lewington will be back for a while,' she added.

He continued to stare at his plate, at the now cold and congealing meatloaf.

'Are you OK?' he heard Mrs Tremain asking. 'You look like you're not well. It's not the food, is it?'

'No. It's great,' he replied. 'I – I just . . .' He just couldn't sit there any longer having a conversation with a woman whose daughter he was going to have to kill eventually. 'I have a headache,' he said, standing up so fast he upset his glass of water. His hand reached out to catch it but Evie got there first, righting it before even a drop spilled onto the tablecloth. Their fingers touched and she pulled away as if she'd been burnt. He pretended not to notice.

'I might go and lie down,' he said, stepping away from the table. 'Have an early night.'

'Oh, OK then,' Mrs Tremain said, looking at the sad pile of untouched meatloaf on his plate. 'Goodnight.'

'Goodnight,' he said.

He looked quickly over at Evie and saw she was staring at him, suspicion clouding her eyes.

'Goodnight,' he said, trying to overcome the indifference in his voice.

She gave him the slightest nod and then started eating again.

As he walked up the stairs he heard her mother lean over and say, 'He's such a lovely boy, I think you could try a bit harder to be polite. I've no idea what's got into you. It's not like I'm encouraging you to marry him. I just think you might have a bit of fun.'

He found himself clutching the banister harder than he needed to and felt himself scowling. The shadows on the landing stretched like the bruises on Evie's skin and he melted into them.

11

Evie stormed into the diner and marched straight over to where Victor was sitting, Danish pastry half raised to his mouth.

'I could have died! I want you to know that,' she announced.

He glanced up at her and, sighing, put the pastry down, looking around to see if anyone else in the diner had heard her. Joe was staring at them, obviously curious to know why she had stormed in as if the end of the world was nigh, but he didn't seem to have heard.

'You're alive, aren't you?' he said quietly, taking a sip of his coffee. 'I told you, if your new lodger was Unhuman we'd know about it.' He raised an eyebrow sceptically. 'And hopefully so would you.'

'Listen, we need to talk about this whole instinct thing,' Evie said, sliding into the seat opposite him. Her instinct was flinging itself around like a compass at the north pole. She had no idea which way was true north any more.

'Why aren't you at work?' Victor suddenly asked, looking at his watch. It was a Wednesday, she'd said she worked at her parents' hardware store on a Wednesday.

'My mum fired me. She said I was working too many jobs and needed some time off.'

Victor smiled. 'Well, that's handy.'

'I'm not going to get time off, am I?'

'Do you want it?'

'No,' Evie said, sitting back in her chair. 'I want to get going. I want to start today. I read that book. I have questions and I want answers.'

Victor didn't respond. He merely raised his hand and Evie wondered what on earth he was doing but then Joe appeared at the table.

'Can I get this to go?' Victor asked, indicating the coffee and Danish in front of him.

Joe grunted and took the cup and plate away with him, muttering hello to Evie as he went. She kicked herself. She still hadn't spoken to him since starting her new job.

The door clanged open and the sound of laughter poured in. Evie looked up absently. It was Tom and her chest immediately constricted, pain shooting up her arm. Who would have thought that guilt felt so similar to a heart attack?

But who was that with him? She twisted to get a closer look, having to blink several times to convince herself that she wasn't seeing things.

That was Kaitlin Rivers from the class below. What on earth was he doing with Kaitlin Rivers?

The two of them hadn't yet noticed her. Evie watched in dawning horror as Kaitlin mock-punched Tom in the shoulder and then ducked out the way, giggling, as he nudged her back. She felt sick all of a sudden and dipped her head, letting her hair fall over her shoulder, shielding her face from view. She could feel Victor staring at her, though, and when she looked up saw he was watching her with a curious smile on his face, his eyebrows flashing upwards questioningly.

'So, ready then?' she said, getting up before he could ask anything.

Victor took his time sorting through his pockets for change and she waited impatiently, keeping her back to the rest of the diner, tapping her foot, acutely aware of Kaitlin's infuriatingly screechy put-on laughter coming from behind her. But then she heard a sound so familiar it made her gut clench. And it shocked her so much it made her foot stop tapping. Tom was laughing. It was a sound she hadn't heard in such a long time.

She supposed Tom hadn't had much cause to laugh these last six months.

The laughter cut off and she heard footsteps approaching cautiously.

She whipped around, expecting Tom, but found Kaitlin in front of her, all bouncy and shiny-faced.

'Hey, Ev,' she said.

Evie felt her jaw tighten. She hated people she didn't know or didn't like calling her Ev. She hadn't even answered before Kaitlin swept on to her next conversational gambit.

'How are you?' she said, tipping her head to one side as though the muscles down the right side of her neck had given way. Her slushy brown eyes stretched wide with faux sincerity. She reminded Evie of a poodle.

'I'm good, thanks,' Evie said, looking over at Tom who pointedly turned away, ignoring her.

Great, Evie thought. She so needed to talk to him and explain that she now believed him about the accident but her stomach revolted at the very concept. She had no idea how to approach him or what to say, especially now this sophomore wannabe Prom Queen was standing in the way.

'So, there's like a party tonight,' Kaitlin prattled, 'and we're like all going and were wondering whether you wanted to come. It's down at the swimming spot on the river.'

Evie wondered why Kaitlin was asking her. Tom clearly wasn't happy about it, judging from the sulky face he was pulling, and it wasn't as if she was friends with Kaitlin. Actually, it wasn't like she was friends with *anyone* in town these days. She kept as low a profile as her role of cheated girlfriend, best friend of dead girl and poor old Ed Tremain's daughter allowed her to keep. She worked three jobs – two now, she reminded herself, thanks to her mother firing her – and in-between studied hard so she could get the hell out of town when the time came. Not that she now needed to study so hard. But the long and the short of it was that she had become known for her solitary ways – a polite term for moodiness – which is why she became immediately suspicious at Kaitlin's request that she come to this party.

She was about to say thanks but I'm busy, when Victor opened his mouth and spoke for her. 'Yes, she'd love to come.'

Evie spun around, open-mouthed, but he totally ignored her.

'What time does she need to be there?' he asked Kaitlin

'Um, eightish, I guess,' Kaitlin stuttered, staring up at the enormous bulk of Victor and wondering in her wide-eyed poodle way who he was and whether she'd accidentally invited him too.

Evie suppressed a laugh at Kaitlin's horrified expression. 'Yes, I'll come,' she said, looking at Tom, hoping he'd heard, praying he'd react in some way. But he didn't. He just glared at her coldly and she found herself longing to see him smile again.

Maybe tonight would give her chance to get close to him, speak to him.

She turned and smiled tightly at Victor. 'Shall we get to work, then?' she asked lightly, as though she was suggesting tea and cake and not a lesson on demon-killing techniques.

He flashed a smile at her in return as though he'd read her mind and took her arm. 'Let's,' he said.

Once they were inside the store over the road, Evie immediately sat down in one of the red chairs and pulled the book from her bag. She looked up, ready to start firing questions but Victor was standing over by one of the rails, flicking through the clothes. She watched him with frustration, what was he doing? They had work to do. She had history to learn and questions burning holes in her brain.

'Here!' Victor announced, pulling a navy blue dress off the rack and holding it up.

'What?' Evie asked, thinking maybe she'd put it in the wrong place and like it mattered anyway.

'I thought you might like something new to wear tonight. You can't possibly wear jeans or a variation on jeans every day of your life,' he said, nodding at her cut-off jeans.

Evie glared at him. Then stood up and took the dress. 'What is this? Your version of danger money? Are you trying to sweeten the Hunter deal by throwing in some designer clothes?' She glanced at the tag. It would be the most expensive thing she'd ever worn by a very long margin. She would accept the sweetening.

Victor took the dress from her hands and held it up in front of her. She looked at herself in the mirror. 'Guess I'll be dressed to kill,' she muttered under her breath to her reflection. Her reflection didn't look amused. Though the colour was flattering – it made her eyes bluer.

'Right, now that's sorted,' Victor said, draping the dress over the back of the chair, 'let's get to work.' He took a seat. 'What have you read?'

'Everything, like I said. But it doesn't say how it all began. You said before that this war has been going on for hundreds of years.'

'Over a thousand.' Victor nodded.

'Well, how did it begin?' Evie asked

Victor reached over and took the book. 'Did you see this?' he asked, flipping to the back pages.

'Yes,' she said, getting up and crouching down by his side so she could peer closer at the spidery scratches – black lines branching and dividing hundreds of times across the page. 'But I couldn't make head or tail of it,' Evie said.

'This is your family tree, Evie,' Victor said. 'Look. Here . . .' He pointed to a dark smudge on the page and she leant in closer. 'There you are.'

'I need a magnifying glass to read that,' she said.

Victor went up and rummaged through the trunk lying open in the corner. He returned with a magnifying glass. Of course there was one in there. Why wouldn't there be?

Her name leapt out at her from the page and she drew in a breath.

Evie Rose Hunter b. 1994 d. -

She stared at the tiny blank space after the dash and felt her heart do a kick.

She forced herself to trace her finger upwards to her parents.

Megan Alice Boissinot Hunter b.1970 d. 1996

'She was French? Was my mother French?' Evie looked up, startled.

'Yes.' Victor nodded.

She felt her chin lift, her shoulders straighten. Somehow she felt chicer all of a sudden, empowered. French. That was pretty cool.

James Henry Hunter b. 1969 d. 1996

'And my dad? Where was he from?' she asked, half hoping it would be somewhere equally exotic or European.

'He was born in America. The east coast. But the Hunter roots can be traced back over a thousand years. Look, see here,' he said, moving the magnifying glass in her hand to the top of the page.

'*Aylen*,' she read out loud, the single name written there in fading ink. '*Born c. 997.*' She looked up at Victor. 'Is that missing a 1?'

'No. That's your great-great-great-times-fifty grandmother.'

Evie stared at the name. 'Wow. So she's where it all began. Who was she?'

'She was the wife of a Native American chief. Legend has it that one day she discovered him and their youngest child slaughtered, their bodies being fed on by an Unhuman. Some say it was a Thirster, others that it was a Shapeshifter in animal form.'

Evie stared at Victor rapt. She was part Native American too. She could live with this.

111

'She swore revenge and with her remaining sons began hunting down the Unhumans – demons as they called them then – living in the land at that time. She became a fierce leader, a warrior of her people. The Unhumans scattered over the continent, seeking shelter, looking for places to hide, and Aylen and her sons would hunt them down. They only started using the Hunter surname in the fifteenth century, though by then there were Hunters spread out as far as Europe.'

'Hang on, hang on, why were the demons looking for shelter here in the first place? Why didn't they just go back to their own realms if they were being hunted? It's the same today – why are they still here? What's so good about this world?'

'The other realms are not all like here. The Shadowlands, for example, are wastelands.'

'The Shadowlands?'

'Where the Shadow Warriors come from,' Victor explained.

'Yeah, about them,' Evie said. 'I have no idea how I'm supposed to fight one of them.'

'OK, we'll come to that,' Victor said, raising his hands to hold her back from the questioning. 'Let's just get through the history lesson first. We don't know why the Brotherhood was originally formed. Early histories say it was to suppress the Originals.'

'They're the really old Thirsters, right?' asked Evie.

Victor nodded. 'We think the other Unhumans all had to unite to fight the Originals and afterwards they formed a Brotherhood to protect the realms and try to take control of this one too. Did you read about the Sybll?' he asked.

Evie nodded. She had read about the Sybll last night. A clairvoyant Unhuman. It had made her wonder why the

Unhumans got all the powers and supersonic strength. What did the Hunters get? Faulty instincts and a love of fashion?

'The Sybll are psychic,' Victor carried on. 'It means the Brotherhood sees us coming. Though their visions seem a little hazy at the best of times. So we are able to surprise them occasionally.'

'They see the past *and* the future?'

'Yes.'

'So they must see us coming every time, then?'

Victor's brow darkened. 'Yes and no. The Sybll only get flashes. They need contact with a person, to touch them or hold something that belongs to them, in order to see into that person's future. Some kind of connection. And they only see decisions as they get made so if you can change your approach at the last minute it confuses them. It's how we managed to destroy the last Brotherhood.'

He flipped to the page with a picture of a Sybll. The picture showed a girl with long white hair. She seemed as human as any of Evie's classmates, except her face was longer and her eyes bigger, as round as saucers.

'What do these mean?' Evie asked, pointing to the strike marks in the corner of the page. 'They're on every page.'

'I was wondering whether you'd noticed those,' Victor murmured. 'Those, Evie, are the reckonings.'

'The what?'

'The reckonings record how many of each species we've killed.'

Evie counted the strikes. 'Eight Sybll,' she pronounced.

'Yes, over the years. Eight's not many. They're tricky to get close to.'

Evie swallowed and looked at the girl on the page. She looked so young and – well, wide-eyed.

'And these?' she said, flipping the page back onto the picture of the Scorpio demon. 'What does this mean?' She pointed to the number 23.

Victor paused. 'That's the number of Hunters the Scorpio demons have taken.'

Evie considered his choice of word. 'Taken? You mean killed?'

Victor frowned, but nodded. 'Yes.'

'And my parents? Where are they? What killed them?'

Victor gently took the book from her hands and turned the pages. He handed it back to her and she looked down.

'A Shadow Warrior? A Shadow Warrior killed them?'

'Yes.'

She looked at the number in the corner, saw that the paper was rough where it had been rubbed over and a new pencil mark made.

'Thirty-three? They've killed *thirty-three* of us?' she said, in a shaking voice.

'Yes.'

'And we've killed just one of them?'

Victor nodded.

She slammed the book shut. 'When do we start this training?'

Victor took the book and laid it carefully on the counter. 'Tomorrow. Today we keep learning, for that's where the knowledge to fight them lies. In the past.'

'Why are they so special? These Shadow Warriors?' she demanded.

'They're silent and they're invisible.'

'So how do I find one? And how do I kill one when I do? It must be possible. We got one, didn't we? How did we do that?'

114

Victor smiled wryly. 'You need to learn to see them first.'

Evie looked at him with interest. 'But how? You said they're invisible.'

'In shadows it's almost impossible. Almost. But *you* have the ability to see them.'

He was definitely overestimating her, but Evie kept quiet.

'Tomorrow, when we train, you'll start to understand how to use that instinct of yours. We need to unlock it, so you can start to sense things better.'

'Right,' Evie huffed. 'But what if I can't sense anything? What if I'm deficient, sense-wise?'

Victor snorted with laughter.

'Seriously,' Evie snapped. 'What if my instincts just aren't up to scratch?'

On the periphery of her vision Evie saw a blur of movement and ducked as something whistled past her ear. She looked up from her crouching position. A dagger hilt was vibrating wildly where it was buried in the wall just behind her head. She turned back to Victor, her mouth agape, disbelief scrawled across her face.

'Your instincts are just fine,' he said, before turning his back on her.

Quicker than thought, Evie crossed to the wall, yanked the still vibrating dagger out of it and chucked it hard and straight at Victor's head. As it left her hand she yelled, realising what she had done but too late to stop it. She watched in horror as the blade soared through the air.

Victor reacted fast. He stepped lightly to the side and the knife flew right past him. But when he turned to face her, his fist was closed around the hilt and she could only stare at him in confusion, wondering how on earth he'd caught it and what he was going to do with it now.

A spark seemed to have ignited his irises, making him look dangerous for the first time, but all he said with a light smile was, '*Touché.*'

12

Evie walked in the door clutching the book and the dress in her arms, and the smell hit her first. Leather and dirt and peaches and dying summer days. Her stomach clenched at the memories that the warm smell of leather dredged up but the smile died on her lips when she remembered it couldn't be him because the only person who ever dragged the smell of horses and leather into the house had been dead for over a year.

That's when she heard her mother's voice, all sunny and breathless, coming from the kitchen. She inched forwards, already knowing, and dreading, what she was about to find. And she was right. There was her mother fussing around Lucas, pouring him tea from the good china teapot and laying out freshly baked cookies on a plate in front of him like he was the President come to call and not their paying lodger. When did Evie – who wasn't a paying lodger – ever get fresh cookies and tea from a pot? Not even Mrs Lewington had ever got cookies.

Lucas Gray had his back to her. Sweat had stuck his T-shirt to his back in patches and his dark hair was unkempt, as though he'd recently pulled off a hat and run a hand through it. When he reached for the tea Evie saw his arms were dirt-streaked, the muscles well worked, his hands strong and sure in their movements. She couldn't take her eyes off his hands – her mind going places it really shouldn't . . .

He turned and caught her staring and she tossed her head to indicate indifference and stepped into the kitchen as though she'd just arrived and hadn't been thoroughly checking him out.

She placed the dress and book on the table and, ignoring him and only nodding at her mother's hello, went over to the sink for a drink of water. She was buying time. She actually had no idea why she was still treating him like this. She only knew that she resented him for being in her kitchen at that moment. She resented the way her mother was fussing over him and she resented the way he smelt. She couldn't tell if she was still suspicious on top of being resentful – she was alive after all. He hadn't murdered her in her sleep last night.

So if it wasn't suspicion that was needling her, then what was it? His coolness? His indifference to her indifference? The sense of him watching her, even when he wasn't even looking remotely in her direction? Like now, she was sure she could feel the weight of his gaze on the back of her neck but when she turned he was laughing at something her mother had said and pouring himself some more tea. He wasn't even facing in her direction. And there was the needling again – only now she wasn't sure if she was annoyed by the fact that he was laughing with her mother or by the fact that he hadn't been looking at her. She gave herself a mental slap.

Then her mother interrupted her crazy mind chatter by letting out a cry. 'You paid *how much* for this?'

She was holding up Evie's new blue dress.

'Keep your hair on, Mum,' Evie said, putting her glass down. 'I didn't pay for it. It was a gift.'

'A gift?' Her mother's voice rose a notch, coming out like a screech.

118

Evie squirmed, knowing exactly what her mother was thinking. She should have anticipated this one and removed the price tag before she walked in the door.

'Excess stock,' she said, 'and I'm supposed to be selling the clothes, so wearing them is actually a marketing strategy.'

What was she talking about? She had no idea but her mother seemed to have fallen for it because now she had switched her attention to the hem length.

'Well, I'm sure it will look lovely on you, dear.'

Evie caught Lucas – she actually caught him – looking at her. And he didn't look away, he held her gaze and it was somehow unsettling. She shuffled from foot to foot, aware that she felt the same way when Victor was watching her – like she was an opponent in a wrestling ring and he was trying to figure out whether to bet on her or against her.

Lucas's grey eyes seemed darker today – iron ore, she thought – the words popping inexplicably into her head. His expression was cool, detached. He seemed to warm up around her mother but with her he maintained an absolute aloofness. Well, she *had* tried to smash his head in with a baseball bat, so it was fair enough she supposed. And who was she to talk anyway? She was an expert at aloofness – she could offer him lessons in how to take it to the next level if he wanted.

'I'm going to wear it tonight,' she said, retrieving the book and taking the dress from her mum.

'Why? What's tonight?' her mother asked.

'There's a party on at the swimming hole, the one down by Jay's Creek.'

Evie left it at that but she could see two pink spots of pleasure start to glow on her mother's cheeks.

This would be her first social foray in six months and she could see the effort it was taking for her mother to hold back from hugging her and telling her how glad she was to see her finally making an effort. At what? Evie thought – normality? That would be a wasted effort. There was no more normality.

She backed away, heading for the door before her mother could say something embarrassing in front of a stranger. Too late. Her mother opened her mouth and Evie prepared herself for the fact that yet another person would soon know the intimacies of her life and the reasons for her lack of social life, but actually what her mother said was even worse than she had anticipated.

'Why don't you take Lucas with you?' she asked.

Evie had been caught off-guard and so had no lie prepared as to why she couldn't take him. And Lucas had been looking at her, suddenly alert, almost daring her, a smile on that overly perfect mouth of his which rendered her momentarily speechless. Her mother had taken her open-mouthed muteness for agreement and switched her attention to Lucas, telling him he had to go and what a wonderful opportunity it would be for him to make new friends, and then shot a conspiratorial glance over his shoulder at Evie – why hadn't she just winked while she was at it?

Evie felt her face getting hotter and hotter and her anger starting to bubble up, because she didn't want Lucas coming along. She had enough to deal with navigating what would be the most awkward social scene of her life – friends she'd basically ignored for six months, acquaintances who only knew her as the dead girl's friend and an ex-boyfriend who the whole world knew had cheated on her, but from whom *she* needed to beg forgiveness.

And here she was tapping her foot at the top of the stairs,

waiting for Lucas to appear. Because what she really needed on top of having to do all of the above was to have to babysit too.

'Are you waiting for me?'

She looked around. She hadn't heard him. He had appeared out of nowhere, freshly showered, wearing a white shirt open at the neck, rolled up sleeves and clean blue jeans. She surveyed him with what she hoped was impassivity though her insides were definitely reacting actively. He was just too good-looking, goddamn it. Without a word, she headed down the stairs.

He stepped aside to let her pass. Was that a frown she saw?

She led him through the kitchen out onto the back porch. They headed across the orchard, Lucas following silently behind. All the time she was aware of him there, out of sight, stepping silently in her footsteps, eyes burning into her back.

Once they reached the river and the path beaten through the grass alongside it, she stepped out of the way and let him go first. She felt uncomfortable letting him have the advantage. Was that another little frown she saw when he passed her?

'It's about half a mile upriver from here,' she said to him. But being behind him only made her even more uncomfortable. He moved so swiftly and so silently she could barely keep up, and she couldn't stop staring at his back, at the ridge of muscle running along his shoulders, the tan line on the back of his neck – but mainly, it had to be said, at his butt.

At one point Lucas stood back to hold a branch out of the way for her and their eyes caught. He seemed to jerk back from her, looking away quickly. There was something about his expression . . . she couldn't work it out. She remembered what her father had once told her about peat fires, about the heat gathering underground and rippling out, the flames hidden from view. That's what Lucas made her think of. He seemed so aloof but there was something going on underneath it all, something burning under all that cool.

Damn it, she thought, swiping at some long grass, why did she even care? She was over boys. Done with them entirely. And besides, she had a million things to deal with right now. If she even tried to list them she'd be here all night. Off the top of her head she was worried about her mother and she was distinctly worried about training tomorrow. And she was angry, too, she knew that. The numbness had melted completely away in the last day and a half. Now she was angry again. She was angry at Victor for destroying her reality and she was angry that she was the one expected to protect a world she actually hated. Did no one get the irony? Did they not see that maybe she didn't care what happened to the world? Except she did care what happened to her mother.

And there Lucas was again, holding back another branch, doing it almost absently, not to charm her with chivalry.

'I've got it,' she said, pushing past him once more. Better his eyes on her back than the other way around because he was a distraction and that, she realised, was *really* why she was so angry at him. It wasn't because she was suspicious of him, because there was no way he was an Unhuman. It was that he was too big a distraction, and she didn't need or want one of those right now. As far as she could tell nothing good ever came of falling for a boy.

It was twilight by the time they made it to the spot by the swimming hole. The party was barely a gathering. There were less than a dozen people, nearly all of them from the year below her at school. Evie sighed inwardly and hovered on the edge of the pool for a moment, tempted to drop into the water and sink like a stone. She used to come here with Tom a lot last summer and that's exactly what they would do, strip off to their underwear and dive in, their hands finding each other in the murky depths.

She looked up, spotting Tom immediately. He was staring at her from across the water and she knew he was thinking the same thing she was, remembering old times. But he didn't return the smile she offered him. She tried to make it placatory, an olive branch, but he just stared stonily at her and then turned back to the group of people he was with and threw his arm around someone. Kaitlin Rivers, to be precise.

Of course. That's why Kaitlin had invited her tonight. To her and Tom's old hang-out spot. It was a *Look, he's mine* statement of where things stood now. Why didn't she just tattoo his name on her face? Evie really felt like turning around and walking back the way she'd come but she could sense Lucas behind her, waiting patiently for her to get it together, and there was no way she was giving Kaitlin the pleasure of seeing her upset. And besides, she needed to speak to Tom whether she wanted to or not. She owed him that much.

She looked over her shoulder, found Lucas standing still as a rock, observing the little party, and said, 'Coming?'

He nodded and started following. He didn't look any happier at the prospect of making new friends than she did at renewing old ones. They strolled around the pond and Evie suddenly became aware of the hush that had descended. The girls sitting at the edge of the pond, with their legs dangling in the water, were watching her. She was used to being stared at, so she just pressed on, trying to force a smile onto her lips. And then she stopped short, realising they weren't actually staring at her. They were staring at Lucas and every single one of them was open-mouthed. Then they pulled themselves together and she

123

watched one toss her hair behind her shoulders, saw a second –
Josey Grunsmith with the oversized chest – giggle and nudge the
girl next to her and Vicki Handsworth clutch the hand of the
girl sitting beside her.

Evie felt her jaw set. She was drawing level with Tom and he
was staring over her shoulder at Lucas, and she caught the scowl
he gave him before he remembered he was supposed to be looking
stony-faced.

How dare he be annoyed at whatever conclusion he'd jumped
to? Evie thought. He was the one standing here with his arm
around Kaitlin Rivers. Though now she saw his arm had actually
dropped away and Kaitlin was anxiously trying to press into him.
Why didn't she just lift a leg and spray him? Evie wondered.

'Tom, can we talk?' Evie finally managed to say.

'What about?' Tom asked.

Evie glanced at the silent group of listeners around them.
'Anna,' she said.

That stilled them, made them glance hurriedly away. Two
people took the hint and backed off. Evie looked pointedly at
Kaitlin.

'Kaitlin,' Evie said, when the girl showed no sign of peeling
herself off Tom, 'this is Lucas. Lucas, this is Kaitlin.'

Lucas hesitated a beat and then stepped forward, holding out
his hand. Kaitlin looked like no one had ever offered her a hand
to shake before and giggled before taking it.

'Pleased to meet you,' Lucas said, his voice so low and sure and
seductive Evie was certain she saw Kaitlin's whole body quiver in
response.

She took the opportunity while Kaitlin turned to putty to
indicate to Tom a space just a few metres away. It was the start of a

path that if you followed it for twenty seconds, opened into a little area between the trees where in the daytime the sunlight sloped through. You could dry off there in-between swims. Tom followed her, knowing exactly where they were going. She remembered the last time she had come here with him. How they'd walked through the long grass arm in arm.

A screechy laugh broke through the trees behind them as they walked. She recognised it as Kaitlin's and froze, wanting to turn around and demand to know what was so funny – what Lucas had possibly said to make her laugh like that – but then she forced herself to keep walking. What Lucas was saying or doing was none of her concern. He could be skinny-dipping with every girl at the party for all she cared.

More laughter. Followed by a splashing sound and a few screams.

Evie turned her attention to Tom, who'd stopped on the path, as though unwilling to enter the old space of their shared memories. His arms were crossed stubbornly over his chest. 'What do you want?'

She frowned at him. Why the sudden change? Their roles had switched and she didn't like it. Was this how it had felt for him the whole time he'd been trying to convince her it was an accident?

'Tom,' she said, her voice faltering. 'I'm sorry.'

He looked taken aback. She saw the flash of pain or hurt, or maybe just surprise, in his eyes before the cold expression descended once more.

'I was too hasty blaming you for the accident,' she blurted.

His eyes widened. 'Oh, so now you *do* think it was an accident?'

'Yes.'

'Why the sudden change of mind?'

'Um, well, I . . .' She couldn't find the words, stammered to a standstill.

'Well, when you figure it out, let me know,' Tom said, turning away.

She grabbed for his arm, her voice breaking. 'Tom, don't be like this. Please. I've said I'm sorry and anyway it still doesn't excuse the fact she was in your car in the first place.'

He turned to face her. 'Why? Would you rather it had been you?'

Her hand dropped from his arm. He saw she wasn't going to answer and started walking away.

'Yes, sometimes I do,' she whispered to the ground.

He whipped around. 'Well, it wasn't. So stop acting like the victim in all this, Evie. It didn't happen to you. It happened to Anna and to me. *You* don't have to live with it.'

He was shouting into her face and she was stunned. And then she had the weirdest sensation, like the world was shrinking around her and all the sounds in the universe had reduced to just the hush of her breathing and the noise of a leaf cracking in the undergrowth. The air around her seemed to be buzzing with static and she was back in the moment except she was sitting on the ground with her legs collapsed under her. And it wasn't Tom's face in front of her. It wasn't his hands wrapped around hers. It was Lucas who was crouching down in front of her, his eyes dark and fearful, his lips just inches from her own, asking her if she was OK.

She stared vacantly into his eyes, which were now darting over her shoulder into the woods behind, wondering how he'd gotten there because a second ago she'd been alone here with Tom – hadn't she? And she could see the concern on his face and she thought it was a little odd. But what was she doing on the ground?

'What the hell are you doing?' Tom was shouting.

Lucas ignored him. 'Are you OK?' he asked again, his eyes back on her now, his voice so soothing she wanted to reach out a hand and stroke his lips and make him keep talking.

'I'm fine,' she whispered. But was she? What had just happened? She stared to her left, into the wide circle of trees that marked the edge of the clearing, and couldn't shake the sense of something or somebody watching her.

'Leave her alone. Who said you could touch her?'

Her attention was drawn back to Tom. He had put a hand on Lucas's shoulder. Lucas looked up at him through his thick lashes. Then he stood slowly. Tom's hand dropped to his side. They were both tall, though Tom had a couple of inches on Lucas. But he was less muscled, and the way Lucas seemed to handle himself, with such confidence, the way he moved without almost seeming to be moving, was making Tom uncertain.

'I think it would be better if you went back to the party,' Lucas said calmly.

Tom raised his eyebrows. 'Oh you do, do you?'

Lucas cast his eyes around the clearing then looked back at Tom. 'Yes.'

Tom's eyes widened and he let out an incredulous laugh.

Evie could see suddenly exactly where this was going and staggered dizzily to her feet.

'Tom,' she said, putting a hand on his arm. 'Drop it. I'm going. *We're* going,' she said, nodding her head at Lucas.

Tom frowned at her. Then with a final glare at Lucas he stomped off back down the path. She felt a warmth in the small of her back, heat flowing through her dress, and realised that it was Lucas's hand, pressing her forwards, down the path after Tom. They walked silently past the others. She noticed Kaitlin and another girl glaring evils at her as they passed. The laughter had ceased and the woods were only punctuated with the sound of muttered whispers. Evie heard the words *Lucas* and *boyfriend* and *fight* and wished she'd never come.

As they walked out of sight into the darkness offered by the trees, she could still feel the heat of all their eyes. Lucas kept on glancing backwards over his shoulder, no doubt checking to see if Tom was following them. She still didn't understand what had caused the dizzy spell. It had never happened before. Her hearing and her heart rate still felt amped up too. She wondered if she might be coming down with something. They kept walking. Lucas not saying a word.

'Thanks,' she said finally, to break the silence. 'But I didn't need rescuing.'

Lucas laughed under his breath.

'I really didn't,' she said indignantly. If only he knew who she was. She wasn't a damsel in distress. She was a kickass Hunter they sent to rescue damsels.

'Well, *I* did,' he finally said. 'You left me with a pack of crazed schoolgirls.'

She smiled despite herself. 'Yeah, it really sounded like you were struggling.'

He didn't reply, just kept ushering her forward and she kept moving because she didn't want the heat of his hand to fall away.

They were back in the orchard. The lights of the house were glistening through the branches. His hand finally dropped from her back and she felt a light shiver travel up her legs.

'Why do you wish you'd been in the car?' he finally said.

She drew in a breath and stopped. She hadn't realised he'd heard that part of the conversation with Tom. What had he been

128

doing in the clearing, listening in? She paused. Strangely, she didn't feel cross.

'I – I just sometimes think it would have been a whole lot easier that way,' she said with a sigh.

She was glad it was a new moon, barely a sliver, and it was so dark he couldn't see her face. She couldn't make out his expression either, though his eyes were shining silver in the light. But she did see him nod. And then she remembered what he'd told them the night before. About his mother.

'Were you in the car with her?' she asked tentatively.

13

He was flung back there – to the scene in the woods. Back to the place where his mother had died while he watched. Holding her hand as the pool of red sunk into the ground around him. The blood-spattered leaves hanging off the tree dripping onto the back of his head, anointing him in red. When the paramedics finally arrived they'd strapped him to a gurney thinking he had a head injury. When they finally figured out he was fine, just paralysed by shock, they called it a miracle.

Not a miracle. Fate. Or luck. If that's what you wanted to call it.

He nodded in the darkness, felt Evie's fingers brush his own, accidentally or not he couldn't be sure.

'I'm sorry,' she said.

He couldn't see her properly, the moonlight was dim, barely penetrating through the branches of the trees around them. He could only see the translucent gleam of her skin. Her eyes looked even inkier than normal, her body narrower in the sheath of her dress.

'I'm sorry about your father,' he said.

He heard her breathing run more ragged, as though it was snagged in her chest.

'What happened?'

She took a breath. 'He was helping a neighbour fix a leak in their roof. And he slipped.'

Life was so precariously balanced, he thought.

'And just six months later Anna died.' She was whispering now. 'It's so weird. I thought I'd go numb like I did after Dad died. But I didn't. I just got angry.' She looked up at him. 'I'm still so damn angry. You know?'

Did he know? He had to force his lips together, clench his jaw shut.

'And I prefer the numbness. I want the numbness back,' she carried on in that slightly husky voice of hers.

'Stick with the anger,' he finally said.

'Why?' she asked, bewildered at his response.

'Because it will keep you going. If you're numb you can't fight.'

As soon as he spoke the words he wished he could take them back. Why was he giving her advice to stay angry and to fight? It would be a lot easier if she was broken and in pieces when it came time to kill her. What in this world was he doing?

A footstep through long grass. His attention snapped to the present.

Someone was out there. The same person he'd sensed stalking Evie in the wood by the river. Definitely Unhuman. But it was too dark and Evie's scent was blocking the smell of whatever was out there so he couldn't tell who or what it was.

He tried to focus. He could hear the sound of dry leaves rubbing together and a tread – heavy, a boy's tread. And a swish, like the wind cutting through leaves. Except it was a windless night.

It was a tail, not the wind. His eyes flew to the trees.

Damn Caleb, what was he doing here? He narrowed his hearing

to one segment, fifteen metres or so behind them. There it was again. The swishing noise, the sound a blade makes when it falls.

He turned to Evie with a smile. 'Let's get inside, it's cool out here.'

Once inside he waited until Evie was upstairs and out of the way before he headed back downstairs to hunt Caleb. Lobo was pacing the back porch anxiously, pausing now and then to howl at the moon. Lucas stopped to stroke him and whisper in his ear that he could relax now, he would see to it. The dog whined just once and then stopped pacing, taking up sentry duty in front of the door instead. Their last line of defence – and a pretty useless one against a Scorpio.

Lucas darted into the shadows of the trees and circuited the house, but there was no sign of Caleb.

What had he been doing here? Why had he followed them to the river and what had he been planning to do? If he hadn't scented him and disturbed him, would he have attacked Evie in the clearing? Was that his plan? Was it sanctioned by Tristan? Surely not. If it had been the others would have come too. And Tristan would have warned him.

Lucas slipped back into the house, one thing still puzzling him. How had the Hunters let Caleb through the net? There were three of them patrolling the perimeter of the town. Lucas had to go the long way around to the Del Rey ranch every day just to avoid the one with the red hair. Even though he doubted any of them could pick him up, he wasn't going to go rubbing their noses in him. He couldn't believe that Victor and three other Hunters wouldn't notice an Unhuman as easy to sense as Caleb.

He took the stairs noiselessly and hovered outside Evie's room. No light shone from under the door. He turned the handle and the door opened freely. No more chair in the way.

She was sleeping, wrapped tight in her covers like they could cocoon her from the outside world and all she feared in it.

Yet what she feared most was right here in the room with her.

The baseball bat was lying across the sheets. He walked over to the bed and looked down. Her hair was half covering her face, her arms locked around her knees which were drawn up to her chest. She looked like she was desperately trying to hide from something. It was so different to how she appeared normally – yes, she was always a little defensive and on guard, but she never seemed to be hiding. In fact, she always seemed the opposite, to be standing so tall, facing everything head on.

He frowned. He wasn't here to look at her and wonder at her fears. He scanned the room. There was no sign of the book she'd been reading the other night – the one he'd heard her turning the pages of. God only knew where she kept it in this riot of a room. This would be a handy time for Grace to appear and help him out, but he was on his own. As he'd wanted it, he reminded himself.

The blue dress she'd worn earlier, the one that had matched her eyes so exactly, had been discarded on the floor. He picked it up and felt the featherweight of it run through his fingers – and felt the same panicked sense of something slipping away inside him. A moaning sound made him turn back to the bed. Evie was crying. In her sleep. The tears were rolling down her cheeks, but she stayed locked in the foetal position even as she cried. He reached a hand out and stroked back a strand of damp hair, wiping away a tear. A small sigh escaped her lips and he drew back his hand, staring at the teardrop on the end of his thumb.

Then, with a rush that caused Evie to pull the sheets even tighter around her, he left the room.

14

He took a blindfold out of his pocket and Evie backed away from him.

'No, don't use the blindfold, Victor,' the woman with red hair said. 'Let her try without it first.'

Evie glanced between them. Victor was looking cross. Earl, the short and squat and mostly silent one, just looked bored. He kept staring around at the cornfield they were standing in as though expecting the Brotherhood to arrive any second. He was armed to take them though, she thought, what with the two swords crossed on his back. He looked like some crazy-eyed Viking. By comparison she felt quite naked and defenceless in her jeans and T-shirt. Victor had told her to quit the jeans but she'd had a feeling training was going to involve running and sweat and possibly blood so she'd stuck with denim.

She did another double take at Mrs Lovell, still not believing she was a Hunter. That the woman in the plaid skirt who'd come into the store and told her not to quit her diner job, the woman who'd babysat her as a child, ran the knitting circle, and who could rival her own mother for nosiness, was a Hunter who'd been placed in the town to protect her.

Evie couldn't get her head around the fact that she was that important. She felt incredibly guilty that she'd sentenced someone to fifteen years of tweed and small-town politics for the thankless task of keeping an eye on her. But Jocelyn, as she was asking Evie to call her now, hadn't seemed in any way resentful, rather she'd walked right up to her and given her a huge hug. She seemed relieved that the charade was over, had even swapped the sensible shoes and plaid skirts for tight leggings and running shoes. She looked fifteen years younger. And had very good legs too, Evie noted.

The third Hunter she'd been introduced to was a girl aged about twenty.

At first Evie had been stunned. For some reason she'd expected them all to look like Victor – tall, middle-aged and built like brick houses. And Mrs Lovell and Earl were both about forty, she guessed – which gave Evie some comfort on the life expectancy front – and they both seemed to be pretty militant in the stature department. So to be confronted with a girl shorter and slighter than her, wearing sheer black tights underneath hot pants and heavy Doctor Marten boots, had thrown her.

Victor had introduced the girl as Risper. She hadn't offered her hand. In fact, Risper had barely lifted her chin in greeting. She had long black hair and blunt-cut bangs that hung down to meet her eyes, which were a churning dark brown colour.

Evie had expected some level of friendship from among her fellow Hunters. A slap on the back, maybe, a welcome to the fold – at the very least a smile or a word of encouragement. But no, only Mrs Lovell had bothered to smile at her and make her feel slightly less nervous about what was coming. Though now Evie caught her chewing her lip anxiously and darting little glances her way.

It wasn't making her feel any more optimistic about the training that was about to kick off.

'OK, Evie, this is designed to develop your instincts,' Victor announced.

A snort from Risper?

Evie whipped her head in her direction but she was just staring sullenly at Victor.

'I want you to stand here. And I'm going to give you these.' He held something in his hand but Evie couldn't work out what they were. 'The others are going to come at you and the idea is for you to hit them with one of these before they can touch you.'

'So a bit like tag, then,' Evie said lightly, staring around at the two-metre-wide corn circle they'd made in the middle of the field. The farmer would think he'd had alien visitors when it came to harvest.

'Yes, I suppose.' Victor shook his head. 'You can try without the blindfold first.' He handed her what was in his hand.

She looked down at what looked like little darts with pointed ends. 'Won't these hurt?' she said, looking up at Victor.

A little smile fluttered around his mouth. 'Only if they make contact.'

She stared at him hard. What was he suggesting? That she couldn't hit them? Right. She pulled her hair back and fastened it in a ponytail. She'd show him.

By the time she was done, the others had disappeared. Victor was standing on the far side of the circle observing her.

'Concentrate,' he told her.

She furrowed her brow in reply and tried to block out the sound of the corn swaying and the chirrup of crickets. She could hear an airplane droning overhead. She spun in a circle, trying to catch the whisper of movement, her arm raised, dart poised. When she spun back, he was standing in front of her. Earl. The silent one. She glared at him as he placed his hand gently on her shoulder.

'OK, out,' Victor called. Earl went to stand next to him. Evie huffed out a breath and tried to concentrate again. She closed her eyes, struggling to pick out a break in a corn stalk or the tread of a foot on uneven ground. There. Just there. She spun and threw her dart. The surprised expression in Mrs Lovell's eyes showed Evie she must have hit her. She looked down and spied the shaft of the dart sticking into the top of her thigh.

'Oh God, I'm so sorry, Mrs Lovell,' Evie said, dashing forward.

'Evie!' Victor yelled.

She turned around, confused as to why he was yelling at her, and was thrown backwards, slamming into the ground, the air knocked out of her. She was too stunned at first to understand what had happened but then Risper's boot came down hard on her chest, pinning her to the floor. She writhed underneath it like a bug pinned on a Petri dish, feeling a sudden surge of hatred towards this girl in her ridiculously short hot pants. Risper snarled something unintelligible and stepped away at Victor's order.

Mrs Lovell helped her to her feet and brushed her down. She'd pulled the dart out of her leg and handed it over. 'Good shot, well done,' she said.

'OK, again,' Victor shouted.

'What?' Evie rounded on him, nursing her bruised ribs.

'This time, you're blindfolded.'

She started to blurt out something about him obviously wanting to see her killed and why not just give them all sniper rifles while he was at it, but he wasn't listening. He twisted her and tied the blackout cloth over her eyes without another word, leaving her nose and mouth clear. Then he spun her into the centre of the circle.

'You have to learn to concentrate, Evie. You need to block out the other sounds, focus on your instincts. Focus!'

She tried to follow his orders and focus. There was no way she was going to let that girl Risper floor her again. She breathed out and urged her senses to take over. She breathed in, smelling the air, Victor's aftershave, something more floral from behind her. Then she felt it, a rush in her head, a sensation in her gut that made her duck, all at once, folding herself flat to the floor. She heard the grunt as someone landed awkwardly off to her right and she twisted around, her hand ripping a dart forwards.

'Excellent. You got Earl.' Victor's voice boomed through the clearing.

She felt the elation in her head, the smile break across her lips, heard Earl's footfall as he went to join Victor. She tried to get her bearings, stood slowly, turning in a circle, sniffing the air, letting her instincts guide her. She could hear the melody of the wind through the branches. It had a rhythm, and then the rhythm broke. There was the floral scent again. She threw a dart without even thinking, straight ahead of her. There was no sound in reply to indicate if she'd hit anyone, but a gentle hand touched her on her shoulder.

'Nearly, Evie. You just missed Jocelyn.'

Evie frowned under her blindfold. That left Risper. She concentrated hard, letting the darkness sink into her, letting her instincts rise to the fore. The noises were secondary she was realising, helpful, as were the smells, but really it was like she was being guided by some completely new sense. Which if she could learn to trust it could be bigger and better than all her other senses put together. Only it was evasive and she was scared to give in to it. It was like throwing herself into an abyss.

She took a step. Then suddenly she felt it – her body screaming at her to move – and she threw herself in a wide arc as something whistled by her. She heard Victor shout a warning, 'Risper!' Whether he was warning Evie or yelling at Risper wasn't clear.

But it was too late. Evie was running on instinct. She dropped to the ground and rolled as another thud landed right on the spot she had been standing on and, with a flick of her wrist, threw the final dart sideways.

She was rewarded with a scream.

She tore off her blindfold. Risper was clutching her arm. She yanked the dart out as Evie watched and flung it to the floor. Victor came up and put a restraining arm on her but his grin was aimed at Evie. Mrs Lovell and Earl were also smiling at her from behind him. She smiled back.

'I think I found my instincts,' she said.

'Finally,' Victor replied. 'OK, one last time for today.'

Evie started pulling the blindfold up. Now she had it, she couldn't wait to go again. Maybe this time she could put a trio of darts in Risper.

'No, no blindfold this time, Evie,' Victor said. 'This time we use weapons. You'll need your eyes.'

'Wait, wait, what? Weapons? What do you mean?' she asked, grabbing for his sleeve.

'Here,' he said, handing her a gun. 'It's loaded with blanks. They explode with coloured paint on impact so we can see if you actually hit anything. The others are armed too.'

She turned around. Mrs Lovell was clutching a bow and arrow and Evie burst out laughing before catching herself. Because no one else was laughing. Not even Mrs Lovell. Earl had his two crossed swords. She forced herself to keep a blank face as she turned with a sense of foreboding towards Risper. She saw immediately that she had been right to be afraid.

Risper had two circles of steel in her hand with serrated edges. Her father had stocked something similar in his store. They were the blades from a circular saw.

She spun back to Victor. 'Are you serious? And you're only giving me blanks?' Had he not figured out yet that Risper was a maniac and was clearly planning on embedding those round metal discs in her skull?

'You'll be fine,' Victor said, brushing her off. 'They won't hurt you. It's just to up the ante a little.'

Up the ante? This wasn't some gladiator arena with Victor casting himself as Emperor Augustus. This was madness. They all had weapons that could kill and she had a gun that fired blanks. How was that fair?

'I can't . . .' she whispered to Victor's retreating back. She whipped around, feeling herself suddenly alone. The circle was empty.

She hesitated for only a second before her automatic pilot kicked in and she cocked the gun. She held it like her dad had taught her, in both hands, pointing dead ahead, and then, aware she was a fish in a barrel in her current position at the centre of an open circle, she slipped between two rows of corn and disappeared.

15

Lucas kept circling the cornfield. At one point he'd had an uninterrupted view of the circle with Evie stood in the centre blindfolded. He'd watched Victor give the orders and the others converge. He knew Victor, of course, and he had heard about Earl, a long-standing member of the Hunters, recognised him by the baldness and the crossed swords on his back. The older red-headed lady, Jocelyn, lived in town. She was the one he had to avoid every day on his way to the Del Rey ranch. The fourth one, a girl called Risper, was an unknown. He didn't think even Tristan knew of her. And clearly she was not a fan of Evie's.

He decided to follow her, keeping his distance. He didn't want to give himself away but they were all concentrating so hard on sneaking up on Evie in the centre of the circle that they weren't paying any attention to their own instincts or the fact that an Unhuman was stalking them. But he didn't want to throw Evie's instincts – as delicately balanced as they were – she needed them all focused on Risper's whereabouts.

Because he didn't want to distract her, he had pulled back, just far enough to see the attack – Risper springing out of the corn straight at Evie, Evie ducking and rolling blind, spinning out of Risper's way, narrowly avoiding a roundhouse kick to the ribs and firing a dart blind but hitting Risper's arm.

He had smiled despite himself but now he was stalking Risper, who was stalking Evie, and his eyes were on the metal circles she was holding between her thumb and forefinger. He had no doubt that Risper intended to use them, no matter what Victor's warnings had been, and his curiosity was piqued. Someone else with vengeance on their mind? Or was there some other drive? Either way it was strange for Victor to have her in the field. Mind you, it would save the Brotherhood a job if he just sat back and let her get on with it.

He felt Earl to his left – the man was light-footed for his size, but the sound of him unsheathing his swords was a dead giveaway. Luckily Evie heard it too. She froze and he watched her close her eyes and take a deep breath. When she let it out she started running full tilt and he had to sprint to keep pace with her, running a parallel course, getting flashes of her dark hair flying. At one point she came to a skidding stop, her blue eyes darting towards him, and he realised that she could sense him. Could she even see him? He had dived backwards well out of range, almost to the edge of the field, and waited until finally he heard a bullet crack and Earl shout, 'I'm hit.'

Lucas couldn't stop from smiling this time. Good hit. He wished he could have seen it. He edged further into the field, still anxious to keep an eye on Risper. It was easier to find Evie, he knew her scent by now, the strong smell of the lavender shampoo she used and the softer, more subtle scent of her skin. She was running at a crouch now, weaving in-between stalks but on a clear path, as though she was being drawn somewhere. He saw the wire on the ground a split second before she did and had to stop from yelling at her to jump. He didn't need to. She saw it in time and leapt over it, diving onto her back with the gun pointed into the air. When she saw no one there she looked confused. And that's when the red-haired woman stepped out from behind her, and tapped her on the back of the neck with the tip of an arrow.

Silently she bent down and offered her hand to Evie and helped her up. Then she took Evie's gun and fired it at the ground, making sure she got the wet paint on her shoe.

'I'm out,' she yelled, her eyes not leaving Evie's the whole time. She then pointed with her arrow into the corn and whispered, 'Watch your back.'

Evie nodded silently and moved off. Lucas followed.

Risper was almost as silent as he was. Almost as undetectable. Almost.

Lucas picked her up first. She was stalking them, circling around Evie to come at her from behind. Lucas dropped back and hovered just out of range but Risper was like a panther, focused only on dropping her prey and not on the Unhuman right beside her that could drop her at any moment if he chose. He found his breathing was running rapid, his hands reaching for his father's blade, and he had to force himself to hold back. There would be another time. Not right here. He wouldn't stand a chance if he blew his cover taking out a girl who wasn't even his target.

Risper was about ten metres to Evie's left when he caught the circle of silver glinting in the sun. Evie paused too, as though suddenly alert to the danger, and Lucas watched as Risper drew back her arm.

He had to choose. And in the instant that Risper brought her arm forward, Lucas chose. He ran straight at Risper, knocking the wind out of her, managing to jolt her arm as she let the disc fly. She tore around, her eyes desperately searching for whatever had bumped her, but he was gone before she could piece it together. Her reaction would be panic, her senses screaming at her that there was an Unhuman out there, but maybe there was doubt too. No Unhuman would be stupid enough to enter a space with that many Hunters in it – would they? He tracked back to Evie, who was crouched down, her eyes fixed on the disc lying on the ground by her side.

An ear of corn lay next to it. She picked up the disc and turned it over, seeming to realise that it had been a kill shot but not understanding fully how she had avoided it. She got to her feet and started running, silently. She reached the clearing and dropped to her knees, her head bowed, her eyes shut.

Lucas felt himself tense, his ears tuned to the sound of Risper heading this way. What was Evie doing? He took a step towards her, instinctively wanting to shield her, realised what he was doing and stepped back into the shadows. Evie's eyes suddenly flew open. She was staring right at him but then she frowned before screwing her eyes shut again. He melted backwards and when she opened her eyes again he saw the confusion as she stared at the empty space around her.

And then in a move he couldn't have foreseen she hurled the circular blade right at him. It grazed the air a millimetre to his left. Damn it. She was aware of him. She was feeling him. And he was endangering her more than Risper by being here.

And then he saw Risper stepping into the circle between him and Evie, levelling the blade and hurling it with force. He felt the wind still and heard the single whisper of steel cutting air and it felt like he was waiting for it to slice into him.

'Hit!' Risper yelled.

He stepped forward into the circle of light, saw his shadow

145

fall ahead of him, announcing him. He heard the footsteps of the others running full tilt towards them and he stepped back into the shadows as they burst into the clearing.

And then he turned and vanished.

16

She could not believe she was missing a body part. And she really could not believe that Victor had done nothing more than tell Risper to pick up the blade and get lost. As far as she was concerned, Risper deserved banishment from the Hunters altogether, or imprisonment at the very least. She was quite obviously bat-shit crazy.

Her ear was stinging like she'd thrown herself head first into some nettles. The very tip was missing and that was going to be impossible to explain to her mother. And would mean wearing her hair down for the rest of her life. She was white hot with anger when she burst into the kitchen, blood trailing down her collar, her hand against the side of her head, holding Victor's cravat in place over the remainder of her ear.

She wasn't expecting Lucas to be leaning against the wall in the kitchen, arms folded across his chest, an anxious look on his face, or for him to head straight over to her when she slammed through the screen door.

'What happened?' he asked, his eyes seeming to register both shock and relief at the same time.

She faltered. 'I, er – there was an accident with a coat hanger.'

He laughed under his breath and stroked the hair back away from the bloodied cravat she was holding over her ear. She felt a shudder all the way to the soles of her feet.

'Who won?' he asked. 'I hope the coat hanger is lying in pieces somewhere.'

'Not quite,' she answered tersely.

He ushered her straight over to one of the stools and before she could resist had pulled her hand away from her ear. She winced and felt the blood flow freshly. He headed to the sink and doused a cloth, brought it back and held it to the side of her head. She relished the coldness. And the heat his body was relaying to hers. He was standing close enough that she could make out the individual lashes that framed his eyes and the smoothness of his skin. He smelt nice too. Fresh citrus overlaid with that worn leather smell. The pain was dulling. She felt all floaty suddenly. She remembered seeing him in the cornfield – or a mirage of him, just before Risper had sliced her head open, like he'd come to warn her. Maybe her instinct took on the form of a person. Odd, very odd, that she should choose him, but at the same time if her imagination wanted to conjure him she wasn't going to complain too loudly.

'What are you doing home?' she asked, trying to pull herself towards some kind of coherence.

'I got off early,' he murmured, turning away. 'Where d'you keep the Tylenol?'

'In that drawer over there,' she said, pointing.

He filled a glass and brought her a pill, which she took and swallowed, all the time looking into his grey eyes. He was really quite amazingly hot – with such incredible cheekbones and wide-set eyes. And his lips – his lips . . . She fell forwards off the stool towards them and he caught her by the top of the arms.

'Are you OK?' he said, setting her to rights on the stool again.

'Yeah, sorry, light-headed. Blood loss,' she said, avoiding

looking at him. But she *was* feeling dizzy all of a sudden, her head had pins and needles, her ear was throbbing.

'Maybe you should go and lie down,' he said, sounding concerned.

'Yeah, maybe I should,' she answered. But really she didn't want to lie down, upstairs in her bed alone. She wanted to fall forwards into his arms and have him hold her for a while. That would be nice. Maybe it would stop the infernal buzzing in her head.

She pulled it together enough to stand up shakily. Lucas's hands hovered around her waist, ready to catch her. She had to have some dignity in the situation, she realised, as she pushed his hands away. She didn't need his help. She could make it to her bedroom. It was only a bit of blood and as a Hunter she was going to have to get used to getting hurt and she was going to have to get used to picking herself up and fighting back. She wasn't going to let a girl with too much attitude and a lame-ass throw get the better of her. It was just an ear. Not a leg. Still, she would definitely be finding a way to pay Risper back – an ear for an ear, so to speak. Or maybe an arm for an ear.

She made it to the bottom of the stairs before she felt the walls crushing in on her. She fell against the banister, gripping it tight. Maybe she did need help after all.

'Lucas?' she said, turning to him.

'Yes?' he answered and she saw the flash of irritation on his face. Registered he was standing with one hand on the handle of the back door as though he'd been just about to leave.

She hesitated. 'Nothing,' she said.

17

By the time he reached the Mission, the last rays of sun were hitting the road. The building had a deserted air. There was only one telltale sign that anyone was even living there. On the second floor Lucas saw a dim, flickering light.

Joshua would still be asleep. But the others would be awake. He drove in through the gate, past the *Trespassers will be shot* sign, and parked in front of the main entrance.

There was no point going about this subtly and trying to sneak in. They would all sense him. Grace had probably seen him coming.

The hallway was empty, and his footsteps echoed across the marble floor. Straight ahead was the chapel but he took the staircase to the second floor and strode down past the weapons room, to the room at the very end, the one designated as a recreation space. Inside, in the heavily curtained gloom, watching television with his feet kicked up onto a leather stool and his tail resting along the back of the couch, sat Caleb. He looked up when Lucas entered. The light from the television was casting an eerie glow onto his face.

'The warrior returns,' he muttered, before turning his attention back to the football game playing on mute.

Lucas stepped in front of the screen, blocking his view. 'What were you doing there?'

Caleb looked up, a smile curling his lip. 'Where?' he asked in an innocently mocking tone.

Lucas heard the roar in his voice. 'Don't.' He took a step forwards, became aware of Caleb's tail pricked up and lowered his voice. 'You were in the woods the other night. You were following Evie and me. Why?'

Caleb didn't answer, just kept smiling.

Lucas ignored the swishing tail and bent down so his face was just an inch away from Caleb's. 'You come near her again,' he said, feeling the fury burning in him, '– *us* again – and I swear I'll kill you.'

Caleb arched an eyebrow. 'And break your oath?'

Lucas straightened up. To kill another member of the Brotherhood would lead to instant exile from all the realms and a death sentence on his head.

'What's going on?'

Lucas looked over. Shula was leaning in the doorway and it didn't look like she'd bothered to change since he'd been here the last time. Apart from to accessorise her silk nightgown with a fuchsia-pink feather boa.

'What's going on?' she asked again, her eyes narrowing at the sight of Lucas standing over Caleb. 'What are you doing back here? I thought you were out playing undercover Shadow Warrior.'

'Caleb almost blew my cover.'

Shula stepped into the room. 'Ooh, naughty, naughty Caleb,' she laughed. But her eyes were as venomous as her skin. Probably at the thought that Caleb had done what she hadn't thought to do.

'You went without us,' she said, circling around Lucas, her fingers trailing up his shirtsleeve, not quite touching him. Like a snake, he thought. It was like having a cobra wind its way around his limbs.

He stood his ground, though his natural reaction was to remove himself from strike range.

'You'd all have gone back there without me if you'd had the chance,' Caleb said, referring to Shula's original plan to ditch him and go back with the others to kill Evie.

Shula wasn't going to be diverted. She acted like Caleb wasn't even in the room. 'And anyway, how did you manage to swing that one, Lucas? How'd you get Tristan to agree when he flat out refused the rest of us?'

Lucas shrugged. 'Because I'm half human, Shula. They don't sense me in the same way they sense you. I'm the only one who can get close.'

Caleb snorted from the couch. 'Yeah, he's getting close all right.'

Lucas felt the anger rising in him. He spun around and found Caleb grinning at him, his eyes glinting. He knew from Shula's silence and the fact that her hand had fallen to her side that she was studying him for signs that what Caleb was saying was true. Damn them both.

'Where's Tristan?' he asked, before Shula could get a word in.

She paused before speaking and he met her eye directly and unflinchingly because he had nothing to hide. He was getting close to the girl because that was his job.

'He's with the Elders,' Shula finally said. 'Explaining to them about you.'

So Tristan was back in the Shadowlands. Lucas felt a huge sense of relief. Right now he didn't think he could face the older man. He'd needed to come back to see Caleb – to warn him off – but he hadn't wanted Tristan to know. He'd done what he'd come here for and now he wanted to get back to Riverview. He nodded at Shula and left the room, heading back down the corridor.

Suddenly Shula appeared at his side. 'What are you hoping to pull off?' she asked.

Lucas didn't look at her. He kept walking towards the stairs. 'The end of the Hunters. For good.'

Shula jumped in front of him, blocking his path. 'Is that it?' she demanded. 'Is it really about your little revenge? Or is it about something else?'

Lucas stopped walking and turned to face her. 'What are you talking about?'

He saw Shula's expression shift, the hardness drop away for a second, exposing something raw and sad underneath the venom. Was that even possible? That she felt anything other than pleasure at exploiting other people's misery?

'She's human, Lucas,' Shula said softly, the sadness in her voice now, as well as her eyes, 'and she's a Hunter.'

'What are you getting at?' he replied through gritted teeth.

She looked at him for a moment longer, then shook her head and turned away, the familiar hardness descending. 'Nothing.'

They kept walking. At the top of the stairs Shula spoke again – the old Shula returned, her voice spiky, her smile mocking. 'So you're not going to ask how we all are, then?'

'How are you all?' he asked without a smile.

'We're great, thanks for asking. Joshua's such a degenerate I'm thinking of locking him in his cell permanently and painting the walls with garlic. Nothing changes there. Grace keeps going off into tranceland but says she can't see anything so who knows what she's doing. I think she's a dud, personally, and is making it all up. We should ask the Sybll for a refund or something.' She was ticking them each off on her fingers as she went. 'Neena's spending more time as a bird than as a person.'

Neena – about the only person in the Brotherhood Lucas actually liked.

'You know, I think she could try being more attractive, don't you?' Shula asked in a hush, leaning in conspiratorially.

He made a non-committal sound. Neena was fine the way she was.

'At least less *feathered*. If I were a Shapeshifter and could look like anyone,' Shula said, throwing her boa over her shoulder, 'well, I'd look like me, but maybe she could try Angelina Jolie or something.'

Lucas studied her, the way her green skin gleamed under the reddish light in the hall, the head thrown back as she hooted with laughter.

'Why'd you always have to be like this, Shula?' he asked.

Her head snapped back. 'Oh you think anyone will ever look at her? You know,' she said, lowering her voice, 'I think she has a thing for the fangs. I've seen the way she checks out Joshua. I think she's letting him taste her, on the sly.'

Lucas gave her a look. It wasn't even worth contesting. Neena would sooner spend her life shifted into a cockroach than let Joshua touch her.

'Someone should tell her it's impossible,' Shula said, ignoring his look. 'She's a Shapeshifter. He's a Thirster. It's about as tragic as a Hunter and an Unhuman hooking up. It can only ever end in tears.'

He moved fast, backing her into the banister. 'What are you getting at?' he asked, keeping his voice low.

Shula held his gaze. 'Don't forget what you are, Lucas.'

'What am I?' he demanded under his breath.

'You're one of us. One of the Brotherhood. As your father was before you.' She reached a hand out and laid it against his chest where his amulet lay under his shirt. Her touch burned even through the cotton of his shirt. 'Don't forget this,' she said.

Then she was gone, half dancing, half skipping down the hallway, her feather boa floating behind her. He stared after her blankly for a second. Why had she felt she had to remind him of what he was? He knew exactly what he was and exactly *who* he was. The oath was stronger for him than for all the others. He carried his vengeance with him, for him it was personal – for the others a game, an honour, an allegiance with fools, a cross to bear. For none of them was it a fight for justice. Just for him.

So how dare Shula and Caleb question his loyalty to the Brotherhood? Imply he was – what? Falling for a Hunter? Was that really what they meant? What they believed? Damn Caleb for seeding that in Shula's head. If it got back to Tristan he'd be hauled back here and have to explain. Maybe lose his chance once and for all. But his chance for what, exactly?

To discover the secrets of the Hunters? What massive secrets had he uncovered? There was the identity of that new Hunter, Risper, with her homicidal agenda. He'd seen something of the way they trained – but that could have been guessed at. He'd learnt that Evie was strong with natural instincts when she bothered to listen to them. But when it had come down to it, when he could have sat back and let Risper kill her, he hadn't. And he didn't know why. And he also didn't know why he was so angry at himself for distracting Evie in the cornfield. She'd been hurt because of him, and when he pictured her with blood pouring down the side of her face he felt himself wince. But why for all the realms did he even care?

He was so bursting with fury as he jumped down the steps that he didn't see her until he was right in front of her. It was like she'd been waiting for him, expecting him at just this point, in just this place.

Well, of course she had.

'Hello, Grace,' he said.

Grace stared at him blankly. Her blonde hair was tied back and her big eyes were dull and glassy, as though she'd OD'd on tranquillisers.

She reached out a hand and took his wrist. Her eyes suddenly became luminously clear. And very, very afraid.

He tore his arm out of her grip. 'What is it, Grace? What do you keep seeing?'

'Nothing, Lucas,' she said, shaking her head.

'Yes, you do. You're seeing something.'

She sighed. 'It's nothing you can change, Lucas.'

He put his hands on her shoulders gently and saw the confusion and then the pain in her eyes. She shut them, as though trying to block whatever she was seeing. 'Tell me,' he asked again.

She slowly opened them. 'I see you dying.'

His hands dropped from her shoulders. He took a step back, tried to laugh it off, even though it was what he'd been expecting. 'We're all going to die, Grace.'

'Yes,' she said sadly, 'but you die soon, and you die because of the choice you make.'

'When I chose to join the Brotherhood, Grace, I knew dying was par for the course. It's the only way out of this.' It was true. When he joined he knew he was signing away his life, but it seemed a small price to pay – even the right price to pay.

'It's what you choose to die *for* that changes, Lucas,' Grace said, walking away.

She left him gazing at the floor, at the patterns of the marble tiles, trying to figure it out. He thought about going after her and asking her to explain. What choice?

And surely if he knew the particular choice he was going to make, couldn't he unmake it? Choose differently? But she had said it was nothing he could change. Why not? Was fate so set in stone?

He stumbled out to his car, revved the engine and tore through the gates back onto the freeway, back to Riverview. Back to the Hunter.

18

Somehow Evie managed to drag herself out of bed and to the diner for her shift. Mainly because she didn't want to have to answer any questions from her mum and because she didn't want Victor to come by, not find her working and assume she couldn't handle a few hours of running around a cornfield blindfolded with a bunch of trained assassins trying to kill her.

Her ear was still stinging and her head and back ached from all the falls. She had a bruise the size of a DM boot on her chest and a general sense of unease. The training had gone OK but she now had to watch her back not just for psychotic Unhumans about to take her out but also for Risper. She suddenly understood what was meant by the saying, *Keep your friends close and your enemies closer.*

When she set foot in the diner she was surprised to see Mrs Lovell, back in her sensible plaid skirt and lace-up shoes, sitting at one of the booths at the back. She hurried around the counter towards Joe and took her apron.

'How've you been, Evie?' Joe asked.

'Yeah, um, good thanks,' she replied. It was the first time they'd talked since the night of the parking lot attack, her first shift back at the diner since then.

'How's the new job working out for you?' he asked with a cheeky smile.

Evie tried to smile back but she just couldn't. 'It's OK,' she said, taking her order pad and heading over to Mrs Lovell's table.

'Hi, Mrs Lovell, what can I get you?'

'How's your ear?' Mrs Lovell's face was a picture of worry.

'Missing in action,' Evie answered, surreptitiously flicking her hair over to hide it. 'This feels weird,' she whispered, ducking her head. 'I still can't get over the fact that you're not actually Mrs Lovell.'

Mrs Lovell smiled faintly.

'Do you actually knit?' Evie asked.

Mrs Lovell let out a small laugh. 'I do now. I've been in town almost fifteen years. It's my home, Evie. As it is yours.'

Evie wrinkled her nose. 'Did they make you come here?'

Mrs Lovell's eyes dashed to the counter. She held her menu up to look like she was ordering. 'They didn't need to make me, Evie. I wanted to come. I wanted to make sure you were safe.'

Evie's mouth fell open. Why would anyone do that for her? Before she could ask another question, Mrs Lovell took her hand and squeezed it.

'Evie, I knew your real mother. She was my best friend. More – she was like a sister. You look like your dad but you have your mother's smile and her eyes,' she said sadly. 'You're like her,' she said, suppressing a smile. 'She was just as brave as you.'

Evie felt her knees shaking. She had to swallow repeatedly before she could open her mouth without fear of choking on a sob. 'You knew them?' She shook her head. 'How did they die? Victor won't tell me.'

Mrs Lovell pulled her hand away. 'Can you come over to my house later?' she said quietly. She looked up suddenly. Was that a

159

flash of fear Evie saw in her eyes? 'Don't let anyone see you,' she said.

Evie nodded, wondering who she was so scared of. Why the secrecy? Maybe she just didn't want her cover blown.

'Just a coffee, thanks, Evie,' she said in a louder voice for Joe's benefit, putting the menu down.

Mrs Lovell's house was a small clapboard one not far from Evie's own, on the road north out of town. Evie parked further up the street down a dirt track and backtracked on foot, coming around to the rear porch and tapping quietly on the door.

Mrs Lovell let her in, ushering her through into her front room and down onto a couch laden with throws and cushions. Then she sat down next to her. 'Here,' she said, handing something to Evie.

Evie took it. It was a photograph of two girls. The girl on the left had big earrings and red hair in a ponytail springing from the top of her head. The girl on the right was grinning widely, and had brown hair swept over one shoulder and blue eyes. Evie recognised the smile because once upon a time she used to grin like that. There were photos to prove it.

'Excuse the fashion,' Mrs Lovell said, 'early Eighties. We were going through a punk phase. That's when we met your father. You should have seen him.'

'How old were you?'

'Sixteen,' Mrs Lovell answered, 'a year younger than you are now. We'd just started training together. Alongside your father. He was rather gorgeous. We all had our eye on him it must be said.'

'How did they die?'

Mrs Lovell took a deep breath. 'They died protecting you.

They were trying to save you from something very bad.' Her eyes flashed to the door as though the bad thing was just outside, lurking in the shadows. 'And we placed you with the Tremains to keep you safe.'

'Why did the Hunters come back for me?'

Mrs Lovell bit her lip before answering. 'We didn't come back for you. Some of us never left you.' She sighed. 'I don't think you realise who you are, Evie. How important you are.'

Evie stared at her blankly. Mrs Lovell reached over and took the photo from her hands. 'You're going to be much stronger than any of us, Evie. Much more powerful. It's why Risper doesn't like you.'

'Doesn't *like* me?' Evie laughed bitterly. 'Understatement. She wants to *kill* me.'

Mrs Lovell shook her head. 'She doesn't. She can't kill you.'

'Er, she tried to plant a saw blade in my head.'

'Believe me, she won't kill you,' Mrs Lovell reiterated.

'She took half my ear off,' Evie said, flicking her hair over her shoulder to better display the blood-soaked Band-Aid on her ear.

'Well, Victor's had words. He's told her to back off.'

'Words?' Evie gaped. 'Why is she even here if she hates me so much?'

'Because,' Mrs Lovell said, sighing, 'despite her attitude she's good to have onside. She'll train you well. You'll just have to ignore the anger. She's jealous.'

'But *why* is she jealous of me?'

'You're the child of two of the most powerful Hunters there ever were. And you're a direct descendant of the original Hunters.'

161

'So? Why would anyone be jealous of the fact I'm an orphan with a family tree heavily branched with murderers?'

'Because, Evie,' and now there was an urgency, a seriousness in her voice that made Evie sit up, 'you could be the one who ends this. That's what the prophecy says.'

'Prophecy?' Evie asked. 'I thought we left the clairvoyancy to the Unhumans.'

'It's an Unhuman prophecy. From a Sybll. Laid down many, many hundreds of years ago. The legend has it that the prophecy was broken into pieces and spread out by the Sybll, who didn't want the realms fighting pointlessly over what would be and could never be changed. The Hunters have tried for centuries to gather those pieces, hoping they would reveal the identity of the child. We have one part.' She stopped, looking frustrated by Evie's blank face. 'Did you not read the book Victor gave you?'

'Yes,' Evie said, nodding vaguely.

'Did you read about the prophecy of the White Light?'

Evie thought back. 'Yes,' she said. 'You mean the bit that went on about a White Light ending a war by severing something? Yada yada. I skipped that bit. I thought it was a metaphor for something.'

Jocelyn smiled. 'It is. It's a metaphor for you.'

'The White Light.' Evie was the one smiling now. 'Yeah. You've known me all my life, Mrs Lovell.'

'Jocelyn.'

'Jocelyn.' Evie sighed politely. 'Does that sound like me?'

'Yes.' Jocelyn nodded more emphatically. 'You didn't know your real parents, Evie. But if you had you'd maybe understand better why we all believe it. They were incredibly special. Completely in tune with each other. The most exceptional fighters we've seen before or since, though I think in time you might match them.'

But they both got killed, Evie thought, but didn't say. How exceptional at fighting were they really?

'Well, surely there must be other Hunters that spew out children together. I can't be the *only* child of Hunters. Maybe one of the others is this White Light.'

'No, the prophecy spoke of a pure-bred hunter. A child of two who remained. You are the only child of two warriors.'

'What do you mean?'

Mrs Lovell's voice had dropped. She was stroking the edge of the photograph she was holding. 'You're the only one left, Evie.'

The only one left? But the family tree was vast, with so many branches they started to look like thorns.

'How can I be the only one left?' she asked. Was the death rate that appalling?

Jocelyn looked at her sadly and shrugged. That wasn't the answer Evie had quite been looking for.

'You don't have a family,' Evie said, after a moment's pause. It was more a statement than a question.

She'd always thought of Mrs Lovell as an old spinster, but in the photograph she'd just shown her she was young and pretty and, even now, she was still attractive. Not half as old as Evie had thought her to be, once you removed the bun and took away the plaid. And she'd been alone half her life. Maybe *all* her life. Evie swallowed, a sudden vision assaulting her of sitting in a kitchen surrounded by hundreds of cats, her face all wrinkled, her joints arthritic from too much running around chasing down Unhumans. If she even made it to forty – the odds weren't in her favour. She glanced around the room. It was warm, cosy even, but

163

there were no photographs on the mantelpiece, no children's toys lying about, nothing to indicate love or family.

She looked around for the cats.

'It's too dangerous,' Mrs Lovell said quietly, interrupting Evie's stream of thought.

'But what about you?' Evie burst out. 'What about me? What if I want children one day?' Admittedly, up until this point in her life she'd never given children a second thought. But now she was having to consider *not* having any she felt as though something had been stolen from her. Plus she was outraged at the enforced celibacy that Victor had happily failed to mention.

Mrs Lovell stood up. Her face had hardened to fury. She rounded on Evie. 'Would you want to bring a child into the world – knowing what happened to your parents – and knowing what would likely happen to the child – *knowing* that they'd become a Hunter too? That this would be their life?'

Evie blinked up at the older woman. No. She wouldn't. Jocelyn was right. She would never bring children into the world if it meant giving them this life. A future like hers. She winced. Why was she even thinking about it? Having a child would require her to start trusting people again, to actually have a relationship. It would require getting close to someone. *Very* close to someone. And that was definitely off the cards. But even as she thought it she felt her chest constricting. The memory of warm hands on her back, fingers stroking her hair. It felt like that Mixen was there in the room burning her all over again. She closed her eyes, scrunched them tight.

'This life sucks. I—' She didn't finish before Jocelyn dropped onto the couch next to her and took her hand, the fury seemingly dissipated.

'Don't get close to anyone, Evie,' she said. 'Look what happened to Tom. And Anna.'

Evie's eyes flashed open at the mention of their names.

'Tom could have died too. Think about the future. Do you want to be responsible for any more deaths? Of children or friends or lovers?'

Evie shook her head vehemently. At the same time feeling the raw edges of the wound tear open – so it wasn't just her who thought she was responsible for Anna's death. Jocelyn did too. And she was right – she *was* responsible. No matter what Victor tried to tell her about blaming the Brotherhood.

She was responsible, so there was no way she was going to let anyone else get hurt. She closed her eyes again, trying to imagine what that might mean. What shutting herself off to everyone might actually entail.

But the only person in her head, filling the space which should have been filled with friends and phantom children, was Lucas.

19

Evie walked with dead steps and an even deader heart down the hallway to Lucas's room, unsure what was drawing her there. He wasn't in – neither was her mum. The house was deserted and she felt like an intruder, walking through rooms that no longer belonged to her.

She opened the door to his room and hesitated, feeling the ghost of his presence. She felt a shiver travel lightly up her body and fade away in the emptiness that surrounded her.

She found herself trailing her hands over the bedcover, along the seat back, standing in front of the photograph, wondering at the coincidence that they were both orphans. The little boy in the photograph with the shining eyes, unruly hair and wicked grin looked so happy and free standing between his parents. She wondered if Lucas had ever felt that way since or if he would ever feel that way again. Was it even possible? Wasn't that happiness destroyed alongside his innocence? With the knowledge of death and the acceptance of loss?

She turned in a circle. What was she doing here? What was she looking for? She didn't know. She only knew that the sense of longing ignited in her wouldn't go. It just kept burning. She crossed to the wardrobe and threw open the doors, ran her fingers through the few shirts hanging up, leant in and breathed in the smell of his skin. The sense of familiarity rocked her – how could he be so familiar to her? She went and sat on the bed trying to gather her thoughts.

She couldn't. She could only grasp at the smoky edges of them. She lay down, drawing her legs up to her chest, and closed her eyes and for an instant imagined Lucas's arms wrapped around her. Imagined herself folding into him, pressing her face to his neck and breathing in deep. And then came a wave of confusion – why him? Why were her thoughts – even her feet – dragging her towards him? She barely knew him. Had never confided in him or touched him apart from one brief moment when he'd been in front of her, bringing her back to earth, and she'd felt a jolt of something but his face had stayed impassive. What was she doing? She hadn't even kissed him. But she was grieving for him as though she had and as if he was now dead or something.

She saw it then clearly for the first time. She saw that she was right. She *was* grieving – for the fact that she would never be able to get closer than this to him, curled up in his empty bed, breathing in his fading scent, imagining his arms around her. This was as close as she would ever get ever again to anybody. It wasn't just about him, she didn't think, it was the vision of loneliness stretching out ahead of her – a life like Mrs Lovell's, with no love in it. And although she'd forsaken the idea of love after what happened with Tom, now she couldn't have it, she realised how much she wanted it. The power of the sob that broke her was so strong it was more like a convulsion. But it was noiseless, an empty scream from the depths of her that contorted her body in passing.

There was nothing she could do but ride it out until her body stopped heaving – and then she lay there quietly, staring at the wall opposite, boxing up all her memories of the past: Anna's raucous laugh; Tom's lips, their first tentative kiss; her mother brushing her hair into pigtails as a kid, her dad raking leaves in the yard and then burying her under them; her real parents smiling at an unknown photographer and, finally, the memory of Lucas, his hands holding hers, his grey eyes holding her tighter. And then the phantoms from her future: the children and ghosts of kisses that would never happen.

She boxed them up, every last one of them, and put them away, locking them somewhere deep inside where she knew she would struggle to find them again. Where she could leave them to rot and crumble to dust.

Lucas had said that she needed to stay angry, to keep fighting, but there was no fight left in her. Not even anger. The numbness had returned and even as she lay there with the warmth of the comforter beneath her, she could feel bony fingers gripping her, pulling her down. Once, in the heart of winter, Tom had dared her to jump naked into the swimming pond and she had, because back then she'd been impetuous and free and that had seemed like the craziest thing they could ever imagine doing. She thought of it now, how the icy tentacles of weeds had wrapped around her feet and legs, tugging her down, and though she had kicked and struggled with frozen limbs to haul herself to the surface there had been a tiny part of her that had wondered what it would feel like to give in to them. That was how she felt now, poised between kicking her way to an overcast sky above and sinking into the quiet dark. It was so much better, so much quieter, down there in the dark.

But she couldn't put her mother through any more pain or suffering. If she only managed to do one more thing it would be to protect the only person she still loved from any more hurt. So, she guessed she'd better start kicking.

She sat up straight. Smoothed back her hair. Stood. Straightened the cover on the bed and walked down the hallway to her room.

It seemed like a stranger lived here, as though she was surveying the remnants of a dead girl's room. She hurried to the desk and pulled the book out of the drawer. Then she sat on the bed and opened it.

The page fell open onto the prophecy about the White Light. She read it.

> Of two who remain a child will be born,
> A pure-bred warrior, the fated White Light
> Standing alone in the eventual fight
> Severing the realms and closing the way

She read it several times, frowning at the page. She still couldn't see how she was the White Light. It could be talking about anyone. It could be talking about Lobo. Of two who remain? How was that definitely her parents? If it was a real prophecy why hadn't they given a name and made it easier? There wasn't even a date for when this so-called White Light would be born. It was ridiculous. Why did everyone put such stock in it?

She flicked impatiently to the back of the book, to the family tree, and for a long time stared at the barely-readable names written there. Her own, with that little dash after it.

Everyone else had a death date filled in. There was just her, still alive. For the moment. She wondered what date would eventually be recorded there, and by whom? Victor?

She stared at the dates next to the other names. Jocelyn had been right. She was the only direct descendant left. By the 1900s the branches were thinning. A thousand years ago they had been spitting out children. But her parents had just had her. And mortality rates hadn't decreased. She realised that most of her ancestors hadn't made it past thirty-five. Maybe that was another reason for the shrinking birth rates.

Then she saw the name at the edge of the page with a line through it. She peered closer.

Margaret Hunter b. 1974 d.

She realised she was gripping the book tighter. Why was this person scored out? And why was there no death date? Was she still alive?

She jumped up at the sound of a car pulling into the driveway. Lobo's howl brought her to the window. It was Tom's car. She let the curtain fall back and stood there with her eyes shut, wondering what to do. She couldn't face a conversation with anyone right now, couldn't stomach even seeing another person, least of all Tom.

He rang the doorbell and she held her breath. Maybe he would just leave. What was he doing here this late anyway? There was a pause and then she heard footsteps crossing the porch, going down the steps. She waited for the sound of his car engine revving, but instead she heard the squeak of the screen door on the back porch. He'd circled around the house, hoping to find the back door open like it usually was.

'Ev?' she heard Tom call. 'Mrs Tremain?'

She headed for the stairs. She would have to face him at some point. Best get it over with. She threw the back door open, startling him.

Tom took a step back, tripping over Lobo who was busy trying to thrust the ball hanging in his mouth into Tom's hands. 'Hey,' Tom said, 'I wasn't sure if you were in or at the diner.'

Evie didn't answer. She caught the stupid dog's collar and dragged him inside the house.

Tom frowned. 'Can I, er, come in?'

Evie looked up. She didn't want him in the house. She stepped outside, letting the screen door swing shut behind her. Lobo howled. She saw the confusion cross Tom's face at her abruptness.

'What is it?' she snapped.

He looked at her carefully. Then he surprised her completely. 'Do you remember Junior Prom?'

Her mouth fell open. She'd just spent the last hour packing away her memories, and he'd just gone and levered open one of the boxes. With a rush she was back standing in the same spot three years before, dazed by excitement as a fourteen-year-old Tom attached a corsage to her wrist. That had been their first official date. Why'd he have to go and pick that memory out of them all? She suddenly remembered the way he'd looked back then – taller than the other boys his age, with a football scholarship in his future and stitches in his eyebrow from a tackle the week before.

She looked at him now and her eyes found the faint scar over his right eye, the shallow crease in his cheek which deepened when he smiled, the soft curve of his lips. She remembered with a start the way they tasted. How tentative they had been when he had leant down for that first kiss, right here on this porch. And how gentle, and how surprised she'd been that that's how a kiss could feel.

He took a step towards her. 'I love you, Ev. I never stopped loving you.'

She blinked in astonishment. Hurled straight out of the past and back into the now.

It took her a second to gather herself. 'And Kaitlin – does she know this?' she fired back.

He winced. 'That's nothing. She's just—'

She shook her head. 'It's too late, Tom.'

'Why?' he demanded, stepping closer, so close that she would only have to hold her hands up and they'd be flat against his chest. 'It doesn't have to be.'

She couldn't look up at him. There was no way she could meet his eyes. 'Yes. It does,' she mumbled to her feet.

She heard him take a breath and she broke in, knowing if she didn't then every single word he uttered would tear the lids off the rest of her memories.

'I don't feel the same way.' There she had said it. She dared to look up at him, made her face as blank and indifferent as possible. She wrapped her arms across her chest and watched her words as they hit home.

He took a step back as if she'd pushed him. 'What happened to you?' he said finally, shaking his head slowly at her.

'You have to ask?' she demanded.

'No,' Tom said. 'It's more than the accident – than me and Anna. It's more recent than that. You were angry, yes, but in the last week you've gone from hating me to wanting to make up with me to hating me again. But now it's worse. Last night you looked at me like you might still feel something, but now it's like you can't bear the sight of me. What's going on with you?'

She turned her head away. The thing about Tom, the thing about having been so close to him once, was that he knew her inside and out and he knew exactly when she was lying. 'Nothing,' she said. 'I'm just tired.'

'Is it him?' Tom asked.

She knew immediately who he was talking about.

'Who?' she asked, as if she didn't.

'Him. The guy you brought the other night. Lucas – is that his name?'

At the sound of his name Evie felt her heart trip up. She swallowed. 'What are you talking about?'

'Is it him?'

The jealousy in his voice was enough to rile her. As if Tom had any right to be acting hurt or jealous after what he'd done to her. She laughed under her breath.

'Do you love him?' he asked.

Evie stared at him, speechless. She'd been about to bawl him out about his right to act like the victim but his question stopped her in her tracks.

'Don't be ridiculous,' she snapped, pulling herself together. 'I barely know him. He's renting a room from my mum.'

Tom shook his head. 'I saw the way he looked at you, Evie. I'm not blind.'

'What way? When?' She felt panicked all of a sudden, as though the porch were suddenly too small, as if the sky was falling and crushing her beneath it – her breathing was too fast.

'When we walked off together he looked like he couldn't bear to let you out of his sight.'

He had? She hadn't even noticed. 'Don't be ridiculous,' she said in a whisper.

'Well, why was he right there then, when you fell? He was so fast. Like he'd been watching you the whole time you were with me. And you should have seen his face. It was like he thought you were dying or something.'

Evie frowned, remembering how he'd appeared from nowhere.

173

One minute she'd felt the world crowding in on her and the next Lucas was crouched in front of her, holding it back. And yes, he had looked concerned, but what was Tom saying? She didn't get it. Lucas hadn't shown any interest in her at all like that – had he? He wouldn't even smile at her. And she'd certainly not shown any outward interest in him. She'd been as rude as possible to him, in fact. She'd practically staved his head in with a baseball bat. It was impossible that he should like her. And he hardly knew her. And anyway, *what did it matter?* She wanted to scream. She felt herself losing her slender grip on togetherness.

'Look, it's fine,' Tom said now, 'if you want to be with him rather than me.'

Evie lost her grip. 'I don't want to be with either of you. I can't be,' she yelled.

He looked at her, confused. 'Why not, Evie? It's not a crime for you to be happy.'

She laughed under her breath – wasn't it?

Tom walked right up to her, his voice so soft that it felt like a caress. He was so close and so familiar. It would be the easiest thing in the world to just lean into him and forget everything. For just five minutes. To just feel warm and safe again.

'I want you to be the way you used to be and I'm sorry that I was the one that did this to you.' His lips brushed the top of her head as he spoke and a spark travelled down her spine.

'No, no it wasn't you,' she said, so tired suddenly of having to push him away. She didn't have the strength for this. 'Please. It wasn't you.'

He stepped back so he could look her in the eye. 'Then who was it?' he said. 'What made you this unhappy? Besides what happened between us?'

Her thoughts flew back to Jocelyn. To her warning. And then she was looking at Tom, into his brown eyes – the first boy she'd ever loved, the first boy she'd ever kissed. And she knew that she could never drag him into the world she now inhabited.

'Nothing,' she said. 'I can't tell you.'

'You used to be able to tell me anything,' he said. His fingers found her face, tipped her chin up so she was looking straight at him. He stroked her cheek softly. 'What happened to you? Where's that Evie gone? You used to smile. You used to laugh.'

Her stomach clenched. 'Tom, don't,' she said, pulling away from his hand.

He paused, letting his hand drop to his side. Then he nodded. 'At least let me do one thing.'

'What?' she sighed up at him.

His lips were suddenly there, against hers, as warm and gentle as they had always been, and it momentarily took her breath away. And then he pulled away and walked off down the porch steps and she realised, as she watched him go, that she had just kissed her past goodbye.

20

It took a while for it to sink in and when it did Lucas had to turn away and lean against a tree and wait for the feeling that was choking him to pass.

But when he turned back to look, Tom was stroking a finger down her cheek and it took every ounce of control in his body to stop from sliding out of the shadows, crossing the short distance between them and pulling him away from her and – he frowned to himself – and doing *what* exactly?

He had stood there frozen, unable to name it at first – this feeling of hate and anger that reared up blackly inside him. And then when he saw Tom lean down and kiss her, saw her head tilt back and her lips part slightly, it felt like a knife had been slipped between his shoulder blades. Then, only then, did he understand that what he was feeling wasn't hatred. It was jealousy and it was so unexpected and so unfamiliar that it hit him like an iron hammer smashing into his chest.

At the same time he recognised the feeling for what it was, he also understood, without a shadow of a doubt, that Grace's prophecy would come true.

What Caleb had said to him back at the Mission had only made him so angry because it was true. And the whole way back in the car he'd been trying to convince himself – no, lie to himself

– about why he was coming back here. He'd played out all sorts of reasons and excuses, imagined himself hauled before Tristan having to explain and telling him he felt nothing for Evie except sheer hatred, that he was driven purely by revenge and his loyalty for the Brotherhood – and for a few miles on that darkened road he'd even tried to convince himself that it *was* hatred that he felt for her – it was so intense and all consuming – but even he had seen through that one in seconds. Had started laughing at himself, in fact. If he hated her why hadn't he let Risper finish her in the corn? Why was he so angry at Caleb for stalking her through the woods? Why was he racing back here with his foot flat on the gas to check she was OK?

And why was it that the only thing he was ever thinking about was her? And her eyes, and the look in them from the photograph – pissed off, defensive, defiant – a look he knew well enough from his own reflection. Why was she the image burnt on his retina? When there were a million other ones to choose from if he wanted to stay focused on revenge?

It had taken seeing her on the back porch with Tom to fully realise the depths of what he'd fallen into. Because as soon as he rounded the corner of the house and saw her standing there, pale and bruised and looking as though she'd just faced down an army of Unhumans, he'd had to stop himself from running towards her and pulling her into his arms. When really, his first reaction on seeing a Hunter should have been to take his blade and slit her throat.

When Tom had thrown his name into the conversation – suggested she loved him – Lucas had been as thrown as Evie seemed to be.

And it didn't matter that she felt nothing for him. He didn't want her to. His only priority now – he saw that it had always been his priority, from the moment he'd pushed Shula out of her way – was to protect her from the Brotherhood. Because the thought of Evie being hurt, being wounded, dying, was suddenly inconceivable. From the second he'd seen her in the photograph it had been so, and he didn't fully understand where the feeling had sprung from. It didn't make sense, he hardly knew her. *And* she was a Hunter. It was absurd, he knew that. And he also knew that if he stopped to reason with himself he'd realise exactly what he was betraying. It was far bigger than him, far more dangerous than him, so he didn't. He couldn't.

In the car he'd decided that the only solution was to keep Evie safe and kill Victor. Evie had nothing to do with his parents' death. Victor would pay and whichever other Hunters stood in his way. But he made a vow to himself that Evie would not be harmed, by him or the others. His only priority now was keeping Evie safe.

And keeping her safe meant keeping her strong. He had to make her fight. Right now she didn't look like she had enough fight in her to handle a ten-year-old human. She looked more unhappy than he'd ever seen her and the defiance in her, the anger he'd seen in her from the off, had vanished. The girl who was standing on the porch slump-shouldered, staring into space, was not the girl who'd bashed open his door and come charging in waving a baseball bat. She was no longer the girl who'd fought Caleb and Shula and somehow won. No, for some reason which he couldn't yet fathom, she'd let the numbness back in, and he couldn't keep her alive that way. He needed her to be angry.

He took a deep breath, felt a quiet calm descend, pushed away the memory of his parents that clattered to the fore and turned his attention to the girl on the porch in front of him. Maybe Grace was right – maybe this was fate after all, it was the only way he could explain it, the feeling he had, the actions he was taking, all felt outside of his control. And if fate couldn't be changed then he had no choice but to step up to meet it.

He was on the porch in front of her before she even registered it. A look of confusion passed over her then she seemed to reel, her eyes widening in shock. He was right. With the numbness she'd lost her grip on her instincts. She hadn't felt or heard him. And what if he'd been Caleb? She'd already be dead.

'Where did you come from?' she half-whispered, her gaze stumbling over the back yard and orchard.

'I was out for a walk,' he answered.

She shifted her glance to the trees and back to him and nodded absently. Was she wondering if he had heard the conversation with Tom?

'Are you OK? You look upset,' he asked.

She shook her head, ran a hand through her hair. 'No. I'm fine,' she said.

Neither of them spoke. He studied her in the moth-blown light. She was so pale, her lips a bright point of contrast, her eyes luminous. Her hair was hanging down covering her ear. It reminded him it wasn't just Caleb he needed to keep her safe from.

'Tom was just here,' she said, frowning up at him. Was she remembering what Tom had said about the way he'd appeared in the wood, the way he'd looked at her?

'You and he?' he asked tentatively, not sure what he wanted to hear exactly.

Evie kept talking, absently, as if to herself. 'We've known each other since we were babies. We grew up together. He was the first person I ever loved.' She paused. 'And I just had to say goodbye to him.'

179

'Why?' he asked, swallowing hard.

She didn't answer for such a long time that he thought she hadn't heard his question, but then he heard her take a breath. 'Things change,' she said with a shrug.

He nodded silently.

'And you. Have you ever been in love?' she suddenly asked.

He looked up at her. Her blue eyes were scrutinising him closely. He held her gaze. 'Once,' he answered, almost without thinking.

'What happened?'

He hesitated before answering. 'I had to leave her.'

'Why?' A small frown line had appeared between her eyes.

'Because she needed me to,' he said.

Evie continued to frown at him. But now it looked like she was about to cry and he had to stop himself from reaching out a hand to her, from resting it against her cheek.

But she didn't cry. She just sighed loudly and leant back against the wall post. He heard Lobo howling gently from just the other side of the screen door but he couldn't take his eyes off her.

'Have you ever had to make a choice?' she asked quietly. 'Only, it's not really a choice, it's a death sentence?'

He stared at her, completely thrown, his heart skipping a beat, and then he saw her close her eyes and lean her head back with a sigh, and a solitary tear rolled down her cheek and he understood that she wasn't talking about the choice he had just made, she was talking about a choice *she* had to make.

He lifted his hand and brushed away the tear.

21

The tip of the arrow whizzed past her damaged ear and she barely flinched. It thunked into the board behind her.

'OK, enough,' Victor yelled.

Risper lowered her bow, deliberately slowly, it seemed to Evie.

'Evie, I don't know what's got into you,' Victor said, 'but if you move that lazily you're going to get hurt.'

Evie raised an eyebrow at him. What did he care? If he was putting her up against a heavily armed Risper again then surely that was what he was hoping for.

'This is for your benefit, Evie. The Brotherhood will be back for you. And if you can't defend yourself, well, then . . .' He shrugged.

If he was trying to scare her into co-operating more fully with his weapons training course then he was failing. Right now she didn't care if the Brotherhood breezed into this room, picked up the crossbows leaning against the wall and pinned all three of them to the far wall.

'Evie? Are you even listening?' Victor yelled. 'You need to know this stuff.'

Evie sighed and finally lifted her eyes to meet Victor's. The frustration was all over his face. She caught sight of Risper behind him, smirking at her. She wished even harder for the Brotherhood to arrive.

Victor was standing in front of her smacking an arrow point into his palm for emphasis. 'We fight with arrows because they can pierce skin better than blades,' he was saying. 'They go deeper.'

He held the pointed steel up to her face to show her. She kept her eyes on his face instead.

'And we tip the arrow point with Mixen acid,' Risper said. 'Burns through Unhuman flesh. And human too, of course. Poisons them from the inside.'

Evie glanced over at Risper who had pulled the arrows out of the board and who was now leaning against the wall, one knee bent, the carved hilt of a large hunting knife poking out the top of one boot.

'Blades and arrows will only slow Thirsters, they won't kill them,' Victor continued, heading over to the war chest.

'I haven't tried a stone cutter yet, though,' Risper added.

'UV lamps bring them down,' Victor said over his shoulder, holding up a lamp similar to the one he'd had in the car park. 'Then you have to set them alight.'

'And make sure they burn.' Risper crossed over to the war chest too and got down on both knees, rifling through it like a kid in front of a Christmas stocking. She grabbed hold of something and heaved it out of the box – her mouth falling open in delight. 'Sweet!' she announced, standing up with it.

Evie had no clue what the metal tube was.

'When did you get a flame-thrower?' Risper asked Victor.

'After I saw that Thirster in the car park. If I'd had one on me then maybe we could have taken out half the Brotherhood in one go.'

'We need to get them now, while they're still young,' Risper said, twirling the flame-thrower like a baton over one shoulder. Evie was tempted to show her a trick or two – baton-twirling she knew.

'The Shadow Warrior's the one we need to go after,' Risper said, laying the flame-thrower down and grabbing hold of another weapon – this time a semi-automatic – which she locked against her shoulder and pointed at Evie.

Victor slammed the lid of the chest down and rounded on her, his face livid. 'Enough!' he shouted, grabbing the gun out of Risper's hands. Evie jumped. 'I told you to drop it.'

Evie looked between the two of them. Risper was scowling through narrowed eyes at Victor. After a few seconds of leaden silence she tossed her hair over her shoulder and with one last glance in Evie's direction – a glance that seemed both pitying and disgusted at the same time – she stormed out of the room.

They were in the back of the store, where the stock should have been kept. Victor had cleared the space of everything except for a table, which now held a selection of blades, knives and swords. The wall was covered in targets like something from a shooting range and a huge trunk – dubbed the war chest – blocked the emergency exit. She guessed it wasn't really the time to talk health and safety.

'Do you want to try with the crossbow now? Or hand-to-hand?' Victor asked, shrugging off his suit jacket and turning to face her.

Evie glanced at the bow. She didn't want to touch anything Risper had touched.

'Hand-to-hand,' she said.

Victor went over to the table and picked up two knives. Since when did hand to hand involve sharpened metal? He handed her the slightly less medieval-looking knife. It was long and light-handled. It reminded her of the knife her mother used to carve the Sunday joint.

She hesitated before taking it. Was this who she was going to be? A knife-wielding attacker? She tried to recall her father teaching her self-defence, back when she was a kid. If he knew the danger she was facing right now, wouldn't he be urging her to pick the biggest knife, the sharpest one, and do whatever it was she needed to do to in order to fight back and survive? Hadn't he taught her that if she fell seven times she needed to get up eight? She bit the inside of her cheek and then held out her hand and took the knife.

No sooner had she taken it than Victor started pacing around her in a circle. She felt her heart finally find its footing and start to gallop, the adrenaline flooding her system. She edged around the opposite way, keeping Victor at a distance. What was he expecting from her? Was he actually going to strike? Was she expected to try and stab him? Was that really what was going on here? Would he hurt her or was this for demonstration only? From his expression – challenging, wary, concentrated – she guessed this was for real. Or as real as the cornfield. She knew he wasn't about to kill her but she knew too that if she got cut he wouldn't care that much. And he wouldn't expect her to, either.

He darted forward, she skipped out of his way feeling the energy flowing through her arms. He was predictable. She kept her eyes on his, that was all she needed to do, she saw. His moves were easy to anticipate if she kept watching his face. She hardly broke a sweat, though with a slight smile she saw Victor already had beads forming on his forehead. She kept backtracking, feinting and dodging his every lunge.

'You can't keep defending, Evie. You have to attack too,' he said with a note of irritation, after she'd successfully avoided his twelfth strike.

She felt herself tense and her hand, the one holding the knife, shook slightly. She tried to steady herself. He would parry anything she threw at him, she was sure of it, but she still couldn't lift her arm, couldn't bring herself to attack.

But he was lunging again and again and again and every time he was getting closer and she knew he was backing her into the corner even as she felt her shoulder make contact with one of the target boards. She ducked and Victor's knife struck the board. She glared up at him – damn, how far was he willing to go? Would he be happy to make a point with the rest of her ear? Or was he thinking she could make do without her head?

Why did she have to learn how to use these stupid weapons – wouldn't a gun do? She could fire a gun. Besides, she didn't plan to find herself in a room with just a knife for protection and a Thirster for company. And she sure as hell knew she wasn't going to start walking around town with a crossbow slung over one shoulder and a hunting knife slid down the side of her boot Risper-style.

When Victor's arm came up she dived beneath it and hurled the knife to the floor. It clanged against the concrete. Victor lowered his hunting arm and sheathed his own weapon.

'What's wrong with you?' he asked. 'You need to be better than this if you want to stay alive.'

Evie ground her teeth and said nothing.

He exhaled loudly. 'If we could harness one of your looks, Evie, we could probably do away with weapons altogether. What's going on?'

'Nothing,' Evie answered flatly.

'Then why the attitude? Why the sullenness?'

It felt like the knife had finally pierced her. 'What?' she spat out. 'Am I supposed to be happy?'

Victor's face fell. He wiped a hand over his brow.

'I'm here, aren't I?' Evie shouted, throwing her arms around to indicate the makeshift training room. 'I'm going along with all this. I've done everything you've asked. I've given up everything and everyone I loved. I've accepted everything you've said and everything you've done to me.' She dropped her voice. 'But don't ask me to be happy. Because you never said that was part of the deal.'

Victor nodded once as if he finally understood. Well good, because she was done explaining herself to him.

'It gets easier, Evie,' he said, moving towards her as though about to place a placatory hand on her shoulder.

'Oh, really?' she remarked, hopping backwards. She didn't want placatory. She'd rather have the knife.

Victor stopped mid-step. 'I thought you wanted revenge, Evie?' His brow furrowed. 'I thought you understood the importance of what you are. Of who you are.'

Evie felt her breath quickening.

'We need you,' Victor said, his voice dropping a tone.

'Why?' Evie fired back. 'Because I'm the White Light?'

She saw a look of stunned confusion cross his face before he managed to hide it. 'Who told you that?'

'Why?' she demanded. 'Jocelyn told me. She obviously thought I had a right to know.'

Victor paused, seeming to take stock. 'OK, so you know. You know how important you are to us.'

He waited. Evie said nothing, only continued to glare at him.

'You could end this,' he eventually said – there he was with the weighing face on, scrutinising her reaction.

She lifted her chin in defiance. 'So they say. But no one even knows how.'

'What else did Jocelyn tell you?' Victor asked.

'Not much,' Evie snapped back. She'd already dropped Jocelyn in it she wasn't going to get her into any more trouble. 'Why didn't you tell me in the first place?'

Victor shrugged again. 'It's a lot of pressure. I didn't want to scare you.'

Evie let out a snort. 'From the man coming at me with a sharpened knife. No. Let's leave the scaring to the Unhumans. And Risper.'

'Risper's fine,' Victor said, dismissing her tone with a wave of his hand.

'I don't get why you're bringing her into this. I don't see what you're trying to achieve other than getting me killed. She hates me.'

'She's jealous,' Victor said, as if it was supposed to be obvious.

'So I hear. I'd be really jealous of me too. I mean, what's not to envy? No friends, no family, no future – but it's OK because guess what? I'm the White Light. Well, whoooopeee-do.'

Victor sighed. 'Evie, you have a future,' he said, but she noted the way he suddenly wouldn't meet her eye when he said it.

'Yeah, I have a future as a killer. Because that's what we're here for, isn't it? To learn how to kill.' She gestured at the knives laid out behind her like a museum display of medieval torture implements.

Victor drew in a frustrated breath. 'If you want to look at it that way then fine. But what you're killing isn't human, Evie. It doesn't count. And they would kill you in seconds. Without a whisper of hesitation or a backwards glance as you lay dying. So it's kill or be killed.' He stepped up close, his face looming into hers. 'Which is it to be?' he demanded.

She didn't answer because right now she was going with be killed.

He sighed suddenly and stepped backwards. 'Evie, have you ever heard the saying, *evil prospers when good men do nothing*?'

Oh, so now she was going to get a lecture about Hitler or Stalin. First prophecies, then guilt trips, now he'd moved on to moral righteousness. What would come next? she wondered.

'It's not just a saying, Evie,' Victor went on, seeing her roll her eyes, 'it's what we live or die by.'

She held up her arms and sighed. 'OK, enough with the lectures, enough already. I'll be good. I'll deal with the prospering evil.'

Victor pursed his lips. 'I'm not the enemy, Evie, remember that. Remember who was responsible for your parents' death. It wasn't me and it wasn't you.'

'No?' she burst out.

'No,' he answered firmly.

She dropped it, switched tack. 'Who was Margaret?'

Victor's expression froze before he snapped, 'Who?'

He knew exactly who she was talking about but if he was going to play dumb she would go along with it. 'She's in the book, in the Hunter family tree – probably an aunt of mine or something. Her name is struck through – hers is the *only* name struck through. Who is she?'

'No one,' Victor said turning away.

She felt like yelling *oh please*, but something warned her not to. She bit her tongue.

All he'd done was prove to her that this Margaret was somebody she needed to find out about. She just had to get to Jocelyn before Victor did.

22

Lucas lingered by the bed for a moment before sliding his hand under the pillow. Evie's subterfuge skills needed work. The book was bound in leather, it smelt of dust and dried ink and, overlaid on top of that, it smelt of her, of her fingers that had brushed these pages. He sat on the edge of the bed and opened it, flicking through the pages of hand-drawn pictures – cartoons, almost – of him and his fellow Unhumans. His eyes ran over the curled writing. This book contained everything the Hunters knew about Unhumans – and it was a lot – but not everything.

They knew very little about the Shadow Warriors, which, given that the war had been waging for over a thousand years, was good going on the part of the Brotherhood. He stared at the picture of the half-erased Shadow Warrior – clearly from another time judging by the clothes. It was amazing that they'd even been able to get a visual for long enough to draw one. But it could have been anyone. It looked like a human. There was a faint yellow smudge around the eyes, which suggested whoever had drawn it had come close enough to see the irises of one. Lucas was glad of the human DNA which had turned his own eyes grey instead of yellow. He noted a strike mark at the bottom of the page next to the picture. One line only.

His father.

He drew in a breath so sharp it felt as if Caleb had snuck up behind him and slashed him across his throat with his tail. He even turned to look over his shoulder to check but the room was empty. He closed his eyes, trying to remind himself of what he had chosen to do. Victor, Victor was the one. He needed to keep his focus. He opened his eyes and studied the book once more, no longer sure what he was looking for. He knew all about Unhumans – a lot more than whoever wrote this book. Right now, what he was looking for was what he *didn't* know, which was how to protect Evie. But maybe this wasn't where he was going to find it.

There *was* something here, though. Something about a White Light ending the thousand-year war between humans and Unhumans and severing the realms. He'd never heard it mentioned before. If it was a prophecy he wondered where the Hunters had got it from. It was clearly a Sybll prophecy – he could tell by the riddling way in which it was written. But which Sybll had given away knowledge like that to Hunters? And, more importantly, why?

There were no answers to be found. He flipped impatiently through the rest of the book. A photograph fell out. It was a picture of two people and a baby. He knew instantly that the baby was Evie – from the shock of dark hair and the deep blue eyes. Even as an infant she was staring defiantly at the camera, as if trying to figure out what it was exactly. He dragged his eyes off her and onto the two Hunters with her. Her real parents. Did she remember them at all or had she been too young when they'd died? She was a Hunter – the last of the direct line – yet she'd never known that until just recently, until the Brotherhood showed up.

How did it feel, he wondered, to have lived in blissful ignorance of your destiny and then to have had that ignorance smashed to pieces by a bunch of demons from other realms? Judging by the comments she'd made last night about a death sentence – not so good. For a minute he sat there remembering the way she'd sighed when he'd wiped away the tear. How her eyes had flashed open, two dark blue oceans of light, and how he'd managed to only hold her gaze for a matter of seconds before he'd had to walk into the house. He couldn't stay close to her, was too scared she'd see through him – and it was going to be a problem because he needed to stay close to her if he had any chance of protecting her.

After she'd fallen into a fitful sleep he'd spent the night in the darkness outside, too wired to sleep and too uncertain of Caleb's next move to dare close his eyes. Besides, he liked prowling the darkness better – it was easier to hide. Easier to think.

This morning Evie had dragged herself out of bed hollow-eyed, and driven to the store. He'd followed on foot, watched her park haphazardly on the kerb and stumble through the door zombie-like. He had wanted to follow her inside, had hesitated outside, but with Victor and Risper there he had no chance of not being seen or felt. Victor had twenty years' experience and Risper, well, she was already on alert after the cornfield. He'd figured that with Victor there Risper wouldn't dare make a move, so he'd left.

He turned the photograph over and read the writing on the back:

'We love you more than you will ever know.

You are our Evie – always remember what you mean, to us.

We are sorry we couldn't be there to watch you grow and keep you safe. We hope one day you will understand why and will forgive us.

Above all we hope that you make the choices we couldn't.

We will love you always,
Mum and Dad x

He stared at the words for a long time before he replaced the photo in the back of the book. What choices were they talking about? He flipped to the last page and traced his fingers over the family tree. All those Hunters. All of them killers – and he was about to make another one into a killer.

He stood up fast, the book tumbling to the floor. He bent to pick it up and stopped with his head pressed against his knee, suddenly feeling the weight of what he'd decided fall on him like lead.

When Jocelyn opened the door he saw her blanch bone-white. She wheeled around, flying down the hallway, trying to outrun him. But he was quicker, inside the house and blocking her way before she had even made it three metres. Her eyes flew wildly to the door behind her, panic stretched across her face.

'I'm not here to hurt you,' he said quickly, before she could make another move.

She was poised on the balls of her feet but at the same time she seemed to recognise that she couldn't outrun him. He watched her do the calculation. She was now figuring she had more hope trying to locate a weapon. He wished she wouldn't bother. It would only have taken her a few seconds to guess he was a Shadow Warrior and by the way she was staring at him with such fear in her eyes he guessed she just had. And yes, there was that flash of panic, the roll of eyes that he knew so well from horses – followed swiftly by a heart-piercing resignation. She knew that her chances were almost non-existent of beating him in a one-on-one fight.

'I'm not here to hurt you,' he repeated, holding his empty hands up. He kept his voice as even and unthreatening as possible. His eyes holding hers. He would kill her, without hesitation, if it turned out he couldn't trust her, but he kept that to himself as he watched Jocelyn slowly swallow back her fear and recalibrate the situation. Hope flooded into her eyes.

'What do you want?' she asked, her breathing rapid.

'I want to talk to you,' he said, 'about Evie.'

Jocelyn stared at him blankly as the words sank in and then she was suddenly in front of him, her hands thrusting him back against the wood. He hadn't seen that coming.

'No, no,' he struggled to get the words out with her hands crushing his windpipe. He was scared to push her back off him in case he hurt her in the process. 'I'm not here to kill her,' he choked. 'I'm here because I need your help. I need your help to *protect* her.'

'What are you talking about?' She loosened her hands ever so slightly. 'You're one of them.'

'Yes,' Lucas said. 'But I'm not going to hurt her.'

Jocelyn's face contorted in disbelief. Her hands started tightening again. Lucas forced his own hands up between hers, easing the pressure.

'I promise you,' he said, 'I want to protect her. And I need to know if I can trust you.'

She took her hands away from his throat but kept her arm pressing against his chest.

'I saw how you were protecting her in the cornfield,' Lucas said quickly. 'You care what happens to her. That's why I'm here. I figured you might be the only one I could trust.'

Jocelyn's arm fell away. She stepped back slowly. 'You're almost impossible to sense,' she said, shaking her head.

194

'I'm half human,' he said.

She frowned. He could see her curiosity was piqued by the news that he was only half Unhuman. Everyone knew that Unhumans were forbidden from mating with humans. 'What were you doing in the cornfield?' she asked.

'Making sure Evie was OK.'

She frowned at him, her body still poised for flight. 'Why?'

He swallowed. 'Don't ask me to explain.'

Jocelyn's eyes narrowed to pinpoints then flashed wide open. 'You have feelings for her,' she said, amazed.

He didn't answer.

'I'm right, aren't I?' Jocelyn pressed. 'Do you love her?'

He felt it like a blow. As if she'd physically struck him. He stepped backwards. Love her?

'You can't,' Jocelyn said, seeing his reaction. 'You know that.'

He looked Jocelyn dead in the eye and finally nodded. 'I know that. Doesn't mean I can stop.'

With the words spoken, he felt an enormous lightening – the unhappiness and small amount of uncertainty which had been hiding in him evaporated into the silence that had opened up. It felt easier to hear it from the mouth of a stranger somehow. Simpler. There was no confusion any more. The voice in his head that had been banging on about his sanity had fallen silent. Jocelyn's unquestioning acceptance made his own acceptance easier.

'Does she know?' Jocelyn asked after a minute.

'Know what? That I love her or that I'm half Unhuman?' Lucas answered wryly.

Jocelyn arched an eyebrow in answer.

'No,' Lucas said finally. 'She doesn't know. And don't worry, I'm not about to tell her.' He was only just coming to terms with it himself. Falling in love with the enemy hadn't exactly been part of his plan.

'Good,' Jocelyn hissed, 'because nothing good can come of this. What will you do if they find out? If the Brotherhood know you've betrayed them? They'll kill you.'

'I'm not scared of dying,' he replied. He realised it would have sounded nonchalant to her ears and looked away to avoid her scrutiny. She didn't need to know about Grace's prophecy or the fact that he'd long ago – when he'd first joined the Brotherhood – resigned himself to dying. So long as he had his revenge first. Death was only a passing on, it wasn't the end.

He could feel Jocelyn studying him, though. He shrugged it off. It mattered little what she thought of him.

'She can't get close to anyone,' Jocelyn said after a while. 'She can't ever be with you, you know that, right? Even if you weren't her enemy, she still couldn't be with you.'

Why was she still issuing warnings? He'd made it clear, hadn't he – that it was of no interest to him to get close to her in that way – to be with her? Yet Jocelyn's words stung.

'Evie doesn't know,' he heard himself say. 'She won't ever know. I promise you.'

Jocelyn was assessing him sceptically.

He chose to ignore the way she was looking at him. 'I can keep the Brotherhood away for the time being,' he said, 'but I can't watch her when she's with Risper.'

Jocelyn looked at him confused. 'Risper won't hurt her,' she said.

'I'm not so convinced.'

'It's not Risper we need to worry about. It's the rest of your friends,' she snarled back.

'They're not my friends,' Lucas said under his breath.

Jocelyn stepped towards him. 'Then why are you in the Brotherhood? Why are you wearing that amulet?' she demanded, pointing at the twisted shape of it under his shirt.

He took a deep breath, forcing himself to stay calm and not let his voice betray him. 'I'm only interested in one Hunter,' he said. 'Victor. After that I don't care what happens to the Brotherhood or to the Hunters. My fight is purely personal.'

She stopped. Her lips opening in a silent question, deep furrows running between her eyes and across her forehead. 'Why Victor?' she asked.

'He killed my father and mother.'

He watched the realisation strike. He saw a line of fear draw across her eyes again as she pieced together the puzzle.

He hurried on before she could ask any more questions. 'Evie can't run,' he said, 'because we'll hunt her down. She's the last Hunter. The Elders want revenge. And they want her.' He grimaced as he said it.

'They want her because she's the White Light,' Jocelyn said.

Lucas's eyes flew to hers. 'The prophecy? Do you mean that prophecy in the book?'

She looked up at him, startled. 'Yes. You didn't know?'

He shook his head. 'No.'

'She'll end this,' Jocelyn said.

He was now the one struggling to comprehend, frantically trying to recall what the prophecy had said – something about a pure-blood child being the White Light and breaking the realms apart. He couldn't remember the exact words.

'That's why the Brotherhood wants her so badly,' Jocelyn continued. 'To stop the prophecy from coming true.'

'But how does anyone know it's her for sure?'

'Her parents were among the only Hunters remaining, the only ones to have a child. She's the only pure-bred Hunter – warrior – to have been born. It can only be her. We've been waiting for her for a long time. It's why we went to such lengths to protect her. You should know this if you're in the Brotherhood.'

Lucas shrugged off her last comment. He didn't know why Tristan hadn't said anything. He raised his eyes to meet Jocelyn's. 'The only way to keep Evie safe is to get her to fulfil the prophecy,' he said. 'If the war ends, if the realms are severed, she can't be hurt.'

Jocelyn was nodding.

'But how? How is she supposed to break the realms apart? How's that even possible?'

Jocelyn shook her head slowly. 'I'm not sure. None of us are. The prophecy in its entirety was lost to us. We only have a piece. But we'll find the rest of it. We have to – we absolutely *need* to.'

'It won't matter at this rate whether we find it or not.'

'What do you mean?'

'Evie – she'll need to be able to fight. If she doesn't learn how to fight then she'll be dead way before you figure out how she's meant to fulfill this,' Lucas said with a shrug.

'What do you mean?' Jocelyn asked. 'She *is* able to fight. You saw her in the cornfield. She's fast and intuitive. With a bit more time – with practice – she'll be—'

Lucas shook his head, interrupting her. 'No. She's given up. I don't know what happened but last night it was like she'd lost something. That defiance I saw in her – that anger – it was gone. I don't know why.'

Jocelyn paled again. She bit her lip but said nothing.

198

'If you want her to be this White Light, if we want her to fulfill the prophecy,' Lucas said, 'we need to give her another reason to fight, because whatever reason you gave her before isn't enough. Right now, if any of the Brotherhood came for her she'd be picked off with no more effort than brushing away a cobweb. She thinks being a Hunter is a death sentence,' he said, remembering Evie's exact words and the way she'd looked close to collapse when she'd uttered them. 'But if we can show her it isn't, if we show her that she can fight us and win, if I can help her gain her full power, it will make her truly believe that she is this White Light, that there's a way to end this, and maybe she'll see the point in fighting. She needs to be angry.'

'What are you thinking?' Jocelyn asked.

He told her. Watched her eyes widen.

'Why?' she said, when he had finished talking. 'Why would you die for her?'

He frowned at the question. 'Isn't that what it means to love someone? And besides,' he said, smiling slightly to himself as he remembered Grace's words, 'I'm dead anyway. It's only a matter of time. So I may as well choose to die for something, or someone, I believe in.'

'Yes.' Jocelyn's voice was cracking. 'I watched her parents do the same, you know. They were trying to protect her too. And I would do the same in a heartbeat – not just because she's the White Light but because she's . . .' She couldn't finish the sentence.

Lucas smiled wanly. 'She's something special. Maybe we all see something in her that she doesn't see herself yet.'

Jocelyn nodded, her lips drawn into a white line.

'Jocelyn, I ask only one thing. If the plan works . . .' He swallowed. 'If it works and she does it, if I haven't had a chance to kill Victor before, swear to me that you will do it. And promise me that you'll find the rest of that prophecy. That you'll help keep her safe when I'm gone?'

Jocelyn stared at him wide-eyed before nodding.

He wondered at her lack of hesitation, how easily she'd said yes. But before he could ask why, they both snapped to attention at the sound of a footstep on the porch.

They sensed her at the same time, for Lucas it was like an extra heart beating in his chest, he could feel her that closely, the sound of her breathing. He could imagine her on the porch a metre away, hesitating before knocking. With a glance at Jocelyn, Lucas merged into the shadows and vanished. Jocelyn stepped silently backwards and into the living room. And then the knock came.

There was a pause before they heard Evie call out. 'Mrs Lovell? Jocelyn?'

Neither of them moved. Lucas waited a full minute, until he heard Evie sigh impatiently and stomp back down the porch steps.

By the time Jocelyn crept back into the hallway he had gone.

23

Evie got out the shower and stood in front of the mirror staring through the fogged-up glass at her beaten-up reflection. She did a quick calculation. She was missing a part of one ear, she had purple bruises stamped across her rib cage and back, a livid pink, hand-shaped burn mark on her forearm, deathly hollows under her eyes and a heart that was still beating, albeit somewhat jaggedly, despite everything that had been thrown at it.

She tried to prod the rawness of the wounds inside her – starting off by thinking about Tom. There was a pang but it was a dull one, as though she was on deep medication. She wished she was – she'd thought about going through her mother's cabinet for the sleeping pills the doctor was prescribing for her after her dad had died, but what was the point? When she slept she had nightmares that she was locked in a room with the green-skinned one and that one with the tail while everyone yelled *Half-and-half* at someone she couldn't see in the room. Sleep was even less fun than being awake. At least when she was awake she could watch for Risper and she could try to work out what she was going to do next.

She had thought too about running. Last night, after she'd thrown the knife to the floor and walked out of training she'd gone to find Jocelyn to demand to know whatever secrets the Hunters were keeping from her. Jocelyn hadn't been home and for a moment she'd wavered on the path in front of the house, wondering whether if she just got in the car and kept driving she could outrun this – hide from it. But if the Brotherhood had found her once they would find her again and she wouldn't be protected, wouldn't even be trained.

'You are Evie Hunter,' she said out loud to the shaky-looking girl in the mirror, the one who was trying to look a whole lot braver than she felt. It felt strange calling herself a Hunter. Hunters were killers – was that then bound to be their fate for always? Her fate? All because of a name? Because of who her parents were?

She took a deep breath and thought of Lucas, whom she hadn't seen since the night before last. She hadn't actually stopped thinking about him since then, he'd been lurking in the back of her mind – the memory of his hand so feather-light against her cheek, storm-laden eyes, the way he'd looked away as soon as her own eyes flashed open. A sudden pang hit her and she had to lean forward against the sink and gulp down big breaths of air to try to ease the pressure in her ribcage.

Once she could stand she got dressed carefully, trying to focus on the detail of every moment to distract her from any other thoughts that might cause another attack like that. She threw on a silk top that she'd taken from the store and a summery Marc Jacobs skirt. She figured she was owed. Plus her mother kept going on at her about wearing dresses and she might only have a few months or days left to make her mum happy.

Finally she brushed her hair and let it fall over her shoulders, covering her still tender ear.

Her mum looked up when she walked in and did a double take. 'You look nice, darling, but dear me, are you not getting any sleep at the minute?'

'I'm fine, Mum,' Evie said, turning her back and heading to the fridge before her mum could see the tears stinging her eyes.

'Are you working this evening?' her mum suddenly asked.

Evie steeled herself and looked over. Her mum was busy rooting for something in her handbag.

'I quit my job.'

Her mum stopped rummaging. 'At the diner?' she said. 'Oh, no, why? Are you sure that's a good idea? I mean that boutique's not going to last another month, is it – surely not? I went past the other day when you weren't there and it wasn't even open – but the prices in the window! Oh my good Lord.'

'Mum, it's fine,' Evie said, sitting down at the table with a glass of milk. 'School's back in soon enough. Joe's fine with it.'

Truth be told she'd had the same lecture from Joe, but he'd also promised her he'd hold her shifts for her in case she changed her mind.

Not that she was going to change her mind. She wouldn't be needing any waitressing jobs from now on. What was the point in working every hour, saving money for an escape that was no longer an option, for a future that was definitely not going to happen? New York? Yeah, she'd be lucky if she even made it to New Year. And now they had Lucas lodging – she put the glass down on the table – well, her mum didn't need to worry about money.

Her mum had obviously decided to drop it, though no doubt she'd be straight in to see Joe on her way through town and would demand to know why he'd let her quit.

'Mrs Lewington called,' her mum said. 'Her sister isn't ill at all. Isn't that the funniest thing? So she's coming back next week. I think I might have to ask Lucas if he doesn't mind moving out.'

Evie's head flew up.

'Though between you and me, dear, I think I'd rather have Lucas's face to look at in the morning over my toast than Mrs Lewington's,? her mother continued. 'I feel terrible. I think Lucas will want to stay in town. Janet Del Rey says he's an absolute godsend when it comes to the horses – he's like that Horse Whisperer, you know, Robert Redford – and every bit as gorgeous – though Janet did mention he's not the most punctual. I do hope he stays in town though, don't you?' Her mum rattled on as Evie sat there speechless, clutching her glass of milk.

She made a non-committal grunting noise because her mother seemed to be expecting some kind of reaction. Maybe it would be better, she thought, if he *did* just leave, then he might not take up so much mental space either. Maybe this was a good thing. Maybe.

She realised her mum was asking her something and with an effort focused back in on her.

'Would you mind doing me a big favour?' she was saying. 'Seeing how you're not working today, would you mind trying to fill up a few boxes of peaches? We haven't done it this year – it's the first year we haven't . . .' Her mother's voice faltered for a second before she steadied herself. 'I just thought it might be nice. You know, before they all go bad. I can make some cobblers, maybe some jam . . .'

Evie smiled up at her. 'Sure, Mum.'

It was only once she got outside in her boots that she discovered why her mum was so keen on her gathering in the peaches. Lucas was there already, straddling the lowest branch of the nearest tree. She hesitated on the edge of the porch with a box in her hand, thinking about turning and going back inside, but he looked up just as she was about to and grinned at her and she suddenly couldn't move. She was pinned like a couture-wearing scarecrow to the spot.

'You coming to help or you just going to stand there and watch me?' he called.

She felt the burn score her face, forced her feet to unstick, and walked over to him holding the box across her chest. Her bruised heart was battering so hard she felt it might cause irreparable internal damage. She stood beside the tree looking up at him. He swung himself up easily so he was in the branch above her and then leant down and offered her his hand.

She stared at it for several seconds before she could bring herself to take it. He lifted her as if she weighed less than nothing, pulling her onto the branch where he was standing, and for a moment, with her hand locked in his, standing there, with her other hand thrown around his neck for balance, she felt the world fall away around them – felt completely and utterly safe for the first time in days, even though she was balanced precariously two metres up on some gnarled old tree branch.

Lucas's face was just inches from her own. He had light olive skin she noticed, he wasn't as pale as he had been a few days ago. There was the very finest trace of dark stubble along his jaw and his eyelashes were unfeasibly straight and long. His eyes were lighter today, less hard and metallic, more the colour of a winter dawn, and they were studying her as if she was the most unusual or breakable of objects. He wasn't sullen anymore. In fact, he was beautiful – striking – he reminded her of someone suddenly but she couldn't think who. Maybe a painting she'd seen once, she thought absently before his hand distracted her.

She could feel the heat of it pressed against the small of her back, between that and the hard, straight lines of muscle beneath

205

his T-shirt she was struggling to breathe. Her heart was hammering away as though she was sprinting through a cornfield trying to avoid three knife-wielding maniacs.

He let her go suddenly without warning, reaching above him for a branch, and she felt the tree sway, the ground become the sky for an instant before levelling out and righting itself, and she found herself in his arms, pressed tight against his chest, her hands gripping around his waist.

'You OK?' he said quietly, his lips pressed to the top of her head.

'Yeah,' she whispered into the hollow of his neck, 'just lost my balance.'

'You got it now?' he asked. 'I don't want you breaking your neck.'

'I got it,' Evie said, dragging her hands off his waist and clutching onto the tree trunk.

What was with her? Normally she was far more balanced than this. And how had he managed to keep his balance with both arms locked around her? She slid away from him and watched as he hoisted himself deftly up into the branch overhead. He started handing her down peaches. She watched his arms, lean and flat-muscled, as he worked. Another dizzy spell hit. She clutched the tree and focused on the box and on wedging it in the fork of the tree.

'How are you feeling today?'

She frowned up at him.

'The other night you looked a little worse for wear.'

She looked away and started lining up the peaches he was handing her in the box.

'Yeah, sorry,' she murmured. 'I had a bad night – a bad week, actually.'

'And are things improving at all?' he asked.

She glanced up at him. He'd stopped what he was doing and

was looking at her through the branches, the leaves throwing patterns across his face.

What could she say to that? If she didn't think about the past or imagine anything about the future, if she stayed right here in this second staring up at him gathering peaches then, yes, she was better. She would even go so far as to say she was happy and that was more than she'd ever expected to feel again.

'Yeah,' she said, offering him the shadow of a smile, 'things are better right now.'

He answered with a smile of his own. 'And Tom?' he asked, turning his back to her.

She paused, watching his shoulders tensing, the tendons rippling down his forearms, and felt a dip in her stomach.

'I don't know. I haven't seen him. I'm sorry about the other night,' she added, hearing the tremble in her voice and wanting to kick herself but knowing she'd probably fall out the tree if she tried to. She didn't know if Lucas had seen Tom kiss her. Had it looked like she'd kissed him back?

'Nothing to apologise for,' Lucas answered quickly.

They worked in silence for a few minutes, Evie's thoughts back on the night before last and on Tom and on kisses she might never feel again – either from him or someone else. Her attention wrapped itself around Lucas and his lips, in profile now, and she allowed herself a minute's fantasy of what they might feel like pressed against her throat, against her own lips, before she turned abruptly away, swearing at herself under her breath. What was with the self-flagellation? It wasn't enough that she got tortured by Victor and Risper and a display of medieval weapons, she had to go torturing herself with fantasies of what she couldn't have as well?

'How's the job going?' Lucas asked, interrupting her internal tirade.

'Oh, I quit it,' she said.

He turned around to face her, his arms resting over the branch in front, his brow darkening. 'Why'd you quit?' he asked.

'I got tired of working in the diner.'

His face visibly relaxed. 'But you're still working at that boutique in town?'

'Oh that, yeah,' Evie said. She didn't think of that as a job any more. A chore certainly, but not exactly employment. 'No, I'm still there.'

'How is it?' Lucas asked, studying the peach in his hand before handing it over to her.

'Well,' Evie said, 'it's not exactly what I expected.'

'Any more coat hanger incidents?'

'No, no more incidents with hangers,' she replied, thinking of Risper and the knives.

'Good. Well, there are perks, I see,' Lucas said, nodding at her clothes. His smile returned, lighting up his face.

'Yeah, guess so,' Evie answered, thinking how they weren't so much a perk as danger money.

'You're not working today, though?' Lucas asked, handing her more peaches.

She reached up for them, their fingers brushed and she almost overbalanced. 'Later, this evening. Some kind of stocktake or . . .' She trailed off. Actually she had no idea what Victor had planned but she knew that the only thing being taken stock of was her inability to throw a knife at a person. Her body heaved a sigh.

'What about you?' she asked Lucas, wanting to change the subject. 'Not working?'

'Later,' he said. 'Giving the horses a break,' he added with an amused smile.

She looked up at him curiously. There was so much she'd like to know about him. 'Janet Del Rey says you're some kind of horse whisperer,' she said.

He threw his head back and laughed and she realised how light it made her feel to hear him laugh, how it helped keep the fear at bay.

'No, not a horse whisperer,' he said. 'I guess I just know what scares people and animals and I know how to take away the fear. That's all.'

That's all. She knew it was true as he said it. He did take away her fear but she doubted very much he knew what scared her. Never in all his imaginings would he believe the things scaring her had tails and fangs and could disappear into the darkness at will. It didn't matter, though – it was enough that he could make her *feel* fearless, even if only temporarily, and even if total fearlessness came only when he had his arms around her, which kind of made it an impractical state of affairs.

'Where did you learn? To ride, I mean. In Iowa?' she asked.

'Yes, on my grandma's farm. We moved there when I was five.'

'So that's where you're from.'

'Yes, there and around. I went to high school in LA for a bit. It was safer in Iowa.'

'Safer?' Evie looked up questioningly.

Lucas was busy, facing in the other direction 'Safer than downtown LA.'

She watched him swing gracefully from the branch he was perched on over to the next tree. High school. She could only imagine how many girls must have lusted after him. A stab of jealousy shot through her.

Just then he turned with a grin and threw something her way. She held up a hand to deflect it and felt the squish of a bruised peach slime through her fingers. She screamed out loud and he laughed, then she reached into the box and lobbed a peach straight back at him. He ducked and it flew past his head.

'You'll have to do better than that,' he said, his grey eyes daring her. There seemed to be a trace of sadness in them still, beneath the surface.

She tipped her head in his direction, her eyes flashing, a spark igniting in some deep part of her body. 'You want to fight?' she laughed. 'I can take you any day of the week.' She reached into the box, feeling for the squishiest peaches she could find.

When she looked back up he was smiling right at her.

24

'What are we doing out here?' Evie demanded to Victor's back.

He ignored her and kept walking, along the path she'd taken with Lucas a few days before, following the river. It was pitch dark, the moon still rising, far from full. There was the black static sky and then the solid black of the overhanging branches overlaying it. It was like walking through a collage entitled *Woods at Night*. She could hear only the occasional owl, a faint scuffling in the undergrowth which she supposed must be an animal and not a Scorpio demon or a Thirster because Victor didn't seem particularly on guard.

Or maybe it was just a test for her and it actually *was* an Unhuman and he was waiting for her to figure it out before she got sliced into pieces and served up on a plate.

'Where are the others?' she asked.

'They're not required today,' Victor answered.

Ever since their little showdown in the training room he'd been acting a little stiffly with her. She chewed on the news that it was just the two of them out here in the woods. Was that a good thing or a bad thing? She was relieved there would be no Risper but worried that Jocelyn wasn't going to be there. One friendly face was better than none.

'Where are we going?'

'Stop asking questions and start focusing, Evie,' he came back with. 'What do you hear? What do you feel?'

'I hear the voice in my head asking me whether I'm insane to be following you out here in the middle of the night and I feel tired and pissed off – how's that for focusing on my feelings?'

'Fine. Be pissed off. But listen to what I have to say and learn it, Evie, because time is running out. The Brotherhood will be back for you. They'll want you dead before you're fully trained. So you have weeks if you're lucky, days if you're not, to be able to defend yourself. And to learn how to attack. Are you ready?'

Evie swallowed. 'Ready for what? To kill someone?'

'Some*thing*, Evie. They're not human.'

'Yes,' she said, rolling her eyes. 'Whatever, yes. I'm ready.'

They had arrived by the swimming pond. It was a black mirror, reflecting the starless sky, a faint silver gleam the only sign that water lay in front of them.

'What are we doing here?' Evie asked, suddenly anxious.

'Endurance, Evie, and desire – those are your lessons tonight,' Victor said, looking at her calmly.

'Huh?' Evie looked up at him.

'There are going to be times in the future when you're going to be faced with things that you will feel are beyond your endurance – both physically and mentally. I think you've been dealing with the mental over the last week and you seem to be holding up OK, so now's the time to test you physically.'

Evie glanced at the water, suddenly seeing where this was going. 'You want me to swim?'

'Yes.' Victor nodded.

'And the desire part? Because I have no desire to swim.'

Victor laughed quickly and pulled something out of his pocket.

212

He held it up to her. She peered closer. It was a gold ring. Her eyes flashed to his face.

'What is it?'

'It's your mother's wedding ring,' he said.

Evie reached out to take it but Victor just spun it out of his hand and skimmed it into the pond with a flick of his wrist.

'What the hell did you do that for?' she screamed at him.

'Desire. You need to remember, I think, what you need your endurance for. What you're fighting for.'

She felt her mouth drop open. She slammed it shut and ground her teeth, pulling her sweater off and ripping the belt of her jeans open. She kicked off her shoes, struggled out of her jeans and then waded straight into the water wearing only her underwear, without so much as a backwards glance in Victor's direction.

The shock of the water hit her hard, almost winding her, causing her muscles to lock and go into spasm. She kept wading deeper though, until the water came over her hips and her feet started to sink into the slime of the bank. She slammed her mouth shut to cut the urge to swear, refusing to give Victor the satisfaction. One more step then she took a deep breath and dived.

She swam down into the darkness, her hands outstretched. Down and down until she felt icy fingers stroking her arms. She brushed the pondweed aside, suppressing a shudder, her breath starting to burn in her lungs. Her fingers sank into the mud at the bottom and she kicked against the spongy feeling, making the water turn even murkier as the mud swirled like dust motes around her. She twisted around. How was she going to find it? It was pitch black here and so freezing she could feel her legs turning to lead.

213

She burst up to the surface, her teeth chattering violently, the air hitting her bare skin and making her gasp. 'I can't find it,' she yelled at Victor's silently indifferent form, leaning against a tree.

'Best keep looking then,' he answered.

She gritted her teeth. She knew she should get out of the water before she froze to death but she couldn't give him the satisfaction of knowing he'd beaten her, and she wanted that ring. She needed to find it. Goddamn Victor. She took a deep breath and then duck-dived down again, this time struggling to reach the bottom as her legs had started to seize up from the cold. She tried to still the panic and to focus – to follow her gut and let it hopefully lead her to the ring – but what if she couldn't find it? What if it lay buried beneath the sand and mud she'd kicked up on the bottom? She twisted around and around, kicking out at the icy fingers tangling in her hair, stroking her lips. She swiped at them but she just got more tangled. And now they were wrapping around her legs, gripping them tight, tugging her down, slowly but surely.

She floated for a moment in the warmth, the cold having completely dissipated suddenly – her body felt warmer, the mud beneath her toes soft as cotton. She glanced upwards, saw the shadow of something – probably Victor – just above the water line. If she could just kick once and slip from the bind of the weed, she'd break the surface and be able to curse him out about trying to kill her yet again, but the weed had a good grip of her now, was winding up her thigh and was pulling her downwards. She kicked. She couldn't break free.

25

Lucas had been watching from the trees. He'd heard Victor's little speech about desire and endurance and seen the glint of metal as he tossed Evie's mother's ring into the deepest part of the water, and he'd taken a step forwards, wanting suddenly to confront Victor there and then. He was getting really tired of watching these daily attempts to kill Evie. And these were the very people who were supposed to be protecting her! Did they not see the irony? And here he was, oath-bound to kill her himself yet hell-bent on protecting her from every last psychopath out there. Victor included.

His eyes settled on Victor and he felt the anger peel back the wounds, almost relished it. Then came the flashes through his mind. Victor's face through the windscreen. The car flipping and spinning, much like the ring Victor had just tossed, through the darkness, landing wheels upwards. His mother's fractured face. The blood dripping onto him from the tree branches overhead.

Victor was standing just a metre away from him right now. It would be so easy to come up from behind and kill him. To end all this.

And he should do it. This second, while he had the chance, while Victor's attention was on Evie.

He took another step. This is what his father would have wanted him to do. But suddenly Evie was tearing off her sweater and kicking off her jeans and all thoughts of revenge were temporarily suspended.

He watched her pull her T-shirt off over her head and toss it to the ground and he stood motionless, unbreathing, as she waded into the pond.

Then she was gone, under the water, and the immediate bolt of panic he felt when he could no longer see her grew with every second she stayed under. He was on the point of diving in after her, had kicked off his shoes, when she resurfaced gasping, glowing in the thin moonlight, her hair slick, her lips almost blue and her teeth chattering so hard he thought they might shatter. He wanted to wade straight in and haul her out but Victor was telling her to go back down and keep looking for the damned ring.

By the time she'd dived again, Lucas had his shirt off and was standing barefoot and bare-chested in his jeans. He slid into the water unseen, melting into the cold darkness, leaving not a trace of a ripple across the surface.

It was coffin dark, deathly cold, silence pressing in on him. He felt the cold only as an afterthought. He swam blind, pushing downwards, his fingers sinking into the mud on the bottom in just a few strokes. He turned, trying to peer through the murk – there, something white gleaming. He kicked and swam towards it.

Evie's eyes were shut, her hair streaming out behind her in black ribbons. Her skin so pale it was translucent, glowing like something unnatural under the water. She was floating suspended in the black water, lulled with the current. Then he saw the weed wrapping its tendrils around her legs, holding her in place. As he swam towards her, an eruption of bubbles burst from her mouth and her lips stayed parted, water rushing in to take the place of the air. He grabbed her wrist and pulled against the weed.

Lucas burst through the surface with her in his arms and heard her gasp, choke and cry out. Her arms flailed at the surface, at him, in bewilderment. He was invisible but still solid. He let her go and dived back down, letting the weight of the water press him to the bottom. He swam fifteen metres to the far side of the pond and quietly broke the surface. Evie was still standing in the water, thigh deep, bent over, gulping down air. She whipped her hair back off her face and stumbled forwards, falling to her knees on the bank.

Damn it. Why wasn't Victor helping her? Lucas glanced over at him.

And found Victor staring right back at him. Not through him or behind him or in his general direction, but straight at him. And he was smiling.

26

Lucas was out of the water before Victor could take a single step towards him. His jeans were plastered freezing against his legs. He was barefoot and the night air whipped his skin as he ran. He wove in and out of the trees, listening for Victor bearing down on him, alert to the whisper of an arrow or the sigh of a blade through the still air. He had no weapons, had left his shirt and his father's knife in the grass by the side of the pond. He ran as though he had the devil on his heels, tearing through undergrowth, his feet ripping on stones. He tried to keep invisible, stick to the darker parts of the wood – those stripped of all moonlight – but he knew Victor could see him now anyway.

He had to get back to the Mission. To the others. But he was heading in the direction of the house. He needed the car. It would be quicker. But how could he leave Evie?

What choice did he have? He swore at himself. He could hardly hang out, put the kettle on and sit back with his feet up waiting for her to return from her night-time swim.

He couldn't protect Evie if he was dead. And once Victor told her who he was – then what? She was hardly going to throw herself into his arms, or look at him the way she'd looked at him in the orchard. No, she was going to plant a bullet between his eyes. Which was what he wanted her to do, wasn't it? To kill him?

Damn it. He swore again. How could he win this thing? He didn't even know the rules any more. Or what team he was on.

No, he thought. He'd never been on any team. He'd always been playing the game alone.

So Victor knew about him. It would only be a matter of time before the Hunters came looking for him. His mind flew frantically through the possibilities, thoughts crowding in on him even as he jumped over fallen branches and skidded over rocks. Did they know he was staying at the Tremain house? Had Jocelyn told Victor about him? Or had he given himself away just now, slipping into the water? Why had Victor smiled at him? Why hadn't he been tearing his throat out? Why hadn't he shot at him? He'd had the chance but he hadn't taken the shot. It was as if he'd wanted Lucas to see him.

Lucas stole through the orchard, his heart rate one rapid single beat, water dripping off his hair and running down his chest and back in rivulets. His jeans were sodden and heavy, squelching with every step. His feet were encased in blood-streaked mud. He circled the house, keeping to the darkest shadows, trying to feel whether anyone besides Mrs Tremain was inside – if he would be walking into a trap.

He paused suddenly, put his head to one side and concentrated. Where was Lobo? Where was the damn dog? He was always on the back porch – a canine sentinel. But he wasn't there now. Lucas listened harder and caught a low whining noise coming from the other side of the house. He slipped around the corner, following the noise, his senses straining, certain he was walking into something.

Lucas rounded the corner and the whining became louder. It was coming from the basement. He jumped down the few steps to

219

the recessed door and turned the handle gently. It opened and he peered in. Inside he could make out the shape of the dog curled up in the corner of the room, whimpering. Lobo barely lifted his head to look at him before sinking his head between his paws.

Lucas stepped quickly into the room, scanning the space. It was a workshop, probably Evie's dad's old space; a workbench ran around two sides of the room, with tools suspended from hooks on the walls. A hunting rifle hung over the door.

The dog nudged him with his nose when he crouched beside him.

'What happened, boy?' Lucas asked, feeling along the dog's legs and shank with his hands, checking for breaks or open wounds.

The dog howled when Lucas's hands closed on his neck. Lucas bent closer. The skin around the collar was burnt, the hair singed off. He could smell the acid burn.

He swore under his breath, patting the dog on the back. 'It's going to be OK, boy.'

He stood up. He could feel her now all right. All the time his senses had been alert for a Hunter and the real danger was right here in the house – and it wasn't even human. It was Shula.

Her presence was palpable – more than the smell, wafting in acid notes off Lobo's coat. Now he could really feel her and it was making the hairs on his arms stand on end, sending rivers of revulsion up and down his spine.

'I'll be right back,' he told Lobo, bending low to whisper in his ear.

He retraced his steps out of the basement, jogging up the veranda steps and pushing open the back door, which was only on the latch. He took the stairs two at a time, listening for any signs that Mrs Tremain had woken up, but he could hear the rhythmic sound of her breathing coming from the other end of the hallway.

The door to Evie's room was slightly ajar, the light off.

He pushed open the door. Shula was lazing back against the pillows on Evie's bed, one fishnet-clad leg crossed over the other, hands clasped behind her head. She beamed at him when he appeared in the doorway, though he was sure he also detected a vague disappointment in the tightening of her mouth. Probably, she'd been hoping that Evie would arrive back before him.

'What the hell are you doing here?' he shouted in a whisper.

Shula pouted. 'My, my, Lucas, what a charming welcome.' She swung her legs off the bed and stood up, swaying on three-inch heels. 'I was waiting for you,' she whispered, walking towards him, her eyelids glinting metallic.

Her finger danced a centimetre above his chest. He stood his ground. If Shula touched him, she'd be regretting it for a long time.

She dropped her gaze, her tongue darting out to wet her lips, and took in his sopping jeans. Then she looked back up at him questioningly. 'Been swimming?' she asked.

He ignored her. 'Why are you in Evie's room if you're waiting for me?'

'Oooh, *Evie's* room,' she said mockingly, turning her back. She marched to the window and yanked the curtain back.

Lucas glanced around the room to see if anything was out of place. It looked untouched – but it was such a mess, he couldn't really tell. He looked back at Shula, huffing by the window. What was she doing here? He needed to get her out of the house before Victor and Evie got back. He needed to get *himself* out of the house. They couldn't find either of them here.

Shula suddenly whipped around to face him. Her nostrils were flaring, her teeth bared in a snarl. 'I just don't get it. I don't get what it is about her.'

He felt his heart start to pump again, as furiously as when he'd been running. He wiped his hand across his face, trying to buy time.

Shula's shoulders fell and she turned half away, not holding his gaze. 'I don't understand why she gets to be the one,' she said in a half-broken voice.

Lucas frowned at her, not understanding. 'She's the child of two Hunters, Shula,' he said quietly. 'She's strong. She's—' He stopped. He wasn't going to tell Shula about the prophecy.

Shula looked up at him, shook her head slowly, 'No, Lucas, I meant for you – why is she the one?'

Lucas stared at her. 'I . . .' he finally ventured, faltered.

Shula waited. Then, when it became clear Lucas wasn't going to say anything else, she straightened her back, tossed her hair over one shoulder, thrust her chest out and spoke. 'You can't choose her, Lucas. You can't betray the Brotherhood. You'd be breaking your oath,' she said, her voice regaining its normal level of venom. 'We'd kill you.'

Lucas studied her hard, not knowing how to respond. 'I know,' he said slowly, his eyes holding hers.

She grimaced at his answer. 'Do we mean nothing to you?'

His hand went to his neck. He felt the weight of the cord holding the amulet. A sacred oath. But his oath to the Brotherhood meant nothing at this moment, compared to the one he'd made to himself to protect Evie. He let the amulet drop and looked back at Shula.

'If I break my oath, you can kill me yourself, Shula,' he said.

She narrowed her eyes and frowned at him, unsure of what he was saying – what he meant. 'Tristan wants to speak to you,' she said. 'Now.'

Lucas started. 'Tristan? He's back?'

Shula nodded.

'What does he want?' Lucas asked.

Shula turned abruptly away, avoiding his eye. 'I don't know,' she mumbled.

27

Evie tiptoed up the steps. She was shivering still, despite the sweater she'd pulled on which was sticking clammily to her arms and chest. Her legs were heavy, as though the weed still had a hold on her. Every step took maximum effort.

She'd tramped back from the pond alone, stamping through the crushing dark, angry at Victor for his stupid games, for throwing the ring in the water and for thinking that she was capable of retrieving it – as if she was a human metal detector – and in sub-zero temperatures too. She was more than angry – she was *furious* with Victor for his deluded belief that she was the one. When tonight had yet again demonstrated that she wasn't – in fact, couldn't possibly be. Even Risper got that. How many more times did she have to drown or lose a piece of flesh before Victor got that through his thick skull?

For a moment down there in the peace and quiet beneath the world, floating among the weeds, she'd wanted to let go, or she thought she had. And she *had* let go – hadn't she? And for a single moment there had been nothingness, just sheer blissful emptiness, a beautiful void opening around her and inside her into which she'd fallen before Lucas had reached into the darkness and pulled her out. She had felt his arms around her, his body hard and supple against hers – then she broke the surface and her eyes had flown open and the cold had struck her, hard as the flat of a knife, and the air had exploded into her lungs and she'd been gasping and floundering and kicking and there was no Lucas. There was nobody. He hadn't rescued her, hadn't dragged her to the surface. He was no more than a figment of her dying imagination. The last thing her brain could conjure, just as she'd conjured him in the cornfield.

It was pathetic, really. Yet in a way she still believed he had saved her. Whatever figment he'd been in her mind had saved her, had made her kick her way free, had made her fight. And Victor? What had he done? Victor would have let her drown. Another wave of loathing rose up in her throat.

She hesitated, shoulders raised, teeth chattering. The back door was slightly ajar. Had she left it like that? She tried to focus her numbed attention on her surroundings, tried to listen to whatever her instinct was saying. But if it was saying anything it was being drowned out by the sound of her teeth hammering together like ceramic plates and her breathing stuttering in her chest.

She pushed the door open. Where was Lobo?

It was OK. He was there in the kitchen, she spotted him lying under the table. She flicked on the light and crouched down.

'Hey, Lobo, boy, what's up? Come out. What are you doing in the house?'

He looked up sadly and whined at her. She scooted under the table and reached out to take hold of the dog, pulling her hand back quickly. His coat was soaked, clumps of white stuff sticking to the fur around his neck. *What the hell?* The fingers of her other hand found the matted fur around his collar, the place where it had been singed away.

She fell backwards, scrambling out from under the table,

spinning around the empty kitchen, noticing at once the muddy footprints across the floor. She went straight for the knife block and pulled out the cleaver, holding it between both hands.

That girl, the one with the skin, the Mixen demon, *she'd* been here. She'd been in the house. Maybe she was *still* in the house. Evie took a deep breath and shut her eyes. Silence flooded in as if she was underwater again, compressing around her – only her heartbeat could be heard thumping in her ears.

There was no Unhuman in the house. Not any longer.

Her eyes flew open. Her mother.

Lucas.

She was up the stairs in seconds, following the footprints across the landing. She sprinted down the hallway and pulled up sharply outside her mother's bedroom, heart hammering, too terrified to open the door, too scared of what she might discover. She forced her hand to find the knob and turn it. Her breath stilled in her chest, images flashing through her mind of green outstretched hands.

But her mother was there, sleeping heavily, fogged up on pills.

Evie walked slowly down the corridor towards Lucas's room. His door was wide open, the bed unslept in, the wardrobe open.

She shut the door gently and rested her forehead against the wood panels. Relief flowed through her, making her head feel light and dizzy. Then anger snapped her to. What had that Unhuman been doing here? Why had she hurt Lobo and then left? But not before dousing the dog in bicarbonate of soda? She opened her eyes. Why had the Hunters not picked up on her presence in the town? Victor had told her she was safe, that the Hunters were watching her back. But the Mixen had breezed on in here as though she'd been invited. Was this another one of Victor's games?

226

It bothered her that Lucas wasn't home. It was past four in the morning. Where was he? She turned her back on his room and headed for the bathroom. She had started shivering again, her clothes moulded dankly to her body. She knew that if she didn't warm up her muscles would start to seize and if the Mixen *did* decide to come back she'd be about as useful in a fight as a statue.

She ran downstairs first, collected Lobo and brought him back upstairs, pushing him into the bathroom ahead of her and locking the door.

If the girl wasn't here now, if she hadn't stuck around, it was unlikely she was coming back, she reasoned to herself. She thought about calling Victor.

No, she decided, she was damned if she was going to call Victor about it. She would just have to rely on her senses and on the fact that it was nearly morning – didn't they only come out at night anyway?

She ran a bath with the hot tap on full and sank into it with a groan. Her skin started to thaw and steam. She rested her head back and shut her eyes.

Lucas appeared. Always when she shut her eyes he was there, slate grey eyes searching hers, lips slightly parted, cheekbones razor sharp, eyelashes almost stroking them. She sighed. What was the brain but a massive instrument of torture? She'd better not let on to Victor or without a doubt he'd find a way to use it against her.

She let the water go lukewarm before she eased herself out. She combed out her hair in front of the mirror and carefully examined herself for more injuries. Her skin was wrinkled from the bath and her eyes were hollow. She was rocking some attractive purple shadows under them but other than an extreme

227

ache beneath her breastbone and a dizziness that came and went she seemed to be OK.

The bed rose up to meet her and she fell into it, already unconscious. Lobo jumped up and lay next to her, his body pressed against her side, shielding her from whatever might come through the door.

28

Lobo couldn't shield her from what was already inside her, though. From the minute Evie's eyes closed she was falling. Sinking. Rocketed down into an abyss of freezing black water. She groped desperately for the sides but there were none, she tried to kick up but her legs were bound, weed cocooning her, wrapping itself around her torso, winding its way around her arms and tightening in a loop around her neck. She could feel her lungs bursting, tried to gasp for breath and started choking. This time there was no peaceful floating, no sway and wave with the current lulling her into the void. No, this was pain – burning, iridescent pain, every single cell in her body bursting into flame at once.

She couldn't tell if her eyes were open or shut but then Lucas was in front of her, parallel to her, falling with her, his hands on her shoulders. He wasn't trying to tug her up to the surface. He wasn't trying to untangle her and she couldn't understand. She tried to yell but her mouth was clamped shut.

Lucas's fingers tightened their grip. Her eyes flew to his mouth, silently forming words. She struggled to make out what he was saying.

Wake. Up. Wake. Up.

She woke up screaming, shivering, sweat-slick. The sheets tangled around her legs, Lobo pawing her chest. She was shaking as she fought to sit up, to free her legs. She gulped down air – warm, sweet, musty dog-flavoured air – let it fill her lungs and wrapped her arms around Lobo.

Her gut tightened suddenly as though someone was tuning a string inside her. Her shivering stopped as her muscles tensed completely. Her head turned to the window.

Someone was outside. No. Not someone. Some*thing*. Something Unhuman. Before she could think, she was out of bed, pulling on a pair of jeans and tying her Converse. She grabbed a black T-shirt from the wardrobe and let herself out of the bedroom, locking Lobo in.

She tiptoed down the stairs, then snuck through the kitchen like a burglar, selecting two knives from the draining board as she went.

She was about to step out onto the back veranda when she changed her mind and crossed to the basement door. She unlocked it and headed down the steps into the damp space that used to be her dad's workshop. It was dusty and mildewy down here. Her father's hunting rifle hung above the door. She thought about pulling it down but it had been up there rusting for over a year and she had no idea where the bullets were even kept. She glanced down at the knives in her hand and chose the sharpest, putting the carving knife down on the side.

The door out of the basement at the side of the house was more hidden than the back veranda, down a few concrete steps. It would afford her a better opportunity to sneak up on whoever was out there. If it was the green one she couldn't afford to be cornered. What was she talking about? If it was *any* of them she couldn't afford to be cornered. Should she be wearing a silver crucifix?

No. Victor had said all that was rubbish. A Thirster was a

Thirster and nothing was going to hurt it other than one of those UV lamps and a flame-thrower – which she didn't have on her. She spied a few bits of wood piled in the corner, the leg of a chair that her dad had chopped up for kindling. She pulled it out of the pile, broke it over her knee and stuck the most jagged half down the waist of her jeans. It would have to do. She didn't have any arrows. And Victor hadn't said anything about stakes. Surely a stake through the heart would do the job? She'd seen vampire movies.

She crept up the stairs, feeling the pre-dawn air bite. Her heart rate was even – rapid, but she felt calm. Focused even, despite having been dragged screaming from a nightmare only minutes before. She allowed herself a moment to assess the situation, her back pressed into the wall.

Where were they?

There – over there. She could hear something straight ahead of her in the trees. A footstep. A swish.

She wouldn't be needing the stake, then. It was him. The one with the tail. She could hear the scything of it through the leaves. What was his name? Caleb? He'd have to be quieter than that if he wanted to sneak up on her. She ran on three, diving towards the nearest tree and shrinking behind it.

He had sensed her, she heard his footsteps. She ran, darting along the tree line, putting distance between them. She needed to outrun him, hide, then circle around. The knife was slipping between her hands. She stopped to wipe her palms down her jeans, took a deep breath and edged around the trunk of the tree.

Silence.

An owl hooted overhead.

Leaves crunching. The squeak of leather. He was wearing that damned Matrix coat. His eyes were the weakness and he was slow too – both mentally and physically. She only needed to sneak up on him, blind him again and then – what? She looked down at the knife. Use it, she guessed.

She wiped her hands again, noticed they were shaking.

She needed to do this. He wasn't here to ask her on a date. He was here to finish the job. Maybe they were each taking it in turns. After Caleb, another one would come. They were probably point-scoring to see who could finally kill her.

The thought needled her. She wasn't going to give them the satisfaction. But damn, she wished that Victor had maybe thought about installing a few UV floodlights around her house or equipping her with more weapons, maybe even a panic alarm. A kitchen knife against a two-metre-long razor-backed tail wasn't a great defence.

He was getting nearer. The swish sounded frighteningly close. She peered around the trunk and saw him, about three paces to the left, weaving in and out of the trees, as though out for a midnight nature walk.

She took a step out into the open. Then another. His back stayed turned, his serpentine tail whisking back and forth. His hearing obviously wasn't that great. She darted behind a tree just behind him. He spun around.

Evie crouched down and wrapped her fingers around a peach. A good, hard, unripe one. She lobbed it into the undergrowth opposite her. The Unhuman spun again and Evie felt the wind split as his tail shaved the air in front of her. She flattened herself against the old tree bark and took the wooden stake from her jeans.

One breath, two breaths. She was up, standing in the open,

one arm thrown back, holding the stake. As he turned to her, his mouth twisting into a grimace, his tail arching back over his head ready to strike, she hurled the wooden chair leg at him. It hit him square in the face. His hand went up to deflect it, his tail lashed downwards blindly and Evie somersaulted out of its way.

Just like being a cheerleader, Evie thought, only stakes instead of batons and knives instead of pompoms. She took the knife hilt in her fist, knelt in the soft earth and took aim.

But in the second in which she hesitated before throwing it, the Scorpio's tail lashed out of nowhere, a blur in her side vision. She threw herself sideways, felt the sting and then the scream of flesh splitting, of blood spewing hotly down her arm.

The tail whipped by again and she rolled, her face buried in leaves and dirt. She rolled once more and his tail slammed into the ground a centimetre away from her nose.

With one last yell, Evie wrenched her arm from under her, rolled back towards the tail and plunged the stake down, spearing it to the ground.

His screams broke the night sky. She didn't stop to watch him tug the stake from the ground. She was up and running, clutching her throbbing arm to her chest, feeling the blood soak warmly through her T-shirt, sticking it to her stomach.

She stumbled down the concrete steps to the basement, hearing only her own pounding heart and the rushing sound of static in her ears. The door stood open. She tripped into the basement and slammed the door behind her, bolting it.

Then she turned around. And let out a scream to wake the dead.

Lucas stepped towards her, his face furious, his cheekbones and jaw sharply silhouetted in the kitchen light flooding down into the basement.

'Are you OK?' he asked, his fingers digging into her shoulders.

His face was in front of hers, his eyes searching hers. He glanced down and took hold of her elbow and wrist, examining the gash left by the Scorpio.

'What happened?' he asked, looking up.

She shook her head. She couldn't speak. She couldn't tell him. She glanced over at the door. There was no sign of that thing with the tail but she needed to warn someone. Let Victor know. He would come and help her. Or maybe one of the others would already be on their way. Her head suddenly fogged up and she leant back against the work surface. Her arm was waterfalling blood. She stared at it in fascination, the long thin line, crimson against the white of her skin. It was incredible the way the blood just kept flowing.

Then Lucas was pressing something against the wound, binding it tight, ordering her to hold it upright to stop the blood flow, and yanking her arm above her head so hard that she thought he was going to tear it out of the socket. Her eyes were pulling in and out of focus, his voice sounding distant and then booming. She tipped her head back and looked at him. What was he doing here? Where had he come from? And why was he wearing no clothes? Or no T-shirt, rather. He still had jeans on.

Little dots started to dance in her vision. She glanced at her arm. Lucas had wrapped his T-shirt around her arm to stem the flow but the red of her blood was blotting through it. Her gaze returned to his chest. There was that amulet. The one she'd seen before somewhere. Under the water. No. In her dreams. No. She couldn't have seen it before. She'd never seen him with no shirt on before. She reached out a hand to touch the amulet. Was it real? Was Lucas real? Her fingers grazed his skin and he stepped back as though she'd tasered him.

She looked up at him. The fog cleared away, the dots stopped dancing. 'You were there?' she asked.

He frowned at her, then looked past her, over the top of her head. 'I'm here now,' he answered.

But then he was gone, heading for the back door.

She lurched forward, trying to bar his way. 'No! Don't go out there.'

He turned back to her and she saw that his expression had altered, set hard in a mask of fury, his eyes liquid black and gleaming through it.

She paused, her hand wrapping around his upper arm. 'Please, don't go out there.' Her voice was a hoarse whisper.

The palm of his hand covered her own. 'I'll be fine,' he said.

She watched him pick up the carving knife she'd left on the side. 'No,' she begged again, stepping in front of the door to bar his way. 'You can't go out there. You don't know what it is. It's not . . .' She trailed off, unsure how to finish the sentence.

Lucas's expression softened, warmth running into his eyes, a sad smile breaking on his lips. With his free hand he reached up and brushed a strand of hair back from her face, tucking it behind her bad ear. His fingers lingered there, pressing against the back of her neck, sending waves of heat down her body.

And then blackness descended.

29

Absolute darkness. He was nothing more than a shadow passing across the leaves, a whisper of wind, mistaken for the wing of a bird or the breeze through the grass. And in that darkness, he hunted.

He followed Caleb's scent, mingling dankly, like mould, amid the sweetness of the fallen peaches and the smoky air of a recent bonfire.

It had come to this. He had known that it would eventually come to this – to breaking his oath, to protecting her from the others – but he hadn't expected it to be so soon. He thought he had time. That Evie had time.

And all he was grateful for was that he'd made it back here before Caleb had actually killed her. Because it had been close. The whole way back doing one hundred and fifty down the freeway, cursing Shula for her lies, cursing himself for falling for them. All he could think about was Evie, half-drowned, bedraggled, bare-legged and having to face Caleb alone.

Why had he left with Shula? He gripped the knife tighter – wishing it was his father's paper-light Shadow blade instead – and he upped his pace, weaving after Caleb. The scent was getting stronger now, metallic-tasting, slightly acidic. The smell of Scorpio blood.

As soon as he'd stepped out of the car he'd known something wasn't right. He should have realised then but he hadn't. Instead he'd let Shula lead him to Tristan's study and had stood before his desk staring at the older man for a full thirty seconds, listening to him talk about the Elders and his trip to the Shadowlands, before he realised the symmetry was off. Tristan's voice was pitched too high, his eyes kept flicking over Lucas's shoulder towards Shula. Just as he realised it was Neena and not Tristan at all, she blurred and shimmered before his eyes. Shula yelled, but it was already too late, Lucas was sprinting down the wide hallway and back to the car.

His feet had barely touched the ground as he ran across the driveway, spitting up gravel with his heels. He'd jumped into the car and spun it out of the driveway before Shula and Neena had even appeared at the front door. He'd glanced at them once in the rear-view mirror. Grace had appeared on the bottom step as pale as ash, Shula was scowling, and Neena was still shimmering wildly in the doorway.

He'd kept his foot to the floor the whole way back, thoughts only on what he might do if Caleb had hurt Evie in any way whatsoever, fear feeding on fear, his hands practically tearing off the steering wheel, the engine protesting at every bend. And then he'd found Evie bleeding, hurt, trapped and alone. Whatever fear he'd been feeling faded away, replaced by a fury he'd never experienced before. A fury that filled his veins with ice. Caleb was about to pay.

He jumped the fence at the back boundary and found Caleb crouched on the ground, nursing his tail, trying to wrap something around it to stop the bleeding. Lucas couldn't help smiling. At least Evie had given as good as she got.

He stepped into the moonlight.

Caleb looked up. 'Lucas,' he said.

'Surprised to see me?' Lucas asked.

Caleb looked over Lucas's shoulder. 'Why aren't you at the Mission?' he answered.

'Why aren't you?' Lucas shot back.

Caleb stood up, his tail stretching out slowly behind him. 'I came here to kill a Hunter.'

Lucas took a breath, nodded. 'I think you might have to revise your plan.'

'Why?' Caleb sneered. 'You going to stop me?'

Lucas eyed him carefully – seeing himself reflected in Caleb's sunglasses: nonchalant, shoulders dropped, eyelids half-lowered. He shrugged.

Caleb shook his head in disbelief. 'Shula said it was true but I didn't believe her.'

Lucas felt his stomach tighten.

'She's a Hunter,' Caleb spat. 'We *kill* Hunters or have you forgotten? We don't try and bang them. Though she is kinda cute – I give you that – especially when she's pinned to the ground.'

Lucas drew in a breath, felt the adrenaline start to soar.

'And her flesh slices easy as a ripe peach.'

Lucas took a step forward, watching Caleb's tail flick off to the side.

'You couldn't just bang her and then kill her?' Caleb asked, sucking through his teeth.

Lucas took another step. 'You shouldn't have hurt her,' he said quietly. 'You really shouldn't have done that.'

Caleb frowned at him. 'Are you threatening me? Do you know what's going to happen to you when the others find out – when Tristan finds out?'

Lucas ignored him.

Caleb's eyes dropped to the knife, his tail arching simultaneously over his head, like a scorpion about to sting. 'What are you going to do with the knife?'

'I told you if you came near her again I'd kill you.'

Caleb stepped forward, his coat flapping to one side revealing the full length of his tail.

'Is that so? You'd kill *me* to protect *her*?' he shouted. 'You lay a finger on me, you'll be breaking your oath. Every Unhuman across the realms will be after you. There'll be a blood price on your head.'

Lucas exhaled slowly. His face stayed blank.

'You'll be banished from the realms,' Caleb said in disbelief, but his voice was already taking on a panicked tone.

Lucas shrugged. He'd never been to the realms, so that made no difference to him.

Caleb finally seemed to grasp the reality and his jaw went slack. His voice pitched up a notch. 'She's gonna get killed anyway. That's what we do to Hunters. So what's the point? You can't stop it from happening. Even if you stop me you can't stop the others who'll follow. Because they'll keep coming for her.'

Lucas waited a beat. 'I can try,' he said.

There was a second of silence, broken only by the swish of Caleb's tail.

Lucas's fingers tightened around the hilt of the knife but his arm stayed frozen. He couldn't do it. He couldn't make the first move. What was stopping him?

Lucas was so caught in his moment of hesitation that he didn't see the tail that had been snaking towards him at knee height. Just as he noticed it, Caleb flicked the end upwards and sliced it into Lucas's chest, slashing him clean across the shoulder. He felt the sting even as he felt himself merge into the darkness, becoming it. Blood started to flow, the heat of it washing across his stomach. He ground his teeth, sidestepping silently around Caleb, who was spinning frantically left to right, trying to hear him.

'Play fair, Half-and-half,' Caleb screamed into the trees.

Lucas paused, knife drawn, and then materialised behind him. 'How fair?' he asked.

Caleb jumped at the sound of his voice, spinning around, his tail scything the air in front of Lucas. Lucas raised his arm to deflect it, catching the tip with the carving knife.

Caleb let out a blood-freezing yell and Lucas stepped backwards another two steps, well out of range.

'I'm going to slice you apart like lunch meat and then I'm going to feed you to your girlfriend. But not before I have a little taste of her myself,' Caleb screamed.

Lucas sprang forward, fast as an arrow, throwing his full weight onto Caleb, felling him to the ground. He pinned him there with his tail beneath him.

'Do it then!' Caleb yelled, spit spraying Lucas's face. 'Do it!'

Lucas was breathing hard, his shoulders heaving, blood from his chest dripping onto Caleb's T-shirt, marking out a target-shaped circle above his heart, several inches lower than a human one. Lucas had the knife raised over it. He hesitated.

'What's stopping you?' Caleb spat a gob of saliva out the side of his mouth and it trickled down his cheek. 'You think you can protect her and you can't. You can't hurt one of your own.' Caleb tried to laugh, though the weight of Lucas crushing his chest made him cough instead. 'What's that telling you, Half-and-half?' he choked out.

Lucas bared his teeth at him. Fury and bile rose up in his throat. He raised the knife higher, readying himself.

With a final heave, Caleb twisted, freeing his tail. It lashed upwards, slicing Lucas once more across the chest, just above his heart. He flew backwards, vanishing on impact.

Caleb staggered to standing before him, wiping his leather sleeve over his face.

'You owe me a T-shirt,' he snarled, his head swiftly moving from left to right.

Lucas stared up at him, feeling the heat of the blood pooling under him.

The tail swung upwards and slashed downwards randomly yet straight towards him. Lucas watched it in slow motion, before his instincts took over. He rolled forwards, the knife leaving his hands in one fluid movement, embedding itself silently between Caleb's ribs.

Caleb's mouth fell open. Then he staggered backwards, his hands tentatively tracing the hilt poking out of his chest. He tried to tug at it, frantic all of a sudden, then his head jerked up, his face filled with disbelief.

He fell to his knees, hands still on the knife hilt, watching Lucas appear in front of him.

'See you on the other side,' he said, before collapsing face forwards, his sunglasses smashing against a rock. He vanished on impact.

Lucas stared at the spot where he'd fallen. All that remained was a mound of clothing covered by Caleb's black leather coat and the glasses, broken in two. He kicked the clothes aside. The knife lay buried underneath, tarred with blood.

Lucas bent slowly and picked it up.

30

Evie rolled onto her side with a groan, her fingers reaching to the back of her neck where the faintest pressure of Lucas's fingers still burned. She sat up in the next instant. Where was he? How long had she been passed out for?

Damn it. She couldn't believe he'd knocked her out. Because that was what had happened, right? The last thing she remembered was Lucas pulling her close, his fingers tightening on her neck and then – darkness.

She could kill him. But she might not have a chance, she realised as she hauled herself to standing, because for all she knew he could be lying out there dead already. She swore as she climbed onto a toolbox to reach for her father's rusting hunting rifle. She unhooked the gun desperately, coughing in the layer of dust that settled over her, and then with trembling fingers started ransacking the drawers for bullets. At the back of one she found a grimy old box with two cartridges inside.

She propped the gun up to load it, noticing the smattering of rust speckling the barrel, and started praying that the trigger part still worked.

Blood had started to trickle down the inside of her arm, the T-shirt – Lucas's T-shirt – already soaked through. The blood was dripping onto the butt of the rifle, making it slippery. She ignored it. She had to hurry. Her arm felt leaden and she wasn't sure how she was going to heft the gun with only one arm but it didn't matter, she had to try. She couldn't leave him out there alone. Damn it. Why did he go? She swore loudly – it came out as a sob. If anything happened to him . . .

The door suddenly flew open and she spun around with the gun in her hands, her finger fumbling desperately for the trigger. It took several seconds to register that it was him – that it was Lucas – because at first all she saw was blood, but then she threw the rifle to the floor and stumbled forwards towards him. He stood there, head bent, shoulders rigid, hands raining crimson drops onto the floor, and didn't look up. She reeled backwards as she got close, taking in the lashes across his chest and shoulder. Blood was coursing down over the flat of his stomach, soaking into the waistband of his jeans.

She paused, her eyes flitting over his shoulder to the darkness outside beyond the door, then took his hand, hot and sticky with red, and unclasped the knife he was holding, and threw it into the sink. Then she drew in a deep breath and pulled him inside the basement, bolting the door shut behind him.

'What happened?' she asked, her voice faltering.

'He's gone,' Lucas said flatly, his head still bowed.

Evie felt her heart stutter. Gone? Gone away or gone dead? She was too scared to ask.

She turned around and started raking through the cupboards, her fingers shaking, trying to find something to stem the flow of blood. In the last drawer she found one of her dad's old work shirts. It was clean. She shook it out and tore it in half, passing half to Lucas to wipe his hands with and pressing the other half against the worst wound on his chest.

'Why did you go?' she asked, angry with him suddenly. For doing something to make her pass out – though had he? For getting hurt. 'I warned you.' She pressed harder against his shoulder.

Had he seen that the person he'd fought wasn't human? That he had a tail? Of course he had. He was covered in slash marks. How couldn't he have seen?

She was suddenly blinded by tears. Why wasn't Lucas saying anything? She couldn't look up. What would she say? *Yeah, sorry about that, I should have warned you about the tail.*

But then, it dawned on her. How had Lucas fought an Unhuman? And won? She was the Hunter around here. And she had failed miserably.

She nudged him backwards gently, her hands on his forearms, leaning him carefully against a workbench. He said nothing – did nothing – as she wiped the trail of blood up his abdomen, across his chest, noticing the faint scars latticing his upper body, as though he'd been in fights before. But his skin was perfect otherwise, satin smooth, running in shallow dips over the flowing lines of muscle and rib.

She mopped the worst of the blood up until the two lash marks made by Caleb's tail stood out. She winced but he did nothing as she pressed the clean edge of the shirt against them to stem the bleeding.

After a few seconds she pulled the shirt away. The bleeding seemed to have eased off. Her fingers traced around the edges of the wound, scared to touch him for fear he might move. But he was still as a statue.

Without thinking, she dipped her head and pressed her lips to his shoulder, just above where the first cut started. His skin was burning hot to the touch. She pulled back, suddenly aware of what she'd just done. Her heart stopped beating, her lungs refusing point blank to expand and draw in air. Lucas stayed frozen. She was terrified to lift her eyes to meet his. For a full ten seconds they stood like two statues before each other. Then she caught a slight movement, a shift in Lucas's body, the ripple of muscle across his stomach as he stood.

Her head flew up.

Lucas was looking straight at her, his eyes burning coals, his breathing rapid. And suddenly his hands were on her shoulders and he was pushing her backwards. She bumped against the wall behind, gasped at the shock and his lips cut it off.

His mouth was hard against hers, but his lips were soft, his taste familiar and new at the same time. She felt her whole body jolt and come alive, her bloodied, bandaged arm wrapping around his neck, her fingers knotting in his hair, pulling him closer, until his hip bone was pressing against hers and his chest was crushing her ribcage and there was no air left inside her. Her head was spinning and she felt like she was going to pass out. His hands were stroking up her neck, tracing her spine, his lips finding the hollow of her throat, making her tilt her head back. She opened her eyes to stop the room from spinning, unhooked her hands from around his neck, running them down his chest, stopping just below his collarbone . . . when she felt the silver of his amulet digging into her palm. She heard him take a breath, pause for a moment, but then his arms wound around her waist and her lips found his again, wanting more, her fingers tugging at his waistband.

They stumbled backwards together, slamming into the workbench opposite. He hadn't let her go. The tools on the side went crashing to the floor, the workbench groaned against their weight and something dislodged from the wall behind Lucas and smashed to the ground at Evie's feet. She ignored it all. He kept kissing her until she felt her legs give way but she didn't fall to the ground amid the tools because he was holding her up, his hands around her waist now, binding her to him.

She pulled backwards in his arms and found him staring right at her. She let her fingers stroke along his jawline, trace the curve of his bottom lip – the line of his cheekbone. She stroked his eyelashes and ran a hand through his hair, pushing it back off his face, and all the while he held her in his arms and didn't take his eyes off her. Those deep grey, haunted eyes, so full of darkness and secrets and pain.

And she felt safe. She realised it with a start that made her draw in a breath, which made him frown and move his hand to her cheek, his thumb pressing against her lower lip. This was the only place she would ever feel truly safe ever again – right here, locked into him, with his arms tight about her and the world falling apart around them. And everything Jocelyn had said to her about not getting close to anyone suddenly seemed inconceivable, impossible. Because her whole body and her entire heart were telling her that this was right – there was no way it couldn't be.

When Tom had kissed her she'd sensed his vulnerability, had felt the burden of having to protect him and shield him from what was outside in the darkness waiting to attack her. But when Lucas kissed her she felt nothing but him. Nothing but heat. He made her forget the outside. And he shielded her from the darkness. She smiled up at him, laughing under her breath.

A flash of something crossed his face then – of longing or hurt, she couldn't tell which. And she couldn't decipher the meaning of the smile he was giving her because it was a sad smile and the sadness was reflected in his eyes. He finally opened his mouth as if he was about to say something and her stomach tightened. But then his eyes flew over her shoulder to the stairs and his hands dropped from her waist. She felt the fear rushing back in at the same instant that she heard her name being called.

'Evie!'

They broke apart, Evie looking around at the sound of her mother's voice shouting down from the kitchen above. She smoothed back her messed-up hair, wrapped her arms around herself to cover the blood on her T-shirt and shoved the bloodied knife from the sink underneath a pile of tools.

'Evie!' her mother called again. 'What's all that noise? Is that you down there?'

Evie could feel her cheeks burning, her lips starting to throb. 'It's just me, Mum,' she finally called out, sounding as if she'd just returned from a sprint around the block.

The door to the kitchen opened and her mum peered down into the gloom. 'What on earth are you doing down there?'

'Just looking for something,' Evie answered, still catching her breath.

'Well, there was an awful lot of banging and crashing. And it's very early. Honestly it's not even six o'clock,' her mother said, peering over Evie's shoulder at the tools scattered on the concrete floor. 'What a mess you've made.'

'Sorry,' Evie replied, holding her bandaged arm behind her back, hoping that Lucas had hidden himself on the other side of the room, well out of her mother's line of vision. If she saw him bare-chested and bloody, down here with a load of power tools dangling from their hooks, she'd wonder what was going on.

'Did you find what you were looking for?' her mother asked, looking suspiciously at Evie.

'Yeah, I found it,' Evie answered with a small smile. 'I'll be up in a second.'

'How you found anything without the light on I have no idea,' her mother said, turning her back.

Evie waited until she'd gone and then turned around, grinning. 'That was close,' she said, the words instantly trailing away to nothing.

Because the room was empty.

Lucas had vanished.

31

Evie smacked her fist against the door, almost putting it through the glass. Finally Victor appeared, strolling across the store, pausing to brush some lint off one of the velvet chairs. He finally unbolted the door and opened it.

'You're early,' he said, glancing at his watch.

'Where were you?' she demanded, pushing past him into the store.

'I was out the back sorting out some new deliveries,' Victor answered, looking her up and down. 'I think you'll like them.'

'No. I mean last night,' Evie snapped. 'I almost got killed.'

Victor had crossed to one of the rails and was fingering his way through the hangers. 'I know,' he murmured.

Evie did a double take. 'Excuse me?'

Victor glanced up at her. 'We were there,' he said. 'We were watching.'

Evie stared at him, uncomprehending. 'I'm sorry?'

'We were there,' Victor repeated.

The words sank in. She felt a wave of nausea churn her stomach. 'What, all of you?' she asked, her voice raising. 'You were what? Cheerleading? Eating popcorn? Firing up the grill? What the *hell*?'

Victor made no comment, he just looked up at her with a bemused expression on his face, waiting for her to finish.

'I needed you,' she said.

'No you didn't,' Victor answered. 'You managed, didn't you?'

Her mouth fell open. 'I almost died.'

He shrugged. 'But you didn't.'

'Only because Lucas—' She stopped abruptly. 'Hang on. You let him go out there. You let a human fight an Unhuman? You stood there and watched him do your job? You told me you – we – were here to protect humans. How could you do that?' Her voice was shaking.

Victor crossed to one of the chairs and deposited himself in it, one ankle resting over his knee. 'Evie,' he said, looking at her pityingly.

'What?' she spat.

'Have you really not figured it out yet?'

'Figured out *what* yet?' she yelled. 'That you're a psycho?'

'No,' Victor answered calmly. 'That Lucas is one of them.'

'One of who?'

'The Brotherhood.'

He may as well have taken one of the crossbows and shot her through the chest. The blow sent her reeling backwards, her ribs crushed. '*What?*'

Victor's eyes were marble hard. 'He's an Unhuman,' he said with a trace of a smile. 'The worst of them. He's a Shadow Warrior. Well . . .' he paused, 'half.'

'He's what?' she heard herself asking.

'He's half Shadow Warrior, half human. And he's a member of the Brotherhood.'

The ground seemed to drop away. She had to put her hands on the back of the chair to keep herself from spinning into the abyss that had torn open in front of her.

250

'I hate to be the one to break it to you,' Victor said.

Sure he did. Evie found her voice. 'No,' she said, shaking her head, 'that's impossible. He can't be.'

'Why can't he be?' Victor suddenly snapped.

Evie stared at him blankly. 'Because . . .' She couldn't finish the sentence. He *couldn't* be one of them. He was – he was . . . Her face burnt at the memory. The taste of him – she had kissed him, had felt his heart beating beneath her hand, had traced her fingers across his body, wrapped herself up in him, lost herself in him.

And he was one of them? He was a demon? It was impossible.

'Why can't he be?' Victor repeated. 'Because you fell for him?'

She turned on Victor, furious, rage pulsing through her body. 'You knew? How long have you known?'

'Since he arrived in town.'

Evie blinked, her fingers tearing through the fabric of the chair she was holding on to. 'Whoa, hold on. You let him move in with my mum, with me, knowing he was one of them?'

'Yes.'

'Why?' she screamed. 'How did you know he wasn't going to kill us?' She couldn't keep the hysteria out of her voice.

'I let it happen, Evie, because you needed to learn the first lesson.'

She frowned at him, thrown. What was he talking about? *What* lesson?

'Do you even remember what I told you?' Victor said suddenly, springing up from the chair, standing right in front of her so she had to tip her head right back to see him. 'I told you to trust me,' Victor said. He shook his head, disappointed. 'You never trust me.'

'You give me no reason to,' she answered through gritted teeth.

251

Victor's voice softened. 'I'm just trying to teach you the lessons that will keep you alive. The second lesson I taught you, which you also failed to listen to, was not to trust anyone else.'

It had been a lesson? He'd let a Shadow Warrior move into her house, just to teach her a lesson? He'd let her believe that Lucas was someone she could trust, had stood by and allowed Lucas to—

She closed her eyes. And was immediately bombarded with images, memories, sounds – jumping in front of her eyes. Lucas's sullen expression when he'd first arrived, all the things he'd said about growing up in Iowa, about his parents dying, about having to leave someone he loved, probably some Shadow Warrior in another realm – maybe even another member of the Brotherhood. The way he was there in the woods so fast, appearing out of nowhere, the way he'd lifted her so easily onto the branch of the tree, his smile – always tentative, unsure. The thin traces of scars across his body.

The way he kept disappearing.

She swallowed hard. It was all a lie. All those secrets hidden, buried deep but still visible in his eyes – this was what he was hiding. It all fell into place, crushing her beneath the weight of it.

It was the worst pain she'd ever felt. Worse than the sting of the Scorpio's tail, worse than the acid burn of that Mixen's skin, far worse than finding out about Tom and Anna. She wanted to edge into the abyss and let it swallow her down. She wished she was still floating at the bottom of the pond, oblivious to this.

'Why do you think he was here, Evie?' Victor cut through her jumbled thoughts.

'I don't know,' she said under her breath. A wave of shame drenched her.

252

'He was using you, trying to get close to you to find out what you knew, how we trained you.'

She cast around in her head for something that she might be able to use to refute what Victor was saying but came up with nothing.

'You *cannot* trust anyone.' Victor hammered the point home. 'You *cannot* get close to anyone. Do you understand me?' His voice was a slap. Evie's head flew up. 'It's your weakness, Evie. And it will get you killed.'

She blinked back tears, fought the sob that was building in her chest. A thought finally occurred to her. 'But Lucas went out there. He fought him. I saw. Why did he do that?' She looked up at Victor desperately. 'I don't understand. If he's one of them, why did he do that?'

Victor raised an eyebrow. 'You saw? You saw him fight Caleb?'

'No, I didn't see that, but I saw him come back. He was hurt. There was blood all over him.'

Victor stepped towards her. 'What if it was all a deceit, Evie?'

She flinched.

'It's all been a game, Evie. He wanted you to fall in love with him. It was part of his plan – to get close to you. To make you trust him.'

No. She couldn't believe it.

'How do you know this? How could you?' she asked, shaking her head.

'Why else would a member of the Brotherhood, the only one with a personal score to settle, move in with a Hunter?' He lowered his tone. 'Think about it, Evie. It doesn't take much to figure it out. And you fell for it so fast. You didn't sense him. Not even in the cornfield.'

253

She screwed her eyes shut. He was there? No. No. No.

'He was playing you the whole time. Biding his time until he had everything he wanted and then he would have killed you.' Victor paused. 'He would have tried, at least. We would have stopped him.'

She wanted him to shut up. She wanted to turn his voice off. If he didn't shut up right this instant she was going to scream. She needed to get out of here, get away from Victor. She turned around, focusing on the door and on making her way towards it without tripping over.

'He's gone, Evie,' Victor called out. 'But he'll be back. And this time you'll be ready.'

She turned slowly around. 'For what?' she asked, her voice sticking in her throat.

Victor walked around her, stood barring the door. 'When he comes back you're going to kill him,' he said.

'I can't – what are you talking about?' Tears started rolling down her cheeks.

'Evie, it'll be you or him. Don't you want revenge? For your parents? For what he's done to you? You're a Hunter after all,' Victor said. 'That's your legacy. It's what you do. It's what we all do.'

'But he's a Shadow Warrior.' Evie finally managed to speak. 'How can I kill him? You said it was almost impossible.'

Victor smiled. 'But you can get close to him, can't you? Haven't you already?'

Risper's arrows shot one by one into her heart. Her whole body shuddered at the memory of Lucas's body pressed against hers, his hands stroking up her back, his lips running up her throat.

'Why not betray him like he's betrayed you?' Victor asked, leaning closer.

She shook her head softly. 'I can't.'

Victor straightened up. 'You can. You will. You have no choice.'

She frowned at him. Hadn't he once told her she *did* have a choice?

'Your first kill, Evie,' Victor said. 'That's what gives you your full power. You never asked about that this whole time – you were never curious about how you'd gain your power – but it's by killing your first Unhuman, Evie.'

She froze.

'If you'd managed to kill the Scorpio the other night then you'd already be feeling it. That's why we didn't interfere. We wanted you to make the kill. And if you had you'd be strong right now – no more weakness, no more uncertainty. As it is, you get another chance when Lucas comes back. You're going to be the first Hunter to kill a Shadow Warrior – besides me, that is.'

32

Lucas pulled through the gates just as the sunrise was setting the roof of the Mission alight. Joshua would be going to ground. It would be safer this way, in case he had to fight his way out.

The amulet seemed to burn his skin as though it knew he'd broken his oath and was determined to brand him. He had stopped at a darkened store in a town just outside of Riverview, broken in and taken some clothes, leaving the cash in the register. The lacerations on his chest and shoulder were smarting under the starched cotton.

He stalled the engine and sat in the car, listening to the engine cool, wondering if inside he'd find Tristan waiting for him, knowing of his betrayal. Grace must have seen. Had she told Tristan?

Had Shula? And Neena? She had been part of the deceit – did that mean she knew too?

He had one chance and he had to play it. He couldn't afford to blow it.

The door to the Mission burst open and Shula came tearing down the steps, flying across the drive, her face pale and sickly in the dawn. He climbed out the car and walked towards her. She faltered and stopped in front of him.

'Where's Caleb?' she demanded.

'I don't know,' he answered truthfully. Somewhere his body

was lying in the Scorpio realm, hopefully in the middle of nowhere.

'He didn't do it, did he?' Shula spat into the dirt.

Lucas frowned. 'Do what?' he asked innocently.

Shula looked up at him, calculating, her bottom lip quivering with anger. 'She's still alive,' she said. Her brown eyes narrowed. 'Why are you here?'

Lucas brushed past her. 'To see Tristan,' he said, walking across the gravel towards the Mission.

He gathered from her silence that Tristan was home.

One foot after the other, his heart starting to hammer, his feet echoing across the tiles, not trying to hide.

Tristan was waiting for him, pouring himself a whisky from a crystal decanter with his one good hand. Lucas double-checked just to make sure it was really him this time and not Neena. It was. He nodded at Lucas when he appeared in his doorway and indicated the dark wooden chair opposite.

Lucas shut the door behind him and went and sat down. Tristan sat before him, enthroned on a larger chair with an ornately carved back. He rested his glass on the table and eyed Lucas for a few seconds. He wasn't wearing his contacts and his yellow irises gave him a jaundiced look. Lucas held his gaze, unblinking.

Eventually Tristan spoke. 'Shula tells me that I might have reason to suspect your loyalty to the cause, Lucas.'

Lucas kept his voice even. 'And you trust Shula?' he said softly.

Tristan cocked his head to one side, examining him. 'Should I trust you?'

'Shula has an ulterior motive,' Lucas answered quickly.

'Oh yes,' Tristan sighed, 'and what might that be?'

'She admitted she had feelings for me and . . .' he hesitated, his eyes dropping in embarrassment, 'I rejected her.' He looked back up at Tristan who was staring at him with a curious smile on his face. 'You know how Shula reacts when she doesn't get what she wants.'

Tristan raised an eyebrow sardonically, seeming to find some amusement in Lucas's tale, though whether he believed it or not wasn't clear.

'So you've no idea where Caleb's got to, I take it?'

Lucas shook his head. 'I was in Riverview. Shula came to get me and told me you were waiting. It was all a ruse so that Caleb could go back and kill Evie. The Hunter, I mean.'

Tristan's eyes flashed at the sound of her name. 'And I take it when you got back to Riverview there was no sign of Caleb?' he asked.

'No,' Lucas answered. Images of Caleb's slick hands pulling feebly at the knife hilt sticking out of him flashed before Lucas, but he kept his face neutral.

Tristan stared at him for several seconds and Lucas wondered if he could somehow see the images too, could read his mind.

'Foolish boy.'

Lucas's stomach tensed. He got ready to spring up.

'He disobeyed my orders,' Tristan continued. 'And that's what happens when you disobey orders.'

Lucas sank back into the chair again, taking a surreptitious deep breath.

'I've just had to spend a very uncomfortable day in the Shadowlands,' Tristan said, raising his glass and knocking back the amber liquid inside, 'trying to convince a roomful of Elders that I know what I'm doing – that this last batch of recruits will

258

be able to handle *one little girl*.' He yelled the last three words and Lucas flinched inwardly.

'And now I have to go back to the Scorpio demons and tell them their last offering wasn't up to scratch and please can they supply another one – preferably one a little more open to following orders.'

He stood to refill his glass. 'You know, after the last battle there was very little choice – hence the ignorant baby Thirster and the frankly irritating Mixen in our midst. It's hard to find volunteers for something which is fast becoming seen as a less than glorious career.'

Tristan took another swig and slammed his glass down onto the desk. Lucas heard a crack. 'Damn Scorpio! If she did kill him, which I have to assume she did,' he paused and seemed to be studying Lucas even harder, 'then she'll have her full powers now, which wasn't exactly what I was hoping for.'

Lucas stayed quiet as Tristan took his seat once more.

'And you, Lucas,' he shook his head, 'I've had to explain all about what you were doing there, explain how it was all part of a master plan to bring down the Hunters from the inside. I gave them that little speech about moving with the times, about adapting – and you know what? They were all for sticking with the medieval. So what have you learnt? Because when I go back there I need something good.'

He focused his needle-sharp eyes back on Lucas. 'All this time in Riverview, living with a Hunter, and what has been the point? You told me you could get close to her, learn their secrets. What have you learnt? Anything? Because the Elders are getting bored. And, frankly, so am I. Tell me something, Lucas, anything.'

'There are three other Hunters protecting the town as well as Victor,' Lucas said, speaking quickly.

Tristan rested his chin on his linked hands, looking bored.

'There's a prophecy,' Lucas hurried on. 'Maybe from a Sybll.'

Tristan rolled his eyes. 'The White Light. Yes, yes, we know about that.'

Lucas faltered. 'You know about it?'

'Yes, we know it,' Tristan snapped impatiently. 'But the prophecy is in fragments and no one knows for sure who it's talking about or when it will even happen. Damn Sybll, about as useless as a Thirster with no fangs.'

'Is that why you want Evie dead so much?' Lucas asked hurriedly. 'Because you think she might be this White Light?'

Tristan shrugged. 'Who knows if she is or isn't? But she's a Hunter and we want all Hunters dead. Don't we?' He arched one eyebrow. 'Isn't that what you signed up for? Not having second thoughts are we, Lucas?'

Lucas could feel the tremor in his voice, the shattering noise of blood pounding in his ears as he answered. 'Of course.' He paused. 'Do Sybll prophecies always come true?' he asked.

Tristan seemed thrown. 'No. Not always. Especially when choice comes into it. And humans are fickle creatures. Always changing their damn minds. They change their minds more often than they change their underwear.'

Lucas's mouth was so dry he could barely voice the question. 'So the prophecy might not come true?'

'Oh, it's definitely not coming true,' Tristan answered with a grim smile.

'Why not?' Lucas managed to ask.

The smile broke into a wider grin. 'Because you're going back to kill her. Time's up, Lucas. We're bored of waiting. We need to end it now. She may have her full power but she's not yet the White Light. If she is even the one the prophecy's talking about.'

Lucas's whole body went rigid. He fought against the natural urge to dissolve into shadow, gripped the sides of the chair instead.

'Consider this a test of your loyalty,' Tristan said, standing up and walking to the door. He opened it. 'If you fail this, don't bother coming back. It's either you or her. And if you don't manage to kill her, I'll be sending the others.'

Lucas stood slowly, his limbs sluggish, his amulet scorching him under the shirt. 'Understood,' he said quietly, avoiding Tristan's yellow eyes, and left the room silently.

He was by the car, fumbling for the keys, when Grace appeared at his side. She was almost as silent and invisible as him.

He looked up at her.

'Don't go back, Lucas,' she said.

He ignored her. 'Does she die?' he demanded. 'Is the Brotherhood going to kill her?'

Grace frowned, shaking her head. 'I can't tell. I need to touch her or have something of hers.'

He threw open the car door and reached across the seat for the knife he'd thrown on the floor. The one he'd used to kill Caleb. The one Evie had used to defend herself. She'd thrown it under some tools and he'd taken it on his way out.

'Here,' he said, thrusting it into Grace's hands even as she took a step backwards, her blonde hair flying like a cape behind her, her eyes wide with fear.

He pressed it into her palm and she let out a gasp, her head tipped backwards, eyes rolling skyward.

'What is it? What do you see?' Lucas urged, glancing hurriedly over his shoulder, back towards the Mission.

Grace's head fell forward; there were blue half-moons underneath her eyes as though she hadn't slept in days.

She turned away, his hand falling limply from her arm. 'I see death. I see everyone's death, Lucas,' she said softly.

33

It was still early when Evie arrived at Jocelyn's. She leant with her finger on the buzzer until she heard slow footsteps coming towards the door.

Jocelyn opened the door in her dressing gown. Evie barged straight past her.

'Did you know?' she demanded, wheeling around to face her.

'Know what?' Jocelyn answered wearily, shutting the door.

'About Lucas. Did you know? Did Victor tell you?'

'No, Victor didn't tell me,' she answered, ushering Evie through to the living room.

Evie sank down onto the couch. 'You tried to warn me not to get close to anyone. I'm so stupid.'

'You're not stupid,' Jocelyn said, sitting next to her. 'You needed to learn.'

Evie's head whipped up. 'You sound just like him.'

She caught sight of Jocelyn's jaw locking in distaste. 'It always ends in betrayal, Evie. Always,' she said.

Evie looked away. She realised she was clutching a cushion as if it was a punchbag she was trying to wrestle to the floor. 'A Shadow Warrior. And I couldn't even tell – that's the hilarious thing. I didn't even know. What kind of a Hunter am I?' She tossed the cushion aside and buried her face in her hands.

She felt Jocelyn's hand on her back. 'The feelings you had for him masked what your instinct was telling you. It feels the same – a light-headedness, a rapid heartbeat, an adrenaline spike. That's how it feels to be around an Unhuman. You mistook that for something else,' she said gently.

Evie's breath jammed in her throat. So it wasn't real, then – her feelings weren't real. But if it felt the same, why hadn't she wanted to jump the Scorpio, or Thirster? Her skin started to crawl at the thought. She'd kissed Lucas, she'd seen him half-naked and had thought about him with a lot less clothes on than that. She'd wanted him. She'd wanted him more than she'd ever wanted anyone before. It made the feelings she'd once had for Tom seem childish and innocent by comparison. And he wasn't even human. What kind of an instinct was that? She punched her fist into the seat.

'Don't be hard on yourself,' Jocelyn said again. 'Just learn from it.'

Learn from it? She was so sick of learning from it. She should have stuck to her guns, literally and metaphorically. She'd renounced boys long before Victor even showed up. She'd even spent part of that night lying in Lucas's bed packing up all her memories and saying goodbye to a future involving boyfriends, marriage and babies. She'd waved *adios* to the vision of herself as an old lady on a porch surrounded by grandkids. If she ever made it to being that old, she knew it would more likely be cats surrounding her.

So why had she let Lucas in? Why had she ever trusted him? She was an idiot. Falling for those damn winter sky eyes which looked to hold a lifetime of secrets and hey, guess what? They did. *Surprise!* And that sad half-smile of his? Probably because he wasn't getting to kill her straight up – he was having to wait.

But what had she expected? Why should he be any different from anyone else in her life? She was such a sucker. She may as well walk around wearing a T-shirt bearing the slogan, *Betray me. I'm good for it.*

She looked up with a start. 'He was probably the one who killed Anna!' Her stomach flipped one-eighty. She had let Anna's killer kiss her. She put her fingers to her lips, remembering how greedy she'd been when his lips found hers, how she hadn't wanted to come up for air.

She screwed up her eyes. 'I talked to him about her. I let him—' She couldn't finish. Anger burst out of her in a sobbing cry.

Jocelyn stroked her back. 'No. It wasn't him that killed Anna,' she said soothingly. 'These are youngbloods. It was the members of the Brotherhood before. Didn't Victor tell you that? We got our revenge, Evie. We practically wiped them out.'

Evie stopped sobbing. OK, that was one less thing to worry about then, to feel guilty about.

'Victor says he'll be back,' she said, wiping her sleeve across her face.

'He will,' Jocelyn said with a sigh.

'Why?'

'Because they want you dead, Evie. And they think he has the best chance of getting close to you. You can use that to your advantage too. He doesn't know you know what he is.'

Evie stood up. 'So *I* have to kill *him*. Is that it? It's either him or me?'

Jocelyn stood slowly to face her. 'Don't you want to kill him? After what he did to you?'

She felt the pain as a shard of jagged glass drilling through her abdomen.

'If you kill him you'll get all your power. It's what you'll need in order to defeat them,' Jocelyn said quietly, her eyes locked on Evie's.

Evie took a step backwards. 'So Victor says. Why did no one tell me that? I'm sick of all the secrets. What else don't I know?'

Jocelyn bit down on her lip.

'Why?' Evie shouted. 'Are you going to tell me? *Why* do I have to kill one of them to get my power?'

Jocelyn took a breath. 'It's just the way it's always been.'

'What kind of power are we talking about anyhow?' Evie demanded, her voice full of sarcasm. 'Will I suddenly get super-strong? Super-fast? Be able to fly?'

'No,' Jocelyn answered.

Evie could feel the glass shove deeper, impaling a few organs as it went. 'Will I not hurt any more?' she asked, holding back a wave of tears. 'Will I be able to forget all this? Will this go away?' She banged her chest. 'This pain. Will it stop?' she yelled.

There was a silence before Jocelyn started speaking. 'Yes. It will dull,' she said. 'You will get stronger in many ways. You will heal faster. You'll move faster, your instincts will fire quicker.'

Evie looked at her, still uncomprehending. How could killing an Unhuman make all that happen?

'It gets easier after the first one,' Jocelyn continued. 'The first one you always hesitate over. The second, you don't.'

Feeling less. Yes. She could do with feeling less. Feeling absolutely nothing would work for her.

She sank back down into the couch, spent. 'Does it make you feel better?'

'Better?' Jocelyn asked, standing in front of her.

'Yes,' Evie said, looking up. 'Killing. Revenge. Does it make things better? How does it feel?'

Jocelyn took her time answering. 'It feels like a release,' she finally said.

Evie studied her. A release? Was that the only way of getting it? Release from this pain – from the anger she felt about everything – about Anna and her parents and her father and Tom and, damn him, Lucas. Would killing every Unhuman in this world make her feel better? Maybe it would, because right now she couldn't think of anything else that might stop this pain except—

NO.

Not his arms. Not being in his arms. What was wrong with her brain that it had to think *Lucas*?

Maybe Jocelyn was right. Maybe the only way out of this was through killing.

'I have no way out of this,' she murmured to herself. 'I can't run. They'll find me.'

Jocelyn said nothing.

'And unless I kill Lucas,' Evie carried on, 'or one of the others, I won't get the power I need to stay alive.'

'Or become the White Light,' Jocelyn added quickly, 'and end this.' Her tone softened.

She walked over to Evie and brushed a strand of loose hair behind her ear. The gesture jarred a memory Evie had of Lucas doing the same. She moved backwards, the pain hardening inside her, calcifying around her heart.

'You owe Lucas nothing, Evie. He betrayed you.' Jocelyn paused. 'You have to kill him.'

Evie glanced at Jocelyn, closed her eyes and finally nodded.

34

She turned the photograph over and over in her hands, reading the message on the back and looking at the image of the strangers holding her. She flipped it once more.

Evie, she read for the tenth time. *We loved you more than you will ever know. You are our Evie –* always remember what you mean, to us. *We are sorry we couldn't be there to watch you grow and keep you safe. We hope one day you will understand why and will forgive us. Above all, we hope that you make the choices we couldn't. We will love you always, Mum and Dad x*

'*Remember what you mean to us,*' she said under her breath. *What* do *I* mean?

Make the choices we couldn't.

What did that mean? What choice couldn't they make? And who could she ask? She no longer trusted Victor and she wasn't sure Jocelyn would tell her all she knew even if she made her drink a quart of truth serum and had a gun held to her head.

She looked up at the sound of a car passing outside. Dusk had fallen while she'd been sitting here staring at an image long lost, at words that meant something but which could have been written by a Sybll for all the sense they made to her. Why couldn't they have been more explicit?

Evie sighed and watched the streetlights flash on one by one as the shadows reached out and touched them. Soon. It would be soon.

She got up from the chair and wandered idly over to the rails of clothes, her fingers stroking through the silks and chiffons gathering dust. She picked out a crimson red dress. It was strapless and tight across the chest – reminding her of a breast plate. The skirt was short and full. It was something to wear to a New York Fashion Week party but seeing how she would never be going to one of those, or even to New York, why not wear it for this little showdown? It was a good dress to wear for a first kill. A good dress for dying in too, she thought, slipping it from the hanger and twirling it between her fingers. The blood wouldn't show up too badly.

She went into the fitting room and changed out of her jeans. She glanced at the girl in the mirror. The stranger with the dark hair running in waves over her shoulders and the eyes like a midsummer sky. Who was this girl wearing a dress the colour of arterial blood? The girl who was looking back at her emptily, blankly.

She reached out a hand and pressed it against the glass. The girl reached out her hand too but Evie's fingers only met a hard surface. The girl was cold, unreachable. A faint smile passed over her lips as though she was pleased to be untouchable, then it vanished.

She turned from her and walked barefoot, feeling the swish of cold silk against her skin. She crossed to the storeroom door and unlocked it. Inside Victor had laid out a table of knives and arrows. She spied the UV lamps in the far corner and a crossbow leaning against the wall. Hopefully Lucas would come back alone but she moved one of the lamps closer to the door and checked it for battery life. Then she propped the flame-thrower heavily against the wall nearby just to be safe. The memory of the Thirster coming at her with his fangs bared still made her stomach shrink.

Eventually she walked to the table bowing under the weight of all the arrows and knives lined up in order of size, like so many operating table instruments. She selected the longest one, the one she thought might be fast enough and sharp enough for the job, and she tried not to think about where it might end up. She almost wished Victor had a table of guns. A gun would surely be easier. Or would it? Victor had told her that guns misfired or ran out of bullets while knives became an extension of the person, allowed you to get close, ensured a kill. A knife could never fail you.

She closed her mind, didn't want to think about it. She didn't want to think of anything but the actions she was taking. Walking from the table to the door, walking from the door to the red velvet chair, sitting down in the semi-darkness with the frozen, posing limbs of the mannequins in the window blocking the light from the street and throwing geometric shapes across her folded legs. Then, while she waited, she focused on breathing in, breathing out. She focused on not thinking of anything else but filling her lungs and emptying them, conscious that every rise and fall was bringing her one breath closer to dying or becoming a killer or possibly both.

The door finally pinged.

She looked up and felt the air leave her body in a whoosh.

Lucas stood tall in the doorway. His face blank, his eyes hooded. Slowly, tentatively, he walked towards her, a curious, suspicious smile nudging the edge of his lips as he took in her bare feet and cocktail attire.

Granted, she was going for the dramatic.

He paused, glancing around the store. She watched him, her heart skittering, her breath coming in puffs.

He wasn't human. That was all she could think. And she could feel it. The dizziness in her skull, the lurch in her stomach, the tightening of her gut. He wasn't human. She felt the shudder ride up her spine. How had she missed that? Because he was so damn good-looking. Even now, her heart skipped a beat just looking at him, in his dark jeans and a long-sleeved white T-shirt which moulded perfectly to his shoulders and chest.

He smiled at her warily. 'I tried to find you at the house. You weren't there. Your mum said you'd be here.'

She slipped the knife into the billowing folds of her skirt and stood, her feet clumsy and her palms slipping on the hilt of the knife.

He took another step towards her, giving her a wry half-smile. 'Sorry I disappeared the other night.'

She forced herself to smile back, tried to look innocent. 'Where'd you go?' she asked.

'Just somewhere,' he said, glancing over her shoulder again. More nervous this time.

Was he looking for Victor? Trying to sense him? The Hunters, Victor included, were all out there watching this whole thing play out via the security camera mounted on the wall. She glanced up to check the red light was flashing away.

She imagined the four of them bent over a CCTV screen somewhere – she wasn't sure where. She hadn't thought to ask. Risper was no doubt sharpening her axe or polishing her crossbow. Of course they were watching – they couldn't allow anything to happen to their precious White Light. Or maybe this was a test to see if she really *was* the White Light. If she died, then she obviously wasn't.

But Evie hadn't cared that she was being forced to do this alone. She'd wanted to face Lucas by herself, even if he was a Shadow Warrior. She had needed this moment – had needed to look in his eyes without the others around, to know the truth of what he was.

She stepped towards him, swaying slightly. 'So,' she said, in as seductive a voice as she could carry off while clutching a knife against her thigh and while trying to focus on the place on his chest where she was going to shove it. 'Why'd you come back?'

She stood on tiptoe inches away from him. Her heart was going a million beats a second. Could he sense that?

His voice was low but oddly toneless when he answered, 'Why'd you think?'

He was so close she could feel his heat, could smell the outdoor smell of him, earth and leather and leaves and something warm and citrus. Her stomach clenched against her inclination to lean in further.

Instead she ducked under the arm he was reaching out towards her and spun behind him, pulling out the knife, holding it out towards him like a flaming torch. He turned around to face her, slowly, his eyes dropping automatically to the weapon she was clutching.

'I'm not sure,' she answered. 'To kill me, maybe?'

He finally raised his eyes to meet hers. They were blank as a cement wall. 'You know,' he said, not sounding surprised.

'What? That you happen to be a demon?'

He seemed to smart at the word. His eyes narrowed – became cold and calculating. Then his mouth twisted into a sneer and his expression shifted, the shadows cutting lines across him, making him suddenly look like what he was. Unhuman.

He wasn't Lucas. That boy was gone – he had never existed in the first place. This was who he really was – as sure as she was now the girl in the mirror.

'You want to kill me? You should have done it while you had the chance,' she spat.

His lip curled into a mocking smile, his shoulders tensed. Then he flew at her. She felt herself ram the wall behind, her head smash against the plaster. She cried out and his hands dropped away instantly.

She didn't stop to figure out why. She brought her arm up and smashed her elbow into his chin, knocking him backwards. 'You used me,' she shouted as he stumbled back. 'You lied to me. I trusted you.' She moved towards him, the knife held up.

He laughed even as he wiped away the smear of blood from his lips. 'You were so easy to fool,' he laughed.

She felt herself flinch at his words – tried not to show it. 'Isn't this the point when you disappear?' she screamed. 'Go on, try it. I'll sense you.'

Lucas weighed her, still smiling as he edged backwards towards the storeroom.

'Was it part of your plan?' she asked, advancing on him. 'Making me fall in love with you?'

She saw something in his eyes. A flash of surprise. His guard dropped. She switched the knife into her left hand and threw a punch with her right, just like her father had taught her. Her fist connected with his jaw and his head flew backwards. He crashed into the doorway and she could have sworn she saw the trace of a smile appear on his lips before his face blanked again.

His hands were at his sides. He was making no effort to fight back. And she realised she wanted him to. She wanted him to fight back. She *needed* him to.

'Why aren't you fighting?' she yelled.

He spat some blood to the floor, looked up at her through his lashes, calculating something. She saw him take a deep breath and then, quicker than she could think, he had her pinned against the wall, his hands locked around her forearms. She struggled uselessly, suddenly understanding how strong he was – his hands were hard as steel – and the panic started to invade. She twisted her head right to left, catching the blinking red light of the security camera. How late would Victor leave it before stepping in? No. She'd already answered that question.

Lucas's face was shoved up close to her own, his lips drawn back over his teeth in a snarl.

She let out a cry as his fingers tightened on her arm, the long gash made by Caleb ripping open under the gauze bandage. She felt the blood start to gush red-hot down her arm.

He let her go immediately, as though she might contaminate him, and stepped backwards, his eyes filled with such pain, for a moment she thought she must have impaled him on the end of the knife without realising it.

She glanced down. The knife was still in her hand.

She looked back up, and before he could come at her again, she launched herself at him with a blood-freezing scream.

He did nothing. He didn't attempt to sidestep her or even hold his hands up to block her. He didn't fade or disappear or whatever it was Shadow Warriors did. He just stood there and let her come.

He flew backwards, landing on his back with a crunch. She landed on top of him and pressed her knees against his chest, holding him down with the weight of her entire body, her arm flattening hard against his throat. She felt his ribcage rising and falling fast beneath her. But he made no effort to struggle. He just lay there, breathing fast, his eyes locked on hers – almost daring her.

She brought the knife up. He kept his gaze on her face, not looking at the knife, and there was an expression there that she couldn't read properly. It was like he was urging her to do it. Like he *wanted* her to do it. Her breathing was matching his own, coming fast and jagged. They stared at each other and for a split second the new Lucas vanished and he was just Lucas again – the human version. His face lost the mask – or it slipped for the briefest of moments – and as it did so she felt the familiar head spin as though gravity had been turned off. Her stomach flipped and she wanted to collapse on top of him and feel his arms come around her and pin her tight. She swallowed it away. It wasn't real.

He closed his eyes.

She hesitated, then lifted some of her weight off his throat. 'Why have you given up?'

He opened his eyes and the mask was back on – his face twisted in a cruel smirk. He laughed. She pressed her knee down harder until it turned into a cough.

'Too scared to actually do it?' he managed to say through the crush. 'Can't you kill an Unhuman? The Unhuman who killed your best friend?' He laughed again. 'What kind of a Hunter are you?'

She frowned at him. 'Anna?'

'Yes,' he said with a smile. 'I watched her die.'

She lowered the knife, easing her arm off his throat entirely. 'No, you didn't.'

She felt him tense beneath her.

'Why are you lying?' she asked, noticing that she was no longer afraid, that the panic had subsided leaving only a stillness inside her, an alertness that hadn't been there before.

'Do it,' Lucas growled beneath her. 'What are you waiting for?'

She scrambled back off him, leaving him lying there, and stood. 'No,' she said.

He jumped to his feet. 'You have to do it,' he said, his voice urgent – panicked even.

'Why? Because it's what you want?' She backed away.

What was going on? Why did he want her to kill him? Assisted suicide wasn't exactly what she'd expected in her first showdown with an Unhuman. A part of her brain tried to process that if he was begging her she should just do it – it would be done. She would have her power. But she couldn't – she stepped backwards, putting space between them instead.

'Evie,' Lucas said, and she looked up, surprised. His voice had changed – it was the soft, low voice he used on Lobo, the same one she imagined he used to calm horses and get them to do his bidding. She could feel herself edging forwards with the knife pointed straight at him, but she dug her heels in and tried to tune him out.

'Do it!' He was suddenly right in front of her, covering the space between them so fast he was a blur. He grabbed hold of her wrists and pulled them towards him and she felt the knife slice through cotton and press against bone, against the softer resistance of flesh. He had it poised in the space between two ribs. 'They'll be coming for you soon. This is your only chance to beat them.'

She looked down at the knifepoint, horrified, tried to yank it back, tried to wrestle her wrists from his grip, but he wouldn't let go. A trickle of blood blossomed red against the white of his shirt.

She cried out.

'Do it!'

Both of their heads flew up. Lucas's grip loosened momentarily and she pulled the knife clear, stumbling back away from him.

Victor stood in the doorway.

'Do it!' he yelled again at Evie.

'No,' Evie said, looking between the two of them, edging further away from both of them. 'What the hell is going on?'

Victor took a step forwards. 'He wants you to kill him, Evie. Do it or I will.' He unsheathed a knife that, apart from the iridescent gleam and engraving around the hilt, looked like something that might be used for skewering hogs. He tossed the sheath to the ground.

Evie burst between the two of them, stretching out her arms so that Victor couldn't get past her. 'No,' she yelled. 'You're not touching him.'

Victor stared at her, stunned. She swallowed, just as stunned as he was. She didn't know what she was doing. Why had she gone from trying to kill Lucas to trying to save him, all in a matter of minutes?

'Evie,' Victor said with a sigh. 'He wants you to kill him, so kill him. Does it matter why?'

'Yes,' she answered. 'It does, frankly. When was the last time a Shadow Warrior asked *you* to kill him?'

She turned towards Lucas who was standing, head bowed, fists curled, shoulders rising with each breath.

'I'm ordering you—' Victor's voice bellowed.

'Shut up,' she yelled right back at him. 'I am done with following your orders. I'm done with listening to you. I'm done with trusting you. Right now the only person I trust is myself. And my instinct.'

'Evie,' Victor said, his voice dropping low, conciliatory. He even managed a curt smile.

'No,' she shouted. 'You told me in one of your little lessons that evil prospers when good men do nothing,' she said, cutting him off. 'But you were wrong. Evil prospers when good men don't think for themselves or act for themselves. Well, *I'm* thinking for myself. I don't choose this life. I'm not going to be like you.'

'You don't get to choose your destiny, Evie,' Victor roared. 'It's been chosen for you.'

She squared her shoulders. 'You're wrong,' she said. 'I *do* get to choose. That's what my parents meant. I get it now.' She shook her head. 'They meant for me to know that I always had a choice in who I was.' She paused. 'That's what they were trying to tell me. They were telling me that I didn't *have* to be a Hunter. That I could choose not to be. They said I should always remember what I mean – and for ages I couldn't understand what they were talking about, there was a comma, but it was in a weird place. But I figured it out. They were talking about my name – what it means – Evie – it means Giver of Life, did you know that? I looked it up. They meant for me to choose to be Evie, not a Hunter, not a bringer of death.'

She knew it even as the words formed on her lips. If only she'd figured it out sooner. It was the only thing that made sense about that cryptic message and the wonky grammar.

'You can't,' Victor said again, as if those words refuted everything he'd just heard. As if two words uttered by him would be all it took to make her change her mind.

She raised her eyebrows. 'I can't what? Walk away?'

Victor snorted through his nose. 'You want to know what happened to Margaret – the girl from your book?' he asked. 'The one with the line slashed through her?'

Evie stayed silent.

'She tried to walk away too. *Tried to.*' A smile curved his top lip.

Evie's eyes widened as she took in the meaning of what he was saying.

'So did your parents.'

She stared at him, not following. She sensed Lucas behind her. A shift of his body. She felt the words finally sink in.

Victor laughed. 'They *tried* anyway.'

She froze, her muscles locking, her breath seizing.

Victor spoke with a curious smile. 'You would think they would have heeded Margaret's lesson. But like you, they weren't too good at learning what was best for them.'

Her breath started to come in shallow gasps as though Victor was choking her. He was just observing her reaction with a small smile.

'I was ordered to kill them, Evie, because they wanted to take you and hide you. They didn't care about the prophecy.'

She couldn't answer, couldn't move. She remembered Jocelyn saying how they had died protecting her from something very bad. The something very bad standing right in front of her. Not the something very bad standing *behind* her, head still bowed.

'So you're going to run off then, are you?' Victor asked mockingly. 'Try to make it on your own? Without your full power? With the instincts of a child? You can't run from me, Evie.'

Evie stared at him. She had been right – he was totally psycho.

Then she spoke, her voice sounding braver, surer, than she felt. 'You won't kill me,' she said, tilting her chin at him. 'You think I'm the White Light – you can't kill me.'

Victor's face tightened, his mouth drawing into a grimace. 'Where will you go? Who's going to protect you?' he sneered.

279

'I will.'

She turned at the sound of his voice. Lucas was staring at Victor. His eyes were blazing, his face set into a mask of fury. She flinched.

'You?' Victor threw back his head, hit by an uncontrollable spasm of laughter.

'I've been doing a better damn job of it so far than any of you,' Lucas answered.

Evie narrowed her eyes. What was he talking about?

She saw a blur out of the corner of her eye and turned. Victor was lunging towards Lucas, blade or skewering knife or whatever it was raking the air in a sweeping arc. But she was in the way. She twisted sideways, bringing her knee up at the same time, slamming it hard into Victor's crotch, felt the softness of flesh and his weight as he crumpled, even as the blade came slicing down towards her.

She was thrown clear, and stumbled backwards, arms flailing. When she found her footing and turned, Lucas had Victor flat on the ground. The blade was somehow in his hands, pressed against Victor's neck, and a thin, red line was bubbling against the steel.

35

'Don't!' she screamed.

Lucas looked up at her, his eyes blazing. She could see the fury in his face and she watched the red line on Victor's neck grow thicker, the bubbles start to fizzle against the blade. Lucas's knuckles were as white as Victor's eyeballs, which were rolling like ping-pong balls in his head. He flailed his arms but Lucas was straddling the bigger man, kneeling on his forearms.

'Don't,' she said again, pleading.

Lucas's shoulders dropped. He moved the knife an inch away from Victor's neck but kept his weight pressing down on Victor's chest and arms.

Victor gargled something.

Lucas looked back at him and, without a second's grace, smashed his elbow hard into Victor's temple, knocking him out.

She stared at Victor's lolling head as Lucas stood slowly, the knife Victor had been holding dangling at his side.

'Who *are* you?' she asked, her eyes finding his face, searching for something she might recognise.

'I'm Lucas Gray,' he answered. 'I'm half Shadow Warrior, half human. I was a member of the Brotherhood. This man,' he nudged Victor's inert body, 'drove my mother's car off the road. I was in the passenger seat – I was just a kid. But I was thrown clear.

I sat and watched her die. All because she dared to fall in love with an Unhuman.'

Evie felt a kick to her stomach that made her flinch backwards.

'And then seven years later he murdered my father,' he finished.

She should have figured it. Now she understood. So they had this much in common then. Victor had made them both orphans.

She drew in a breath. 'And everything else . . . ?' she asked.

'Everything else was the truth,' he answered, his voice suddenly fierce.

She weighed him carefully for a second. 'Did you kill the Scorpio demon?'

'Yes.'

'Why?'

'Because he hurt you. And because he would have killed you if I'd given him another chance.' He was standing before her, his arms at his side, his eyes level with hers.

'Were you there in the cornfield?' she asked.

'Yes.'

Her breath caught in her chest again. 'And the pond?'

'Yes,' he answered, in the same steady, low voice.

'Why did you save me? Why didn't you let me drown?'

He seemed caught off guard. He paused, a frown line appearing between his eyes, a questioning smile forming on his lips. 'Don't you get it?' he asked.

'Get what?' she answered.

He laughed under his breath but kept gazing at her with those slate eyes of his. She tried to shake it off – the way he was looking at her. The same person had just shoved her against a wall and looked at her with hatred in his eyes. She couldn't make sense of it.

'How can you not see?' he asked quietly, shaking his head.

'See what?' she asked, unable to mask the irritation in her voice.

'Who you are. *What* you are.'

Her mouth dropped open, but then she recovered and pulled a face at him. 'But you came back to kill me.'

'No,' he said, his voice rising. 'I came here so *you* could kill *me*. If I'd come back to kill you, believe me, you'd be dead.'

She pursed her lips. 'Why? Why did you want me to kill you?'

'Because it was the only thing I thought I could do to save you.'

She snorted out loud. 'How would that have saved me?'

'Betrayal makes you angry,' he said, 'I saw that with Tom.' He stopped and his eyes dropped to the floor, his foot nudged Victor's hand. 'I didn't plan the other night,' he said finally, looking up. 'I never intended for you to . . . feel anything for me.'

He dropped his gaze and she felt her own cheeks start to burn. Oh God, hadn't she admitted something earlier, during their fight, about loving him? Where had that come from?

'I just wanted to make you think I'd betrayed you. I wanted you to have an easy fight. If you were angry enough I thought you could be provoked into killing me. Then you'd get your power.'

She said nothing, her heart still busy pumping all the blood in her body to her cheeks. Her mouth had run dry, her tongue was paralysed.

She looked up at him, something finally dawning. 'You would have died?' she asked, forming the words carefully. 'For me?'

He held her gaze. 'Yes.'

She could barely get the word out. 'Why?'

'Because I believe in you.' He shrugged.

She rolled her eyes. 'Please don't start with this whole White Light crap again. Even my parents didn't believe it.'

283

'Well, I do. You don't see yourself as I do, Evie. You are it.'

She continued to stand there, hands on hips, staring at him defiantly. She didn't want to be it. Did he still not see that?

He took a step nearer. 'I've been saving your ass since the beginning.'

'What—'

He carried on. 'And back then I didn't even know why. I was acting purely on instinct. I had no choice in the matter. I kept telling myself I was coming back here so I could get close to you in order to kill you but it was a lie. This whole time, from the minute I saw you, I've been more interested in keeping you alive than in killing you.'

She stared at him. There wasn't much to say to that.

He took another step towards her, his voice husky. 'And now it seems you've decided not to fight,' he said, sounding both weary and faintly amused at the same time, 'so someone's got to do it for you.'

He took a step towards her and the ground seemed to tilt.

'I will fight anyone who tries to hurt you – human or Unhuman. Monster or demon. I'll do the killing. If that's what it takes to keep you alive.'

She finally opened her mouth and discovered she hadn't lost the power of speech. 'No,' she said.

He paused. 'Look, I'm as good as dead anyway. So I may as well spend whatever time I do have left protecting you. Making sure the prophecy comes true.'

That was the sticking point. She pounced on it. 'Why do you want it to come true so much?'

Lucas shrugged. 'If the prophecy comes true you'll be safe. No Unhumans will be able to hurt you. You can be Evie, like your parents wanted. You don't need to be a Hunter.'

She took that in. He had a point.

'And besides, the war needs to end, Ev. Don't you think it's about time?' She smiled despite herself at the familiar use of her name, but then the smile faded and was replaced by a frown. What he was saying wasn't what she wanted to hear. She'd already decided. She wasn't having anything to do with the Hunters any more, or their stupid prophecy. She'd chosen. That's what the big speech to Victor had been all about. She wasn't a Hunter. And now here Lucas was, undoing it all – making her question once more who she was and what she was doing.

'I have no home any more,' Lucas continued, interrupting her thoughts, 'I'm banished from the realms. I have a blood price on my head.'

'You broke it for me,' Evie whispered, almost to herself.

His voice was suddenly close, sending a shiver down her spine. In the gap between words he'd moved so he was standing just a few inches from her. She could see the individual spikes of his lashes.

'I broke it long before today,' he said softly. 'I broke it the moment I first saw you. When I saved you from Shula outside the diner.'

She tipped her head back in surprise, trying to see into his eyes. He was looking down at her and she could see herself reflected – a crimson slash across his iris.

The word never made it to her lips. But he heard it anyway.

'Because I love you. Even then I think. Not because you're beautiful and wear crazy ball gowns to kill Unhumans, not because your cheerleading moves make for an interesting fight scene, not because you'll jump into frozen water to hunt for a ring, nor because you're the White Light.'

She couldn't help herself. She groaned.

He kept talking, brushing over her protest. 'I love you, Evie, because you make me a better person. For the first time in my life I'm fighting for something other than revenge.'

She felt her ribs expanding and contracting, squeezing her heart tight then tighter still. He put his hand under her chin and tipped her head up so she was looking at him again.

'I'm not sure I fully understand it myself but I know that I love you and that something is pulling me towards you. Fate, destiny, whatever you want to call it.'

She swallowed, staring into his eyes. That was exactly how she felt. And she hadn't even realised it properly until now. How was it possible that he felt the same way?

'It was you that taught me I could choose,' he said softly, so softly she had to lean into him to hear better. 'That I could choose who I was and who I wanted to be. I would die for you, Evie Tremain, because I love you.'

Her stomach lurched into her mouth. Her legs became elastic. She tried to tell herself it was a natural reaction, just a natural reaction. He was an Unhuman.

'Why should I trust you?' she asked in a breathless rush.

His hand dropped away from her chin and she felt untethered by its loss, as if she might fall over.

'You said you trusted yourself,' he said. 'You trusted your instincts. What are they telling you now?' He stepped back, giving her space.

She looked at him – tore her eyes from his and studied his face. That curve of a smile, the straight dark eyebrows drawing together as he waited for her answer. His dark brown hair falling forwards over his brow which she had a sudden urge to brush back. Her eyes skipped down to his chest. She drew in a sharp breath as she saw the bloom of red against the white cotton, where her knife had pierced the skin.

She swallowed again at the understanding of all that had happened, shook her head a little to try to unscramble her thoughts. Her eyes traced his hands, one still holding Victor's blade loosely at his side. Then she looked back at his face.

Could she trust him?

No.

No more trusting anyone. That was the deal. Trusting people just led to situations like this one.

His lips parted softly.

OK, maybe this situation wasn't all bad.

He frowned more, starting to worry at her silence.

She chewed her bottom lip. How could she tell if the dizziness she felt around him, the stomach-pounding, adrenaline-rushing feeling was actually love and not her body telling her to run away fast? How could she decipher her heart? And, she thought, more worryingly, if she trusted him then didn't that mean she would have to believe what he had said about her being the White Light? And then what? Where would that lead her? Lead *both* of them?

Her eyes went to the knife again. Lucas followed her gaze, realised what she was looking at and dropped it to the floor. He held his palms up towards her in a gesture of surrender.

'So?' he asked.

She closed the distance between them in two strides and took in the surprise that flashed across his face before she closed her eyes and kissed him.

The whole world – all the realms included – fell away to nothing. There was just her and him and she was safe. She felt his arms come around her waist as he drew her against him, his lips scorching against hers, lighting a fire deep inside her. And it could have been her instincts but it could just as well have been fear that made her clutch him tight, scared he would disappear.

She finally pulled back; his arms stayed tight around her waist. She rested the palm of her hand against his chest and felt the beat of his heart, hard and fast against it. His amulet was gone.

She said the words before she could think them. 'I trust you.'

His hands found her face, his lips were a tantalising fraction away from her own, when he stopped and pulled back. She froze. Had he tricked her after all? One of his hands dropped from her waist. She started to struggle against the other one, but then she saw he had pulled something out of his pocket and was holding it in front of her face.

She blinked and tried to focus. He was holding a thin gold wedding band.

'I think this belongs to you,' he said.

She stared at him in amazement. 'You went back for it?' she asked, her fingers shaking as she took the ring.

'Yes,' he murmured. 'I wanted you to find it.'

'But how would I have found it?'

'If you'd have killed me my body would have returned to the Shadowlands – at least I think it would have – being half human I'm not sure, some of the lore doesn't seem to hold true – but if my body had vanished, the ring would have stayed here, everything from this realm stays behind – clothing, weapons, rings. You would have found it. And hopefully you would one day have understood.'

She looked at him, marvelling at the fact he'd gone back for it. For her. For a tiny piece of metal sunk into the mud and weeds.

She slipped the ring onto the fourth finger of her right hand. 'Thank you,' she said quietly. Would her parents think she was doing the right thing? She wondered. Would they think she was crazy for believing she could end this war? Or worse, that she was a traitor for allowing herself to fall for a shadow warrior?

Lucas drew a finger along her cheekbone and she involuntarily shuddered. She heard a groan and hoped to God it wasn't her.

But it wasn't. Lucas's hands dropped away and they both turned towards the groaning sound.

Victor was stirring at their feet. Evie stared at him. She felt nothing.

Wrong.

She felt numb towards him. Maybe later there would be anger, fury, hatred, murderous rage, but right now she felt nothing.

Lucas dropped down beside Victor's head and she wondered what he was doing and then she caught the glint of the knife blade in his hand.

'What are you doing?' she screeched, grabbing his shoulder.

'What I've been vowing to do every day since I was nine years old.'

'No,' Evie shouted. 'You can't kill him.'

'I have to. Did you forget what he did? He killed my parents. And yours too.'

She flinched. 'Yes, I know. He's a psycho. That doesn't make it right. I'm not going to let him make me into something I don't want to be. Or you for that matter. I already gave him too much of me. We let him go.'

Lucas stood up from his kneeling position. 'We let him go and he will come after you.'

'And you'll protect me if I need you to, but only until I can protect myself.'

Lucas's lips pressed together, his straight brows drawing together into one line.

She felt the distance between them as a physical thing, recognised the urge she had to close it. She reached out a hand and placed it on his arm. 'Lucas,' she said more softly, 'you just said that you loved me because I made you a better person.' She watched him frown. 'If this is the better you, what the hell were you like before?'

He pulled away, wincing.

She pressed on. 'You said that you believed in me. I don't know if you are right to or not. But if you think I can make this fighting and this killing stop, then I'll do it. I won't walk away. I'll stand and fight with you. By your side. I'll see it through to the end. But I won't kill in cold blood. And I won't kill for revenge and I won't let you either. Because I'm not going to become like him.'

36

Lucas knelt in front of Victor and pressed his face up against Victor's.

Victor's eyeballs were rolling wildly in his head as he struggled his way back to consciousness. He waited until Victor had focused enough, until he saw a spark of recognition, and then he pressed the knife tip against his throat where the line of blood had already clotted.

'This blade belonged to my father,' he said. 'I left it by the pond.' He paused and heard Evie make a sound behind him. 'Do you remember my father?'

Victor's nostrils flared. He tried to turn his head but the knife pressed down and he fell still.

'You killed him, just as you killed my mother. Do you even remember her? Do you remember the boy in the car with her?' He watched as Victor's eyes sprung open in surprise. 'Yeah, you probably should have made sure there were no witnesses left behind.'

He saw the fear drain into Victor's eyes as realisation finally dawned.

Lucas felt the weight of his father's knife in his hands, so delicately balanced it felt like holding a flower stem. The metal so iridescent it was almost see-through and so sharp that if he moved his fingers a fraction it would fall through Victor's jugular as easily as a raindrop through a cloud.

He leant forward even closer, dipping his head so he could whisper into Victor's ear. 'Know that I am saving your life because of her. Know that. She saved you.' He nodded in Evie's direction. '*I* would have killed you.'

He moved the knife away from Victor's neck, replacing it with his knee. 'Get me something to tie him up with,' he said, looking up at Evie.

Evie stood stock-still, staring at him.

'Quickly,' he urged.

She looked around frantically for something – then tore a Chanel dress off the rail and pulled the belt from around its waist, chucking it towards him. He tied a convoluted knot around Victor's wrists and neck, binding him into a foetal position.

When he was done he stood up, noting the wide-eyed relief on Evie's face. His hand found hers and he tugged her towards the back door. They stepped through into the storeroom. Lucas took in the weapons laid out before him, frowning.

'Where are we going?' Evie asked.

'We have to get away from here. They're coming,' he said, letting go of her hand and bending to pick up one of the UV torches. He switched it on and off before tossing it to her. 'Here, take this,' he said.

Then he grabbed hold of the nearest knife encased in a sheath, and handed that to her too. She took it, discarding the one she'd had up until now, the one tipped with Lucas's blood.

'OK, let's go,' he said, taking her hand and sprinting to the back door, which led out onto a back alley.

'Hang on,' she said, pulling back. 'Where are we going? I can't just leave.'

He turned to her, his hand on the handle. 'You want to stick around and have a give peace a chance bed-in?'

She smiled sarcastically.

'Or do you want to stay alive?' he asked, ignoring it. 'The people coming aren't exactly the kind of people who you'd want climbing into bed with you. They don't understand peace. All they know is that you are the White Light and they want you dead before you go raining on their parade.'

'I can't just leave – what about my mother?' she protested.

He opened the door. 'We'll call her.'

She dug in her heels as he tried to pull her through the door. 'What?'

He turned back to her and saw the fear on her face. He wanted to smooth it away, hated that the fear was in some way caused by him. That's when he heard the footstep in the alley, the sound of shallow breathing. He whirled around, blocking Evie with his body.

'Going somewhere?' Risper said, stepping out from behind a dumpster. He caught the silver flash of something in her hand and knew without looking closer that it was one of those circular blades she'd had in the cornfield.

He heard the growl that erupted from his own throat, felt Evie press closer against his back, her fingers digging into his waist.

'Where's Victor?' Risper asked.

'He's tied up.'

Risper frowned at him, her small mouth pursing. She was tiny – barely bigger than a child – but he knew from watching her in the cornfield that she was fast and that she was dangerous.

'We were just leaving,' Lucas said quickly, smoothly, calculating how fast he could reach her and weighing that up against leaving

293

Evie unguarded. 'The Brotherhood are coming. You can stick around for the party if you want but we're leaving.'

His fingers tightened on his father's blade. He wasn't going to let go of Evie. So instead he squeezed her hand and took a step forward, his eyes on the saw blade Risper had brought up to her chest. Just one flick would be all it took and he would be quick enough to dodge it, but would Evie?

Risper danced to the right, blocking their path. 'She's not going anywhere with you.'

Evie pulled against his grip suddenly, stepping out from behind his back. 'Risper,' she said, 'he's not one of them. He's helping me. I trust him. I'm leaving with him.'

'No you're not,' Risper hissed. 'You think I'm letting you go with him you've got another thing coming.' Her voice raised to a yell. 'I've been waiting four years for them to tell you who you are. I've had to risk my life to protect yours when you were too ignorant and too stupid to even know what you were.'

'You tried to kill me,' Evie burst out. 'What do you *mean* protecting me? You've been trying to bury one of those things in my skull ever since you first saw me.'

Risper threw her a look as cutting as the blade. 'I couldn't believe it was you. That you were supposed to be the one to save us,' she spat. 'You – you're just a girl.'

'So are you!' Evie shouted back.

'If you were meant to be it – if you were really it then you would have survived anything I threw at you.' She frowned, her voice dropping. 'And you did.' She glanced at Lucas. 'You did,' she repeated.

'So what? Because you only got a piece of ear and not my whole head you suddenly think I'm the White Light? That it's OK to protect me?'

Risper pressed her lips together, anger coming off her in waves.

Evie opened her mouth to say something more. Then rammed it shut again.

Lucas's eyes scanned the alley. Something. There was something out there. Something coming closer.

'Yes,' Risper suddenly said, her face scrunched up with fury. 'I *do* believe it. Because, despite everything, you're still alive. And if you're it then I'm not letting you out of my sight. You're what I've been waiting for. You're not leaving. You're staying right here and you're fulfilling whatever it is that damn prophecy says you're doing. Because I want out.'

Lucas interrupted her stream of fury. 'Risper, there's no time. I can protect her better than you.'

He felt Evie tense next to him, her back straighten, her hand clutch at his. 'Lucas, I feel something,' she said and he caught the note of panic in her voice.

'They're here,' Lucas said, still staring at Risper.

Risper whipped around, her eyes raking the alley. She spun back to face them. 'They can't be,' she said. 'Jocelyn and Earl were supposed to be holding them off.'

'Well, they've obviously failed,' he said, tugging Evie after him. 'Let's go,' he said as they pushed past Risper.

Lucas paused, looking left and right. Left was a dark, garbage-strewn alley, about one hundred metres long, which emptied onto Main Street. Right was the same, only shorter, running for fifty metres before it hit a brick wall where another alley backed onto it. A yellow lamp illuminated a zone at the far end and he caught the blur of movement beneath it.

'This way,' he called, pulling Evie to the left.

They started running. 'Where's your car?' he asked.

'Behind Joe's diner,' she said. 'Free parking.' She shrugged, seeing his expression. 'Where's your car?'

'Parked on Main Street, one block down.'

It was her turn to give him a look. But Lucas was staring straight past her.

He sensed her before he saw her, felt Evie react too, both of them coming to a screeching halt about twenty metres before the end of the alley. He heard a movement behind him and glanced over his shoulder. Risper had been hot on their heels and had drawn up sharply too. Her eyes were narrowed, her teeth bared, but she wasn't looking at him, she was looking straight past them.

Lucas turned and saw Shula step into the light, feet spaced wide, hands on hips. She was wearing a black catsuit that clung to her body in ways that not even skin could manage. Her hair was swept back off her face, piled high on her head. She was standing in the green light cast by an emergency exit sign and it was making her glow toxic.

'Well, someone's in a hurry,' she announced, with a wink directed just at him.

Lucas stepped forward into the light, shielding Evie. He heard the whisper of steel against steel as Evie unsheathed her knife behind him.

He started edging her backwards, his brain trying to process his next move. If Shula was here the others would be nearby. The best way would be through her and out onto Main Street. It was the quickest route to the car.

He glanced sideways at Risper who had eased forward and planted herself side by side with him. Whatever her motivation, they both had a common interest now.

Risper's dark eyes found his and in that single second he knew she had understood what he intended to do. He faded into the shadows like a sigh, drawing his blade as he did.

Shula's face contorted into panic and fear. 'I sense you, Lucas,' she yelled into the space between them.

Evie's yell brought him back. He materialised as he spun around, his arm flying out instantly, drawing her against him, his eyes darting down the alley in the direction Evie was pointing.

Joshua was advancing silently behind them. As they stepped into the square of light, Evie cried out.

For a second he didn't understand but then he took in the blood dripping from Joshua's chin, the red streaks splashed across his T-shirt. Joshua's face was illuminated, his smile so wide Lucas could make out the drops of blood hanging on the end of his fangs.

'Your Hunter friend was tay-ay-sty,' Joshua said, smacking his lips together. 'Mmmmmmmmm.' He licked his palm, smiling, his eyes fixed on Evie.

Lucas heard Risper swear, sensed Evie's heart rate pounding like a starter pistol.

'Oh, why the brooding, scowly face, Lucas?' Shula pouted. She turned to Evie. 'You fell for this? Seriously?'

'You're not jealous, are you?' Evie snapped back.

Shula looked like she'd been slapped, but then, plastering on a smile, she turned to Lucas. 'So, yawn yawn, blah blah, hand her over, Half-and-half.'

'Don't think so, Shula,' he said, his voice carrying more than a warning in it. 'And if you want her you'll have to go through me to get to her.' He raised an eyebrow as he tipped his blade to catch the light.

'Oh, he's willing to die for you!' Shula clapped her hands together, looking at Evie. 'Isn't that sweet? So romantic. I best make sure he gets to fulfill that. Otherwise it's just oh so many empty words and you'll forever be wondering if he actually meant them.'

'There are three of us. And only two of you,' Lucas growled.

Shula sighed. 'Actually there are three of us,' she said, pointing up to the emergency exit sign. Lucas looked up and spotted the tiny brown sparrow sitting there.

'Neena, get down here,' Shula hissed.

The bird fluttered its wings and flew down, flapping left and right as if not sure where to land. Eventually she landed in a shimmer to Shula's left, materialising straight away into Neena's normal form. She stood there, staring at the ground, her narrow shoulders tensed.

'So that makes three against two because your girlfriend doesn't count,' Shula smirked, looking at Evie. 'I hear tell she can't fight very well. And Grace tells us she didn't kill Caleb after all, so I know she doesn't have her full power.'

He heard the crunch of gravel as Evie stepped forward, and his hand tightened on her wrist, holding her back.

'Power or no power, I seem to remember I smacked you up pretty good last time,' Evie said.

Shula's mouth pursed. 'I was wearing heels,' she said. 'I was at a distinct disadvantage.' She paused. 'You know, I still have coffee stains on that dress. I think you owe me. Maybe after I rip out your guts and decorate your boyfriend with them I'll go shopping in your little store, help myself to something new.'

'I don't think we have anything in your size,' Evie answered back, 'or anything that goes with green, for that matter.'

Lucas sensed movement to his right and whipped around.

Joshua had sauntered forward, a fingernail prising something gristly from between his teeth. Risper placed herself in front of him, a saw blade in each hand, looking like she was judging where to plant the first one.

Joshua paused mid-step and smiled disdainfully at her. A blade like that would barely scratch his skin.

'It's got Mixen acid on it,' Risper said, seeing Joshua eyeing her weapon. 'Might not kill you, sure is gonna hurt.'

Joshua frowned at her moodily, then looked at Lucas. 'What y'all doing fighting with Hunters? You're on the wrong side.'

'Am I?' Lucas replied. He weighed his own blade. It was Shadow steel, strong enough to break through Thirster skin, but if he was fighting Joshua that would leave Shula free to make a move. And then Neena? Would she actually fight? He didn't know but he wasn't sure he could hurt her.

Joshua tugged the gristle free and threw it to the floor. 'I always wanted to taste Shadow Warrior.'

'Come over here and taste it, then,' he said.

The light blinded them all.

'Back the *hell* off,' Evie yelled, stepping forward into the space that had opened up in front of them.

She was waving the torch in her hand. Joshua fell back, his arms flying up to cover his face, his skin starting to sizzle like bacon fat.

Ignoring his screeching cries and Shula's swearing, Evie took Lucas's hand. 'Come on,' she said, 'let's go.'

37

They backed away, their eyes on Shula, steadily, furiously advancing on them. She had paused only to unsheathe the metre long sword slung between her shoulder blades. It looked like something that had last seen battle during the Crusades.

Risper hurled a blade. It cut through the air. Shula dodged it. The second one, following hard on the shadow of the first, took her by surprise and sliced into the flesh of her shoulder.

Shula screamed in outrage, her hand flying to the wound, which started pouring a steady stream of greenish-black ooze. She hefted the sword into her left hand.

'Good job I'm left-handed,' she spat through gritted teeth.

'I've only got one blade left,' Risper said under her breath.

Lucas swore, his hand tightening around Evie's wrist.

'Do something, Neena! The light!' Shula yelled.

Evie took another few steps backwards, tugging Lucas with her, holding the torch high, trying to direct its beam straight onto the Thirster lying on the ground.

She took another step. Something blurred at the edge of her vision, leaping towards her, and she yelped as the torch flew out of her hands, smashing to the ground by her feet. The alley plunged into darkness. The spitting fat noise stopped – became a hiss.

Evie stared at the cat, as narrow and black as the alley, that was standing over the torch hissing at her. Then it shimmered and a girl took its place – the girl with the brown hair and the narrow chin. She was looking at Lucas, her bottom lip quivering. Before Evie could even process what had just happened – a cat becoming a girl – the girl had run over to the smoking Thirster and was helping him up.

Half of his face had melted away, patches of skin hanging down over his jaw like tattered drapes.

Evie felt her stomach contract. His lip curled upwards and she saw a fang appear, razor-sharp, shining white against the black crust of his burnt lip. He took a wonky step forwards, his shoulders rounding, his head tilting in her direction. Through the gap in his cheek she could see the rest of his teeth grinding.

Lucas thrust her backwards. 'Run!' he said.

She staggered a few steps. 'No,' she answered, stepping close and brushing his arm. 'I'm not leaving you,' she said.

'We'll hold them off, just go,' Risper hissed at her.

Before she could answer her, Risper had dived underneath Shula's outstretched arms and hurled her last blade straight at Joshua. It struck him dead centre in the chest. He let out a roar, his head flying back.

Shula turned on Lucas, who stood blocking her view of Evie.

Evie looked at her knife. 'Risper!' she yelled.

Risper turned just as Evie spun the knife, hilt first, straight at her. Risper caught it in her right hand, a smile flashing onto her face. It wouldn't do – it wasn't enough. It was a stupid knife – she needed a crossbow or a flame-thrower. But Risper turned back to the Thirster and stepped towards him and Neena.

'Go!' Lucas roared.

Evie took one last glance at him and then she turned and she

301

ran, her feet skimming the ground. She could see the door to the store still standing open sixty, now fifty metres ahead of her. And inside there was the crossbow and more weapons.

She had to get back there.

From behind her she heard the clash of metal on metal, the shrieking tear as one blade scraped another. And then a scream – a human sound – that shattered the night air. Cut off so suddenly that Evie came to a thundering halt, her heart leaping into her mouth.

Risper.

She looked over her shoulder. And out of the darkness came a shape, bearing down on her fast, the sound of pounding, loping paws overtaking the pounding of her own heartbeat.

She threw herself forwards towards the door. There was a swish, a rush of wind at her side, and in front of her Neena appeared – her face pale, her eyes fierce. Her chin quivered.

Evie felt the adrenaline flood into her body, her hand coil into a fist.

Then the girl opened her mouth, her eyes darting over Evie's shoulder and then back to her face. 'Tell Lucas I did this', she said in a rush. 'Tell him I'm sorry. I hope he's right about you.'

Evie pulled back startled. 'What?'

The girl didn't answer. She just became a blur. A dizzying heat mirage right in front of her. And then his face appeared.

'Lucas,' Evie whispered.

She knew it wasn't him – but it was him. It was exactly him. His grey eyes were staring into her own, and there were the tiny flecks of black around the iris, but the expression in them wasn't his. It was neither fierce nor haunted nor fathomless. It was afraid. And she had never seen Lucas look afraid.

He stepped past her.

She turned open-mouthed, wondering what the girl was doing, and saw the Thirster standing there. Before her eyes his skin was healing, the oozing gaps where the flesh had been seared were knitting up. He raised a hand and wiped the blood from his chin.

She felt her heart ramp up a gear, the sickly spin of panic mixing with adrenaline, making her body start to shake.

'You want the girl you'll have to come through me to get her,' she heard the girl who looked like Lucas say in Lucas's voice – low and threatening.

'OK.' The Thirster shrugged. And he lunged.

His teeth ripped through Lucas's neck as though it was a wishbone. Evie let out a scream. She felt blood splatter warm against her cheek and she screamed even louder. She couldn't stop. And the blood was everywhere, lakes of it pooling around her feet, which she only now realised were still bare.

The Thirster had fallen to his knees and the sound of sucking and of flesh ripping was filling her ears and she was choking and crying even as her instinct was telling her to turn and run. Lucas's voice in her head, screaming even louder than she was, to turn and run.

She turned, her fingers finding the door, and she ran. Inside – she spun around, panicked and wild.

Her head flew back and forth trying to focus. Her hands were shaking as she ran over and picked up the other torch. She hefted it into her left hand and then unhooked the crossbow from the wall. Risper's crossbow. She pulled four arrows from the sheath and then ran back to the door.

In the alley lay a body. Only it wasn't Lucas any more. It was the girl – lying doll-like, limbs splayed, face slick with blood.

The Thirster was gone. Evie glanced up the alley. Where was he? She dropped to her knees, frantically searching for a pulse on the girl's neck. Her fingers slipped. Blood gushed warm over her hand. There was a faint trace, a murmur and then it was gone. The girl's eyes were open, glassy, staring accusingly up at her. And then she disappeared, just some scraps of blood-soaked material left lying on the ground. Evie fell back onto her haunches, her hand dropping away and splashing into the pool of blood she was crouched in. She tried to push the sob back down her throat but it lodged there splinter-like, choking her. Why had the girl done that for her? Or for Lucas?

She couldn't stop to think about it. She was up, running again, her hands bringing the bow up, setting an arrow into place even as she ran. Up ahead she could see the girl, Shula, waving the sword, swirling it around, dancing with it. Next to her, prancing in rabid circles, was the Thirster, fangs bared, arms spread wide. He'd gone back to help Shula fight Lucas, probably thinking she would be easy prey after he was dead.

Between them, discarded next to a pile of clothing, lay Risper's boot. Evie couldn't piece anything about the scene in front of her together. Where was Lucas?

Then the pile of clothing took shape. The limbs were bent so awkwardly she hadn't at first seen it was a body.

That it was Risper.

Her vision blurred and she grasped at the crossbow to stop it falling off her shoulder. It wasn't possible. They were dancing over Risper's body, on top of her, as if she was nothing more than a bag of trash. Evie swung the crossbow back up, blinking away the tears.

She let it drop.

Where was Lucas? She couldn't see him.

The world tipped violently before righting itself. She stood on unsteady legs, her whole body shaking, as the scene in front of her became clear.

She couldn't see him. She could feel him – like an extra heart beating in her chest – but she couldn't see him.

The two Unhumans weren't dancing. They were fighting. They were fighting Lucas. She couldn't see him but they obviously could – or they could sense him.

Shula was spinning like a dervish, wielding the sword in both hands, bringing it down in swinging arcs, her face contorted in rage, but now Evie looked closer she could see sparks flying off the sword.

The crossbow was rammed against her shoulder; she was looking down the sight. She pointed it at Shula.

She couldn't fire.

She couldn't see if Lucas was in the way.

She closed her eyes. What was she supposed to do?

Sense him.

Her eyes flew open. She breathed in, breathed out. Felt a sudden pull as the sounds and smells in the alley dropped away and a calmness – a stillness – flowed through her.

A shadow danced across the alley, a blur before her eyes. The trace of a blade smashing against Shula's sword, sparks raining down.

He took form slowly before her, a dark insubstantial shape made of shadows and flitting so fast she couldn't make the shape whole, could only make out the blade as the light glinted off it as it twisted and fell smashing again and again against Shula's sword even as he had to bend and somersault and dodge the Thirster coming at him from behind.

Evie took aim, waited for the shadow to spring, and then she let an arrow fly.

305

It thumped with a sickening crack into the Thirster's chest and she watched him fly backwards, his feet scuffing the ground, his hands wrapping around the six inches of arrow shaft sticking out the centre of his chest. Then he looked up and saw Evie standing there and let out an ear-splitting roar.

She let the second arrow fly and it thudded into his stomach. Another scream tore from his stretched mouth.

Evie rammed the third arrow home and raised the crossbow once more, sighting it on Shula who was standing, sword clutched before her, sweat pouring down her neck, panting madly.

'Drop the sword,' Evie shouted.

Shula eyed her, eyed the crossbow.

'Lucas, it would help if I could see you,' Evie called.

He appeared, silent as a ghost materialising before her. She smiled faintly. His shirt was stuck to him in places, sweat plastering his hair back, his whole body tensed and his breath coming fast. His father's blade was shining in his hand.

He gave her a look that almost made her drop the crossbow. She felt like she was dissolving – that she needed to run to him, feel his arms around her before she disappeared – before he disappeared again. But before she could take a step or utter another word he had turned to Shula.

He took a step, raising his blade, pointing it straight at her neck. Shula flinched backwards, her sword dropping to her side, grating the ground.

'Lucas,' she pleaded as he backed her against the wall.

Evie clutched the crossbow tighter, aiming it straight between Shula's eyes.

She didn't see the Thirster coming. She was concentrating so hard on Shula and where to place her last arrow.

306

But there he was, suddenly a solid shape behind Lucas, his hands locking around his neck, dragging him backwards, and Lucas was falling, and the Thirster sank his fangs in with a sickening yell and blood was spurting like a fountain, spraying the ground and covering the Thirster's face in a veil of red.

Evie screamed as she let the fourth arrow fly. And she screamed as it pierced the Thirster just above the eyeball, throwing him backwards off Lucas and skewering him to the far wall of the alley. She ran, tossing the crossbow to the ground, stumbling towards Lucas, who was fading, becoming indistinct, even as she flung herself towards him. Her hands were reaching for him – needing to reach him – even as Shula raised the sword like an axe above her head.

And she saw the shadow of the blade fall, felt the gust of wind as it cleaved the air above her. And she scrunched her eyes closed and threw herself forward over Lucas's body.

She waited for the blow to land, her lips tasting blood and sweat and darkness.

Nothing happened.

She opened one eye. Her face was buried in Lucas's neck, her hair covering his face like a sheet. She raised herself on her elbows, her fingers finding his lips, his nose and his cheekbones. He was still here. Still solid. Still real. She felt his breath warm against her hand, then his eyes flashed open and she felt his arm come around her waist. Before she could say anything, he had rolled, and she was underneath him, his weight on top of her pressing her down, and her hands were around his neck wanting to keep him there. But he was up in the next beat, crouching low with his back to her, blade in hand, blood trickling down his neck from the two puncture wounds.

She scrambled up, gripping his shoulder for support. Her mouth fell open.

Shula was spreadeagled on the ground, her head resting on Risper's boot.

Her eyes were splayed wide in surprise and it looked as if someone had taken a marker pen and drawn a fat black circle on her forehead. A thin trail of greenish blood was seeping out of it.

Then Shula was gone as though she'd been nothing more than a mirage. One second her body was lying there and the next second there was only a trickle of green ooze pooling on the ground and a leather catsuit spread diagonally across the ground.

Evie clutched Lucas's arm and looked over at the woman standing over Shula's remains.

'Jocelyn,' she whispered in a husky voice.

Jocelyn said nothing; she didn't even look in Evie's direction. She just re-holstered the gun she'd been holding and walked over to the Thirster lying propped against the wall with an arrow stuck through his brain. Before Evie could say her name again, Jocelyn had struck a match and tossed it onto his chest.

The flame caught and started to crackle. Evie watched as the body suddenly came to life, struggling and writhing against the arrow bolting him to the wall. A long scream tore from his throat as the flames started licking at his flesh, melting it like cellophane.

Evie shrank behind Lucas's back. The scream and the smell hung in the air even after the body had gone. And only when there was nothing left but four twisted and warped arrowheads lying in a pile of dirty ash did Jocelyn look up.

She glanced between Evie and Lucas, then down at Risper. Her eyes finally fell on Lucas, on his hand linked with Evie's and the sleek blade in his other hand.

'You broke your promise,' she said. 'You told her.'

Evie frowned. What promise?

Jocelyn smiled wryly. 'And you're still alive,' she said to him.

Evie glanced at Lucas.

'She refused point-blank to kill me,' Lucas said quietly. He paused, his voice dropping. 'I love her. I will do my best to keep her safe.'

Jocelyn weighed him silently for barely a moment. 'Against the Brotherhood? Against all the realms?' she burst out, anger tipping her voice, a sneer replacing the smile. 'Love won't be enough.' She took a step towards him. 'And your best won't be good enough.'

'Maybe not,' Lucas answered shrugging, holding his ground in the face of her anger. 'But it's her choice.'

'Where's Victor?' Jocelyn asked, ignoring him, looking at Evie.

'He's tied up in the store,' Evie answered. 'He killed my parents.' She swallowed. 'Did you know?'

Jocelyn paused and Evie saw the answer in her eyes even before she spoke it and it was like a slap in the face – a dagger between her ribs. 'Yes.'

Evie heaved in a breath. How could she have known? How could she? And how could she have lied about it?

Jocelyn winced as if she had heard Evie's silent accusation. 'I couldn't do anything, Evie,' she said. 'I was powerless. He's much, much stronger than I am. And if I'd tried and he'd killed me then there would have been no one to look out for you – and I'd sworn to your parents that's what I would do.'

Evie stared at her, speechless.

'You didn't kill him when you had the chance?' Jocelyn asked, turning to Lucas, unable it seemed to stand the way Evie was staring at her.

Lucas shook his head in answer.

Jocelyn frowned at him.

'Come on,' Evie said quietly, pulling Lucas by the hand forward, past Jocelyn, past Risper, without looking at either, without taking her eyes off the road ahead and their way out, past the scorched ground where the Thirster had lain. And she didn't let go of Lucas's hand because it was the only thing that was keeping her from falling, it was the only thing that was real. And holding on to him was the only sure way she knew of keeping him from disappearing.

'Don't come after us,' she said to Jocelyn over her shoulder, 'and tell Victor not to try either.'

'Where are you going?' Jocelyn yelled, her voice echoing like a shot off the walls. 'There is nowhere you can go. They will find you. The Brotherhood . . . Victor . . . you can't run away, Evie! Look what happened to you parents!'

Evie stopped. She turned around slowly to face Jocelyn and felt Lucas at her side, turning with her, his arm brushing hers, steadying her.

'We're not running away,' she said, her voice low and sure, 'we're going to end this. Lucas and I. Without you, and without Victor.' And for the first time since she'd read about the prophecy, and understood her parents' cryptic message to her, she felt absolutely sure of herself and of exactly who she was.

'I'm not a Hunter any more,' she said, smiling. 'I'm the White Light.'

Acknowledgements

Thanks to:

Kerrie, Jamieson, Karen and Tom, whose beautiful house in California provided everything I needed to start this book. And Kadek for doing everything in our house in Bali, enabling me to finish it.

John and Alula for the love and sandwiches. And extra special thanks to Alula for her patience sitting in a car seat for days on end whilst we road-tripped around California.

My brother, whose judgement is always spot on, and who taught me to always trust my instincts when writing.

My mum, for teaching me to trust my instincts regarding everything else but mainly about not getting into cars with strange men.

My dad for pointing out that vinegar's acidic (even the balsamic kind) and suggesting bicarbonate of soda might make a better choice of Mixen anti-venom. I always was bad at science.

Vic and Nichola, as always, for accompanying me on the journey. It makes the trip a lot less lonely.

Tara for her generosity, wisdom, kindness and American eye. And Lindsey for the same . . . as well as for the pizza.

Claire and Paul for letting me be the first guest in their beautiful new house where I found the peace, the Manchego and the red wine required to edit.

Alby Ball and Suki Zoe for making me look good in the photos – bless you and your fabulous talents.

All my lovely blog readers and fans whose emails and reviews and tweets make my days and inspire me to keep imagining and keep writing. Thank you so, so much.

Lobo the dog. I took your name without asking you and hope you don't mind.

My agent Amanda for being generally wonderful. Discussing Shadow Warrior lore and first kisses in the middle of a traffic island in Covent Garden will always rank as a career high for me.

My editor Venetia who has guided this novice writer through two books in a few short months – I never knew editing could be so much fun.

Lydia, Phil and Catherine at Simon & Schuster for providing me with wonderful books, tips on shoes, encouragement and support. You guys rock!